The Charm of a Cowboy

Trena VanHoff

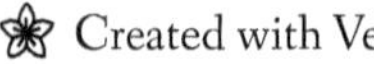 Created with Vellum

Dear Reader,

I can't begin to express how grateful I am that you've taken a chance on me and my novel. Because of you, a lifelong dream has come true —I get to share my stories with the world. I never imagined I'd come this far, and I owe it all to readers like you. Your support means everything to me, and I truly hope this book will touch your heart in some way.

This story is especially dear to me because it's set in the hometown of my great-grandmother, Annie Laura. She was a woman who lived her life with open arms, giving love to everyone she met and shining as a light in our big family. Her kindness and warmth continue to inspire me, and I hope a piece of that spirit finds its way to you through these pages.

Your support keeps me writing, and I'd love to stay connected with you!

📖 Follow me for book updates and behind-the-scenes glimpses of my writing journey: Instagram, Facebook & TikTok: @trenavanhoffbooks

📚 For news on upcoming books and exclusive content, visit: www.trenavanhoffbooks.com

With love and gratitude,
Trena VanHoff

Chapter One

I felt the cab slow to a stop, which would have been normal — except we were in the middle of nowhere. I quickly tapped the glass separating us with my knuckles, trying to get the driver's attention. "Excuse me. Why are we stopping?"

"This is as far as I go." The taxi driver continued to pull the vehicle off to the side of the road, completely unfazed by the panic in my voice.

My heart rate quickened as I took in the empty road and the sprawling, vacant fields around us. "Sir, if this is a money issue, I have more than enough to pay you to take me all the way into town—and I'm happy to give you a generous tip for your trouble. I understand this might be asking a lot, but I am happy to make it worth your effort."

He shook his head slowly, like I was missing something obvious. "Ma'am, I'm a Raleigh taxi service. I've already taken you further than I should. You'll have to get out here."

"The next town is only a few miles away. Could you at least take me there?" My voice shook with rising anxiety. Thankfully, it was only ten in the morning, so I wasn't stranded out here in the dark. But that wasn't the only danger I had to worry about, and we both knew it. "If my phone's right, it's just thirty-eight more minutes to my stop. How much more would it take for you to take me there?"

Without a word, he stepped out of the cab and opened the trunk. Panic surged through me as I scrambled to stop him. I reached out, grabbing his hand as he reached for the first of my three suitcases. His expression was serious, making any protest I could muster feel hopeless before I even spoke.

"Miss," he said, his southern drawl still carrying a trace of politeness, but the edge was clear. "As I told you, I've already gone further than I should."

I hurried to grab my purse and jacket from the backseat, handed him a wad of cash to cover the drive, and took my suitcases from him. I could already feel the humidity hitting my body now that I was outside the air-conditioned car. "How am I supposed to get to Clinton since you aren't going to drive me."

"Dunn is about a thirty-to-forty-minute walk in that direction." He pointed vaguely ahead. "Once you get there, head toward the town hall. Someone there should be able to help you get a ride to Clinton." Without another word, he climbed back into the taxi, flipped the vehicle around, and sped off, leaving a cloud of dust behind him.

I stomped my foot after him, but I knew he wasn't looking back to see it. I threw my purse over my shoulder and grabbed two of my suitcases, while balancing the third on top. The driver said it would be about a forty-minute walk, but I knew it would take me much longer, considering the weight of my luggage and the height of my heels.

Looking down at my heels, which had seemed so perfect at the airport, I couldn't help but feel foolish. They weren't made for anything like this. I didn't have anything better to change into, so I gave one last regretful glance at the disappearing taxi and began my trek toward the nearest town, dragging my bags behind me in a pathetic cloud of dust.

The driver had been optimistic, claiming it would take forty minutes. But over an hour later, the town still hadn't appeared. For miles, all I saw were farms with small houses and barns, each isolated from the road. Every time I checked my phone for a signal, I was met with more disappointment. No service. No way to call for help.

Only one beat-up truck passed me as I walked down the road, and the driver didn't slow down or glance my way. His large tires kicked up dust, sending it straight into my face, where it stuck to the sweat already beading on my skin. The humidity and exercise had me soaked through with no relief in sight.

Relief overcame me as I finally reached the small town that started with a mixture of small shops and houses. It only took a few moments until I got to the main street. Several of the buildings still bore the charm of old homes, but oversized signs planted in their front yards now revealed their transformation into local businesses. These businesses were various lawyers, accounting firms, and real estate offices with a few small boutique shops.

There was a small bench in front of the library, where three older women sat, still dressed in their Sunday best despite the late afternoon hour. As I approached, I couldn't help but notice the disapproval on their faces, their eyes narrowing at my shorter skirt and heels, as if my outfit alone had offended them.

"Hello, ladies, I'm looking for city hall." I set my bags down on the ground and lift my hair off my neck, fanning with my hand to catch any hint of a breeze. The thick, humid air clung to me, making even the smallest effort feel like a chore. "Can you point me in that direction?"

The woman closest to me, wearing a long pink dress, nodded slowly, taking a moment to assess me from head to toe. When her gaze finally returned to mine, her expression deepened into one of clear disapproval, her eyes narrowing as if she had found me displeasing.

"The city hall building is two streets down on the left side. You can't miss it—there's a big state flag out front." Her southern accent was as thick and sweet as I'd imagined, although it did seem almost cartoonish.

I smiled politely, thanked them, and gathered my bags, heading in the direction she had pointed. As soon as my back was turned, their conversation picked up again, and I could imagine they were whispering about me.

The woman's directions were straightforward, and before long, I found myself climbing the front steps of town hall. As soon as I pulled the door open, a rush of cool, air-conditioned air hit me, offering a welcome relief from the oppressive heat. The building was small, with a modest front desk where an older woman sat, and an equally elderly man stood behind her, silently rummaging through a filing cabinet near the window.

The woman greeted me with a warm smile, her accent matching the one I'd heard from the women in front of the library. She shuffled the papers in front of her quickly, gathering them into a neat pile before she let her hands rest in her lap. My gaze drifted to the bright red of her fingernails, the same shade as the lipstick smudged at the corners of her lips—slightly overlined, as if applied in a rush this morning. "Hello, Miss. What can I do for you?"

I dropped my purse onto the counter and pulled my suitcases to my side. "Hello. I'm trying to get a ride to Clinton. I had a cab from Raleigh, but he said he could only take me so far. He dropped me off a few miles outside of town. I've walked over an hour to get here and still have a long way to go." I tried to keep my voice steady, but a hint of frustration slipped through. Rationally, I knew it wasn't her fault I was stranded, but the annoyance still crept in. "So, can you help me get a cab to Clinton?"

I noticed the small badge on her sweater that read "Joan," and her eyes softened as she listened to me. She placed a hand gently to her throat, resting on the pearl necklace she had there.

"My, what a hard day you've had." She smiled kindly, though the faintest amusement danced at the edges of her voice. "I'm so sorry, Sweetheart, but there aren't any cabs outside the big cities. Not much use for them out here." She chuckled lightly, as if this was common knowledge, like I should have known better.

"What about an Uber? Is that an option?" I asked, but Joan just stared at me blankly. I sighed, answering my own question. "No Ubers."

"No, but I bet we can get someone to give you a ride or you can wait for the bus," Joan said, waving her arm toward the back. The man who had been lingering there since I walked in finally looked up. His wrinkles seemed to match line for line to hers, particularly the deep creases around their eyes. Those lines were the deepest on their faces, hinting at a lifetime of smiles or squinting into the sun.

Joan turned to him, speaking as if I wasn't standing right in front of her. "Is Colton heading back to Clinton anytime soon? This young lady here needs a ride." Her tone suddenly laced with snark.

The man scratched the back of his balding head, clearly pondering Joan's question. "I think he was planning on sticking around here for a few days, but I can ask him if he's willing to make the drive—"

I cut him off, already pulling my wallet from my purse and rummaging for the cash I'd stashed there that morning before my flight. "I'll pay him for his time, and for the cost of gas. I know this is an inconvenience for him."

Both of them let out a small gasp, but it was Joan who responded, her offense clear in her voice. "Miss, that won't be necessary. The Sampson County officers would never take a bribe. It's their job to protect and to serve the community."

"It wouldn't be a bribe," I retorted, still holding out my wallet with the cash visible as if it would entice them to see I was serious. "I didn't know he was an officer. This is just fair compensation for his time. I'm sure he has better things to do than drive me around."

Joan's smile returned, the previous snark vanishing without a trace. "Officer Bennett would never take compensation for a good deed. Let's get this figured out and have you on your way." She turned toward the man behind her. "Butch, call Mr. Bennett before it gets any later. We need to get this young lady moving."

Butch reached for the wall-mounted phone and dialed. His side of the conversation was muffled, but judging by the way he kept nodding enthusiastically, Colton seemed agreeable to whatever he was saying.

I pictured a short, stocky cop on the other end of the line, probably with a graying mustache and a voice that carried more authority than his stature should allow. Maybe he had a coffee cup in one hand, a half-eaten donut in the other. The kind of guy who had seen it all but still took his job a little too seriously.

"Why are you heading to Clinton?" Joan asked, raising a curious eyebrow. I understood her skepticism—Clinton was a small town with a population of just over eight thousand, mostly made up of family farms. It wasn't exactly a vacation hotspot, especially for a young woman traveling alone.

I picked at my cuticles, keeping my eyes down, hoping she'd move on if I kept my answer short. "I have family out there I need to see. I won't be staying long, probably a week at most, which is why I'm trying to get there quickly. I would've called, but I don't have service."

Joan smiled warmly, and I was relieved she let my vague answer slide without pressing further. "Well, that'll be just wonderful." She reached over and gave my hand a light pat, her earlier snark seemingly forgotten. "Would you like something to drink? You look a little parched after that walk."

The dryness in my throat was impossible to ignore now that she mentioned it. "Yes, please."

She disappeared into the back and quickly returned with a small paper cup of water. "Why don't you take a seat right here while you wait for Mr. Bennett to get here?" She pulled a stool from beneath her desk and offered it to me.

I took it gratefully, sinking onto the seat as the weight of the day pressed down on me. The walk had drained me more than I wanted to admit.

"Thank you." I downed the water in one go, only to be hit with a bitter aftertaste, something strangely reminiscent of hard-boiled eggs. I swallowed hard, forcing myself not to gag.

Joan watched me with an expectant smile. "Would you like some more?"

I shook my head quickly, fighting to keep my expression neutral. "No, I think I'm good. That was all I needed." In truth, I'd rather make that entire hour-long walk again than take another sip of whatever that was.

Joan simply nodded and returned to her seat, reopening a game of solitaire that I must have interrupted when I walked in. "This is always where it gets complicated," she said, moving her cursor over the screen to indicate two nearly finished rows and two barely started ones, with another row completely empty.

It was clear she was trying to fill the silence, so I offered a brief smile. "Do you play often?"

"We aren't that busy, so it helps pass the time." She clicked a card into place, then sighed. "The hard thing is, I always get stuck at this point. Usually, by now, I run out of moves, and a little animated deck of cards tells me to try again. Thank goodness restarting is easy—no penalty for failure."

I analyzed her computer screen and immediately spotted her next move. "You could move your king of hearts row to the left and create a new panel. There are fifty-two cards in a deck, with each suit having thirteen denominations. You currently know the face of thirty-four cards, and most of the ones you can see are clubs and spades. That means there's a high chance a heart or diamond is behind the king of hearts, which would let you merge the row with the two different heart stacks—or at the very least, support the rows beside it."

Joan gave me a long, calculating look, clearly not expecting such a detailed answer. "What should I do with the ace of hearts in my extra cards at the top?"

She followed my suggestion, moving the king of hearts, and just as I had predicted, a seven of hearts was hiding behind it. She added it to the first stack and managed to connect the row, allowing the game to continue.

"You can click on it, and it will move to the top automatically," I explained. "As more hearts fall into order, add them too. That'll clear space on your board and give you more room to work with."

Joan clicked on the ace of hearts and watched as it effortlessly moved to the top. I could see the subtle satisfaction in her expression as the pieces began to fall into place. "It's all about seeing the bigger picture," I added, "The goal isn't just to move cards, but to create pathways. It's like a puzzle. The fewer cards on the board, the more space you have to maneuver."

She seemed to consider my words for a moment before moving the next card. "I never thought about it that way." Her voice was tinged with surprise, as though it had never occurred to her that the game could be approached with such precision.

"Most people just react to the immediate moves in front of them," I said, my eyes tracking the cards as they shifted into their rightful places. "But if you think ahead, look at what's not visible right now, and anticipate what will happen next, you can make fewer moves and avoid unnecessary ones." I paused, realizing I might have sounded a bit too clinical. "Sorry, I tend to think in terms of strategies."

She chuckled softly, clearly amused. "I can tell. You've got a mind for this kind of thing, that's for sure."

It was true. I couldn't help it. Seeing patterns, anticipating outcomes, analyzing the steps ahead—those things were second nature to me. Sometimes, I found comfort in them. It was simple compared to the chaos of real life, where variables were unpredictable, and control wasn't guaranteed. But this? This game had clear rules, and I was good at reading them.

Joan continued with the game, the cards slowly falling into place as I had suggested. She looked a little more confident now, but I could tell she still needed a little more help to finish it. I didn't mind though; there was something soothing about explaining the strategy, about breaking down a problem into manageable pieces.

I glanced down at my watch and then back at her. Time was passing faster than I realized. I had made the walk here, and now, I was waiting—again. It wasn't something I liked. The waiting, the uncertainty. I preferred to keep moving, keep figuring things out.

A man opened the door to the town hall, wearing dirty, worn-out jeans, a sun-faded red t-shirt, and a black baseball cap. He paused in the doorway, scanning me with the same level of scrutiny I was giving him. My mind automatically cataloged the details and compared them to the average man I would have run into at home. The faded shirt, the worn jeans—it screamed 'hard work'. But then again, what did I expect? This wasn't exactly a city full of luxury.

I couldn't help but think how I probably didn't look much better. A long morning of travel, followed by a sweaty, frustrating hour-long walk, had left me feeling anything but put-together. I briefly wondered how out of place I looked in this town—too polished, too much like someone who didn't belong in a setting like this. Still, I had no choice but to be here.

"Mr. Bennett, thank you so much for coming down here. I hope we weren't pulling you away from anything important." Joan jumped to her feet, her smile wide, the tone of her voice shifting with a warmth that seemed to cross the line into something more. If she were forty years younger, I'd probably call it lust; at her age, it was more likely admiration.

I glanced at the man she called Mr. Bennett and immediately revised the picture I had painted in my head of him. Mid-twenties, fit —his biceps were noticeable even under the loose t-shirt. He was taller than I expected, and his presence had an edge that immediately caught my attention. In my mind, I had expected someone who resembled the small-town cops I'd seen on TV—perhaps a bit rounder, with a mustache that made them seem slightly out of touch. But here, in front of me, was someone who seemed far more modern. Attractive, even. That fact caught me off guard, and I instinctively filed it away without giving it too much thought.

He took off his hat, folding it neatly and stuffing it into the back pocket of his jeans. There was something almost casual about it, but I could tell it was a move he'd performed countless times. At least he didn't seem any more put together than I felt. The heat had clearly gotten to him, too, and I couldn't help but note how much better he wore the sweat than I did.

"I was surprised when Butch called," he said, walking up to the counter. He reached out to shake Butch's hand and leaned down to kiss Joan on the cheek. The gesture was casual but polite, a small-town familiarity that felt almost out of place in the cool, air-conditioned office space.

His green eyes cut over to mine, and the change was instantaneous. The warm energy he had shared with Joan vanished, replaced by something cooler, more guarded. I recognized it instantly—a shift in demeanor that felt like the kind of look someone would give a person they didn't trust completely. The playful glimmer in his eyes didn't fool me—it was a defensive mask, like he was sizing me up without revealing too much.

"Are you the troublemaker in need of a ride?" he asked, his voice laced with light sarcasm, though there was an undertone that made it hard to tell if he was joking or just assessing the situation.

"Troublemaker" seemed a little aggressive, considering none of this situation was within my control. I hadn't asked to be dropped off in the middle of nowhere, and I certainly hadn't planned on walking miles through the heat. If I had been given the option, I would've stayed in that cab all the way to Clinton.

"I suppose I am." I quickly decided to play along, forcing a confident smile to mask the irritation I felt beneath the surface. Rising from my seat, I extended my hand between us, waiting for him to shake it. When he did, I felt the rough callouses that only came from hard, physical labor—nothing like the soft hands of someone who sat behind a desk all day. But it wasn't just the texture that caught my attention. There was a warmth there, something that didn't come from the oppressive heat outside. It was a reminder of the kind of man I was dealing with, he was someone who worked with his hands and someone who likely spent more time on the move than sitting still.

"Ellie Monae," I said, making sure to keep my voice steady. "It's nice to meet you, Colton Bennett."

He seemed to be holding back some sort of quip behind his smile, though he quickly switched gears, delivering the kind of southern gentleman's response that sounded like it had been practiced a time or two. "It's very nice to meet you, Ellie. I didn't realize I'd be rescuing a damsel in distress today, or I would have come better dressed."

I held back the eye roll I was desperately fighting and fixed the practiced smile I'd perfected over the years. "Well, it's a good thing you don't seem to have been busy." The words came out stiff, and I could tell from the slight raise of his eyebrow that they weren't landing the way I intended. I quickly adjusted, recalibrating my tone. "Thank you for coming to give me a ride. I really appreciate you taking the time out of your day to help me. I understand it's an inconvenience."

The shift was subtle but noticeable; Joan seemed to approve, her lips lifting in a smile. I took notice of the smudge of red lipstick on her front teeth. Trying to be discreet, I lightly scraped my own teeth with my finger, hoping she would get the hint. She didn't, though, and instead turned toward Butch with a clear direction. "Butch, why don't you help Mr. Bennett take her bags outside so they can get on their way?"

The men quickly moved into action, Colton grabbing my suitcases while Butch took my carry-on. Colton extended his hand, offering to take my purse, but I declined with a slight shake of my head, tucking it securely under my arm as I followed them toward the door. Joan stayed close behind me, her steps light and quick.

As I stepped out into the bright sunlight, I remembered my manners. Turning back toward Joan, I gave her a warm smile. "Joan, thank you so much for your help."

She pulled me into a tight hug, and I awkwardly attempted to reciprocate, unsure of how to respond to the sudden closeness from a stranger. "Of course! When you're heading back out of town, you should stop by so we can say goodbye to you."

I gave her a gracious smile, nodding as I stepped outside into the blistering sunshine. The warmth of the day immediately hit me, and I couldn't help but think that I would not be returning to this city when I left. There was no point in feigning any more affection for a place that had been nothing but a pit stop on my way to where I needed to be.

Colton and Butch stood in front of a beat-up, rusted red truck, and I couldn't suppress a grimace as I watched them throw my expensive luggage into the truck bed. The soft thud of each bag landing was followed by a thick cloud of dust rising up around them, settling over the items.

As Colton dropped his arms back to his side, I noticed the shiny badge and the steel of his handgun tucked securely into a holster at his belt. He quickly adjusted his shirt to keep it covered, a small motion that seemed instinctive, almost as if he did it out of habit.

"You're in luck, Ellie. The drive to Clinton's only about thirty minutes from here, and traffic seems to be moving smoothly today," Colton said, his voice casual. He'd already angled the truck, so the passenger door was open and waiting for me, his hand extended to help me inside.

The door was open wide enough for me to glimpse the inside: a small pickup truck, with a faded tan bench seat in the front. It was as worn as the rest of the vehicle—dusty and covered in stray pieces of hay, bits of it clung to the upholstery. I didn't let my nose scrunch at the sight, but I couldn't help the fleeting thought that this would be more of a mess to clean off my clothes than I'd anticipated.

I refrained from commenting that the traffic between the two towns was probably always smooth, considering the population here was small enough to make congestion a non-issue. Instead, I took his hand and allowed him to help me into the truck, letting him play the part of the southern gentleman.

He quickly closed the door behind me, and the sound of it slamming into place was followed by the window slipping down a few inches, the result of its obvious lack of secure fit. Colton walked around to the driver's side and climbed in, the cramped cab leaving only enough room for my purse to sit between us. I opted to place it there; if I didn't, I would have ended up with my arm brushing against Colton's, and that was a situation I preferred to avoid.

As we pulled away, I glanced over my shoulder to see Butch and Joan standing at the doors of town hall, waving us off with the same warm smiles one would reserve for beloved family members. Their hands were poised in the air, an almost choreographed farewell. I turned back to face the road as Colton steered the old truck onto the highway.

The small town faded in the rearview mirror, and the reassuring signs marking the distance to Clinton—only thirty miles away— offered me a sense of relief that I'd be there soon. Silence, however, didn't seem to be Colton's preferred mode of travel. Barely a few seconds passed before he broke it with his first question. "Butch said you walked into Dunn. How far did you walk?"

"I walked for over an hour," I said with a wry smile, now able to laugh at the absurdity of the situation. Earlier, I'd wanted to cry. "My cab driver stopped on the side of the road and basically kicked me out."

Colton glanced at me, raising a dark eyebrow. "And what were you going to do if Joan hadn't been able to get you a ride?"

"Keep walking, I guess." I shrugged and turned my gaze out the window. The trees stood tall and straight along the road, their thick trunks unyielding to the heat. Small breaks in the forest revealed paths leading back to homes or farms. Despite Colton's attempt to fight the humidity with the AC cranked up, a small crack in the window let the stifling air seep through. "I only had so many options, especially without Uber service out here. Not to mention the lack of phone service to call for help. I figured if I just started walking, it would be fine. I'd get there eventually. One bright side is that I had no lack of sunlight."

"It is thirty miles; I imagine that would end up being about a six-hour walk. Maybe seven or eight hours, considering the type of shoes you're wearing." He glanced down at my heels, shaking his head with clear disapproval. "Don't you have anything better in one of your bags?"

"No, I didn't come out here expecting to go for a walk. Normally, when you hire a taxi, the driver gets you to your destination." I couldn't resist a quick glance at his boots, a snarky comment slipping out before I had a chance to filter it. "Your heels don't look much shorter than mine. I'm sure your walk wouldn't be any more enjoyable."

He let out a deep, unexpected laugh, and my eyes met his, surprised by the amusement on his face. He held a pleasant smile, though, as he countered, "Heels? Ma'am, these are boots." His drawl stretched out the word "boots" like he was trying to emphasize the distinction

Cowboy boots, in my world, were more of a fashion statement than a practical piece of wardrobe. Based on how beat up and dirt-covered his were, though, I could only assume he saw them as something entirely different.

I shrugged, choosing once again to focus on the view outside the window rather than keep eye contact with his dark green eyes. The way he stared at me made me feel like he could see right through me, like he could uncover all my secrets. "Call them whatever you want," I muttered, still looking away. "They have a flat toe and an extended heel, designed so your foot sits at an incline, with the ball of your foot elevated above your toes. That's technically a heel."

Colton seemed to reconsider his decision to keep talking and reached forward to turn on the radio. An old Blake Shelton song crackled through the static, just clear enough that we could recognize the voice. Without missing a beat, Colton slapped his hand against the dash, a loud bang filling the cab. Blake's voice came through loud and clear, much to my surprise.

He cleared his throat, a sheepish smile pulling at the corners of his mouth. "Sometimes, it just needs a gentle tap to reset it," he said, chuckling nervously.

I smiled, trying to ease the tension in the truck. "It's always good when you can figure out a way to make things work for you." The silence lingered, pressing in on us, and I could tell from his fidgeting that it was bothering him. I decided to break the quiet. "How long have you been an officer? The people at the city office seemed to know you well."

"Five years now." He shifted slightly in his seat, his cheeks flushed with a soft pink. His gaze stayed fixed on the road ahead, as if something might suddenly appear. "There are a lot of Sampson County officers who live in Dunn or Clinton. I just happened to be in Dunn today, and I'd already been by their office this morning to fill out some paperwork. So, they knew I was around."

"And which one do you live in?" The question slipped out before I could stop myself. I wasn't usually one to ponder aloud or pry into other people's lives, but something about Colton made me want to know more.

His smile remained steady. "A bit of both," Colton said, leaning back in his seat. He let one hand drop from the steering wheel into his lap, settling into a more relaxed position. "I grew up in Clinton, and that's where I still have a house, but my parents moved out to Dunn a few years ago when my dad handed over his farm to my older brother, Brendan. They wanted a change of scenery but still wanted to be close to the grandkids. Because of that, I seem to be up at my parents' house a lot to help them with things."

I tried not to scoff at his idea of a change of scenery. In Vegas, most people who retire move to Florida to get a sense of something new. I couldn't see how Dunn and Clinton could offer enough of a difference to warrant a move, let alone be considered "new."

"Does your brother have kids?" We had only exchanged a few words, but I couldn't picture him as a father—more like the fun uncle type, if I had to guess. The lack of a ring on Colton's finger suggested he wasn't married, unless he'd taken it off for the manual work he'd been doing today. Or maybe he was divorced.

He reached into his back pocket with enthusiasm and pulled out a wallet. Flipping it open, he showed me a photo of two young girls smiling in their matching leotards. "Oakley and Wren. Oak's five, and Wren's two. My sister-in-law, Lacy, is pregnant with their third, and the girls are over the moon about the idea of a little sister."

I sucked in a sharp breath, thinking of my own childhood with my sister and how chaotic our house could get. "Two young girls? I imagine that's a handful."

"I'm not sure if my brother will be able to handle it if this one is also a girl, so they're waiting until the baby is born to find out the gender." Colton chuckled, his eyes returning to the road, but it was obvious his mind was lost in a thought that brought him joy. A small smile played on his lips. "But the girls call her belly 'Lilly,' and every night they pray that it'll be a girl, hoping God will hear their prayers."

"I remember begging for a little sister once too. I think most big sisters just want a little baby they can treat like a dress-up doll." My sister Olivia came four years after me, and from the time I was two until the day she was born, I begged for a younger sister. After that, I begged for her to go live at our grandma's house, which never happened, despite my constant pleas.

He seemed to relax now that there was a flow to the conversation between us. "Did you enjoy having a sister?"

I thought of my younger sister, the last time I saw her with purple hair that drove my prim-and-proper father wild. "I do now. When we were younger, we fought a lot—mostly over silly things like clothes or toys. There was enough space between us that we actually missed each other when I moved out for college, which was nice." I turned the conversation back to him, hoping it would make me feel more comfortable. "Is it just you and your brother then?"

"No, we have a little sister too. Paisley. She's a junior at NC State, majoring in marketing with a minor in business." The pride he had for his sister was clear in his expression, just as it had been when he spoke of his nieces. "She's hoping to return and run the farm's marketing team to help further the business... that is, if she can't become a professional barrel racer."

I let the comment about barrel racing sit between us, knowing that was probably further into his life than I should go, considering this ride would be our only interaction. "I also had a minor in business. It'll definitely help open some doors for her."

He seemed to give me another look over, reassessing his earlier opinion of me. "What was your major?"

"Statistics. My father had recommended business for my minor due to the reliability of jobs that would come from having that on my resume." He hadn't been wrong. Working for a research team had been fulfilling and profitable. I could have seen myself being very happy there for a long time, but then my mom had asked me to join her in the small town of Clinton, North Carolina, for what she was considering a relaxing vacation.

"Are you close with your father?" He pushed for more information, his curiosity obvious. I wasn't sure I wanted to give it, but I could tell he wasn't going to drop it.

"For the most part." I pulled my phone from my purse, checking it again for a signal. No surprise there—still nothing. "Is cell service a myth out here?"

He glanced at me sideways, seemingly surprised by my abrupt change in subject. "Well, when you're out here on these back roads, there's bound to be dead spots. Sometimes even in town, it's spotty since we don't have a lot of towers. Lots of folks still have landlines because the connection's clearer."

I couldn't help but raise an eyebrow at that. "I would have assumed landlines were obsolete by now, given the widespread use of cell phones." My words came out with a bit of dry sarcasm, the kind of observation I'd made countless times in a city full of new tech.

He only gave me a look of mild amusement, clearly unbothered. The corner of his mouth curled up slightly, but he didn't comment, simply keeping his focus on the road.

The signs that we were nearing Clinton were like the ones I had seen when approaching Dunn. More farms dotted the landscape, and in the distance, a cluster of buildings indicated the outline of the town.

Colton straightened in his seat, his posture shifting from relaxed to alert. "Do you know where you're going, or do you want me to drop you at town hall? You can use my phone if you're still without service."

I recited the address mom had given me, and I noticed his eyebrows slightly raise. He didn't offer any further commentary on it, instead focusing back on the road, driving with an ease that contrasted with my own internal calculations whenever I was behind the wheel. I decided not to probe further, letting the quiet settle between us as the town came into view.

The house was on the east side of the main town, and I couldn't help but stifle a giggle as we drove past a store labeled *Piggly Wiggly* —it was almost too perfect for a place like this. Colton drove us past a string of small family farms before he turned into the driveway of a white farmhouse with yellow shutters. Matching yellow pillows sat on the rocking chairs of the wraparound porch, completing the picture-perfect scene.

It looked like something straight out of a Hallmark movie. It was so different from the sleek, modern house I had grown up in.

Colton hopped out of the truck and started hauling my bags out of the bed as if they were weightless, unceremoniously dropping them onto the dirt path without any consideration for their expensive labels. I grabbed my purse and scrambled out of the truck, nearly stumbling as my heels sunk into the uneven ground.

"Would you be careful with those?" I rushed over, gripping the side of the truck for support, and grabbed one of the bags from his hand before he could drop it into the dirt with the others. "They're expensive."

He gave me a half-smile, his voice dipping even lower into his southern drawl. "Ma'am, it doesn't matter how expensive your luggage is. Luggage is luggage." Since stepping out of the truck, his accent had somehow deepened, and his usual relaxed demeanor had shifted. The playfulness in his eyes was gone, replaced with a hard edge I hadn't noticed before. It wasn't just the way he stood, but the shift in his posture, like something about being in front of my mom's house had triggered it. "Dirty or clean, as long as the zipper works, it'll keep your clothes the same way."

"You might be right, but it's not exactly courteous to drag dirt into the house if I can help it." The proper part of me wanted to hold onto that polite expression, but it was a struggle. I grabbed the first handle and shifted the bag, so it was on its wheels. "If you just set them down on the grass, I'll take it from here."

Colton shook his head, the stubbornness in his posture evident. His expression remained firm, and the hard look in his eyes didn't waver. "I'm sorry, Ma'am, but I was tasked with getting you here safely. Seems only right that I finish the job."

He didn't wait for me to argue. Without a hint of strain, he lifted my heavy bags and walked toward the front door, leaving me trailing behind with nothing but my purse.

By the time I reached the bottom of the steps, Colton was already knocking on the door. He set the bags down at his feet, standing tall and solid before the wooden door. I couldn't help but take a moment to survey the back of him and found it just as pleasing as the front. His jeans fit his backside like they'd been molded to him.

I braced myself as the door swung open, expecting to see an older version of myself standing there. But as my mom glanced at Colton before turning her gaze to mine, I realized that the reflection I'd once seen in her was no longer there. Mom and I had always been parallels —tall and slender. Since the day I was born, we shared blonde hair and emerald, green eyes. But now, for the first time, I could confidently say I didn't recognize her and couldn't see my future in her eyes.

Chapter Two

"**M**om?" The woman who raised me had always been the picture of perfection. Her hair was always styled, her makeup immaculate, and her clothes were nothing short of high-end—always the latest trends, purchased the moment they hit the runway. But the woman standing before me now had a ponytail that ran down her back, no makeup to speak of, and a worn North Carolina sweatshirt.

She was unrecognizable, a stark contrast to the polished image I had known for years. I couldn't help but stare, my mind struggling to reconcile the two versions of her.

"Sweet pea! I'm so glad you made it. I was starting to get worried."

Never once in my life had she called me 'sweet pea,' but for some reason, with her new look, the nickname felt... fitting.

My mother pulled me into an unexpectedly tight hug, a gesture that felt like more physical contact than we had shared since I was a little girl. I focused on the space behind her head, trying to keep my composure as a man approached and extended his hand to Colton. "Sir, how are you today?"

The reason Mom had moved to Clinton was simple: she'd met a man on a widow-and-divorcee cruise, and in the span of a few days, had a whirlwind romance. With the captain's help, she married him on the spot. She didn't even bother coming home after that; instead, she sent me a packing list and an address to send it to.

In the two years since, we hadn't worried about seeing each other. She kept in touch with empty phone calls and photos documenting the moments she didn't want my sister and me to miss. Only now was I starting to realize how few of those photos had included any pictures of my mom.

"Mom? You look so different." The woman before me had clearly missed a few hair appointments. Her usually blonde hair now had streaks of silver, and the lines beside her eyes were more pronounced, evidence that she hadn't kept up with Botox in the last two years, which was unusual for the woman who once had a standing appointment when she lived in Vegas.

She laughed, as if there were some private jokes I wasn't in on, and the man behind her joined in. Mom reached out and grasped a strand of my hair, twirling it around her fingers like she used to when I was little. For a moment, she felt less like a stranger. "Yeah, I've changed a bit in the last few years. You'd be surprised at how great one feels after spending some time out in the sun."

"Spending the day outside in the sun? I don't think I've ever seen you spend time out in the sun." My voice betrayed the disappointment I felt. The woman who had raised me was obsessed with avoiding sun exposure—self-tanning lotions, trips to the spray tan booth, and layers of sunscreen to shield herself from the very thing that now seemed to be a part of her daily life.

She pulled me to her side, linking her arm through mine and guiding me into the house. "Honey, there's something about sitting out on the porch, legs stretched out in the sun. The warmth of it makes everything feel right."

A basset hound lay lazily on a thinning rug near the fireplace, looking right at home. Mom pulled me further into the house, past a large family room with well-worn leather couches and a television playing a football game. She didn't stop until we reached a spacious kitchen—white cabinets with grey granite countertops, all centered around an island featuring a pitcher of what looked like iced tea and a freshly baked blueberry pie. The scene screamed southern perfection, further cementing the image of a life so far removed from the one I'd known.

"Mitch was so sweet to renovate his house last year so I could design some parts to suit my taste. We kept the family room and most of the bedrooms as they were—this is where he raised his children, and we wanted to keep things familiar for them. It was mainly the master suite that we revamped, but I must admit, the kitchen was my passion project. I just couldn't leave it alone." Mom pulled open various drawers, eagerly showing me the features she had added, including a large sink and a new stove. She gestured to a faucet above the stove. "This is called a pot filler. It extends with hot water, so you don't have to carry a heavy pot across the kitchen. Such a lifesaver."

Mom had never been much of a cook when I was growing up. I could only recall two occasions when she'd tried to prepare a meal, and both times it ended with her ordering pizza for my sister and me after what she was cooking had burned beyond repair.

I could hear Mitch and Colton still at the door, their voices carrying through the house, and I struggled to keep my attention on my mother while the two men were still outside. Somehow, they knew each other—Colton just hadn't mentioned that when I told him where I was headed although suddenly the expression on his face when I gave him the address made a lot more sense.

Mom ushered me toward the seats at the island and pulled the plate of treats closer. She poured the drinks and placed a slice of pie on a plate before me. "Try this. I made it myself this morning in anticipation of your arrival." She reached over to play with my hair once more. "I don't know why you wouldn't let me pick you up. Mitch and I would have been happy to make the drive."

I shrugged, thinking about the adventure I'd had to get here today and how much simpler it would have been if she'd picked me up. A taxi had seemed like the better option when we planned the trip. "I figured I could take a cab and make it here without any issues."

"Then why did Colton end up bringing you here?" Mitch asked as he walked in, with a sheepish Colton trailing behind him. It made me feel better that he looked just as uncomfortable as I felt.

My cheeks flushed slightly. "My cab driver kicked me out just outside of Dunn. He said he'd already taken me farther than he should have and told me to start walking."

Mom let out a small gasp and reached for my hand, clasping it between hers as if to comfort me. "Honey, why didn't you call? I would have come to get you."

I nodded, letting my gaze drift around the pristine white kitchen she was so proud of. But if I had service at the time, would I have called her? She was still my mother, and you're supposed to lean on your mother. But as she held my hand, looking at me with unfamiliar eyes, I remembered—she'd never been that kind of mother.

Colton must have noticed the tension on my face because he jumped in to save me. "Ellie mentioned she didn't have any cell service on the drive. Maybe while she's here, you could look into a prepaid phone for her?"

Mitch flashed a wide smile, his salt-and-pepper hair neatly styled to complement the tan of his skin. "We can do that." He rested a firm hand on my shoulder, the same way a father might with a young child. "We'll run down tomorrow and get one set up for you. Or maybe we'll just move you over to our phone plan—one less bill for you to worry about."

It felt strange, the way he spoke about taking care of me as if we were anything more than strangers. We had met once or twice over FaceTime, but that was the extent of our relationship before today.

"Thank you, Mitch, but I can handle it. I'm only here for a week." I gave him my most gracious smile while subtly shifting my shoulder from beneath his hand. The gesture felt too much like something my own father would have done, and in Mom's new world, that somehow felt... wrong. Like I was being disrespectful to the man who had raised me.

"How did you meet up with Colton?" Mitch dropped his hand from my shoulder and onto the counter, his movements easy and unbothered. Without hesitation, he reached over and sank his fork into my untouched pie, claiming a bite as if the plate belonged to him. "Your momma makes the best blueberry pie in the whole state of North Carolina. You need to try a bite."

This was all so foreign to me. I could barely conjure up the image of my mother pulling cookies from a package, let alone one of her baking homemade pies with expert hands.

I quickly steered the conversation back on track. "I got out of the cab and walked to Dunn. Someone directed me to city hall, and an older man—Butch—called for Colton. Somehow, he just knew that Colton was going to be my hero and get me here in one piece." I watched him carefully, noting the way he seemed to stand a little taller when he was near Mitch, especially under the older man's gaze. As if there was something he needed to prove. "How long have you known Colton?"

Mitch let out a low chuckle and glanced at Colton, the warmth in his expression easing the tension in the younger man's shoulders. "I've known Colt since before he could walk. My wife, Rebecca, was close with his mother, and our boys grew up together. You'll get to meet your stepbrother, Mason, while you're here—they've been best friends their whole lives. Colt pretty much grew up here with Mason."

The shock written across my face was nothing compared to the realization sinking into my chest. My gaze flickered between Colton, my mother, and the man who was now—legally, at least— my stepfather. No wonder Colton had recognized my mother's address.

"I'm sorry, Ellie." Colton's voice was quiet, his expression apologetic. "I should have said something when I realized where you were headed."

I shook my head quickly, forcing a polite smile as I pushed my chair back and stood. "That's great you all known each other."

"It's funny, really," Mitch added, setting his fork down on the plate. "Fate has a way of bringing people together, doesn't it?"

Colton stiffened beside him, but I wasn't sure if it was the sentiment or something else entirely.

"Yeah," I murmured, carefully schooling my expression. "Funny how that happens."

I could spend hours dissecting the irony of it all—how a random cab driver's impatience had rerouted my entire day, leading me straight into the orbit of a man who, by all accounts, should have been a stranger. Instead, Colton was woven into the fabric of my mother's new life, raised like a son to my stepfather, familiar to everyone in this house except me.

Overwhelming anxiety settled in my chest like a weight, pressing heavier with each passing second. The walls weren't actually closing in, but my brain was cataloging every exit, every possible escape from the suffocating familiarity of this unfamiliar place.

I forced a polite smile, smoothing a hand down my shirt as if that alone could ground me. "Is there a bathroom nearby? I'd love the chance to freshen up."

Mom jumped from her seat and walked me to the bathroom, her hand warm around mine. The bathroom, just off the kitchen, had been redecorated to match the space she was so proud of—completely unlike the home I grew up in.

"Just join me in the family room when you're done. We have so much to catch up on." She squeezed my hand again, her smile soft but unfamiliar. Maybe it was the way time had softened her once sharp features, the new lines creasing beside her green eyes, or maybe it was something deeper, something that came with her new look. "Honey, I'm so glad you're here with me."

I returned the hand squeeze lightly before letting go. "I'm glad I'm here too." Not quite a lie.

I stepped into the bathroom, shutting the door between us, and finally exhaled. My hand dove into my pocket, fingers curling around my phone. Relief washed over me as I saw the signal bars flicker to life. I tapped Olivia's name, pressing the phone to my ear, whispering into the receiver like a secret. "Olivia, pick up. You need to pick up your phone."

Her voicemail came out loud and strong in her obnoxiously chipper voice. "Hi, you've reached Olivia Monae, owner of The Velvet Hanger. I'm away from my phone right now, but leave a message and I'll get back to you as soon as I can!"

I clenched my jaw, waiting for the beep before launching into a frantic whisper. "Liv, you need to call me back. Mom is on a whole other planet right now. She's wearing a sweatshirt, her hair is in a ponytail, and she isn't wearing a single drop of makeup. She stopped getting Botox. Let me repeat that for emphasis: No. Botox." My words sped up, each one landing with increasing hysteria. "She's baking pies, Liv. Pies. Like she's been possessed by a Stepford wife. I don't even know who I'm talking to anymore." I exhaled sharply, pacing the tiny bathroom. "Why aren't you here? Why am I the one who feels obligated to show up and play the good daughter? You don't seem to feel that pressure at all. My life would be so much easier if I could just adopt your way of thinking and let go."

I tried to remember the breathing exercises my therapist taught me for moments like this, but each breath I took felt unsteady, as if the air itself was too thick.

"I know why you didn't come. You were clear on your reasons," I murmured, my voice wavering. I focused on my reflection in the mirror, but the person who stared back at me felt just as foreign as my mother. "It's just... I'm freaking out. And it would be easier if you were here, going through it with me." I closed my eyes for a moment, trying to steady myself. "I love you."

I let the phone hang up, tossing it onto the small counter. My hands found the faucet, and I took my time splashing cold water over my arms, then moved to my neck and cheeks. The chill of the water helped pull me back into the moment. When I looked at my reflection again, I felt a little more grounded.

I wiped down the counter and sink, clearing away the water residue before straightening my top and slipping my phone back into my pocket. I hoped that she'd find the message and call me back soon.

Finding my way back to the family room was easy. Mom's voice floated through the air as she tried to convince Colton to stay for dinner. "Why don't we invite Mason over too? Then the two of them can meet, and you can almost be a buffer since you know them both now."

Saying that Colton knew me felt like a stretch, but I appreciated Mom's effort to make me feel comfortable.

"I could probably get Kenna here too if we push dinner back to seven," Mitch said. "That might make it easier on her—so she doesn't feel like we're throwing her to the wolves. We all know the combination of Mason and Colton can be a lot."

I'd met his daughter, Kenna, once—if a brief, almost forgettable phone call even counted as meeting someone. So, no, her presence wasn't going to change how out of place I felt in this group. If anything, it just added one more unfamiliar face to the mix.

As I walked down the hall, I let my footsteps fall heavier than necessary, a deliberate warning before I stepped into the room. Better to announce myself ahead of time than feel like I was intruding.

"Mom, that bathroom is beautiful." I offered a smile that I worked to keep steady and confident. I joined them in the family room, where they were all comfortably settled on the couches. The way they were positioned—relaxed like they'd done this countless times. Even Colton had leaned back into the cushions in a way that suggested he belonged. "And that kitchen looks like something out of *Home and Gardens* magazine."

Her face broke into a proud smile, the kind she only wore when she truly believed in something. Mitch mirrored it, his hand tightly intertwined with hers. "I'm so happy to hear you say that. I know it's so very different from the house you grew up in. I drew a lot of inspiration from the farmhouse's beautiful white exterior, the way the sunshine bounces off it. There's something about it that feels almost... angelic."

She had raised my sister and me in one of the sunniest parts of the US, yet in the past hour, she'd brought up the sunshine here more than once, almost like she was speaking of it as if it had healing powers. It made me wonder if it was more than just the weather—maybe she was associating it with something deeper. The wrinkles by her eyes, which I used to view as signs of aging, now seemed more like the natural growth of tree roots reaching for nourishment in the soil. It was strange, but in a way, it felt like she was evolving in front of me.

"Do you enjoy living here?" I could hear the fake smile in my voice as my brain scrambled to process the image of Jenifer Monae—my mother—baking, redesigning kitchens, and wearing an apron. It felt like a vision out of someone else's life, not the one I'd known.

Her face lit up with a large, genuine smile, and the wrinkles by her eyes deepened, settling into place like they'd always belonged there. "Ellie, I absolutely love living here! I'm so excited that you're here this week. I've wanted to share with you and your sister every part of my life here. It's such a disappointment that she couldn't get this week off to travel with you."

We both knew that Olivia could have taken time off if she really wanted to, but it was probably easier for her to say it that way. It wasn't lost on me that just last month, my sister had gone to Cabo for the weekend on a whim—no real plans, just the freedom to do it since her schedule was her own. It was typical Olivia: spontaneous, carefree, and always a little too detached from the responsibilities she didn't want to face.

"She's definitely missing out by staying home. You look good, Mom. North Carolina seems to agree with you." I smiled as I said it, and for once, I realized it was genuine. "Good thing we can call her often while I'm here. At least we can show her what she's missing."

Mitch clapped his hands together with enthusiasm, a loud laugh following suit. "Now that's the spirit! Alright, tonight we're doing it—a big ol' barbecue. Colton, if you don't mind calling Mason, I'll get in touch with Kenna. Once we get the kids here, it'll be a real party!" He jumped to his feet and headed toward the kitchen to make the call to his daughter. Colton, however, went the other way, his footsteps leading him to the front door, which slammed behind him with a soft echo.

Mom reached over and squeezed my hand tightly, a gesture she'd clearly picked up during her time here. "I love having both of them around, but I'm happy to have a moment alone with you." Her eyes sparkled mischievously. She glanced over her shoulder toward the kitchen to make sure Mitch wasn't about to walk in. "What do you think of Colton? Isn't he just the biggest cutie? Mitch always calls him his bonus son. When Mason's here, Colton's usually not far behind, especially now that his parents have moved to Dunn. It's been nice to have the two of them around. The house can get so quiet sometimes. We often do Sunday dinners after church with the two of them—sometimes Colton's brother and his family come over too."

"That sounds really nice." I could picture the halls of the house overrun with people—kids running around, their laughter filling the rooms. "Colton spoke a little about his family. They seem close."

Mom's expression softened, a hint of regret clouding her eyes. "I wish our family could have been that way. It's been so nice to feel their warmth. I hope you'll get to experience that tonight while you're here."

Mitch returned to the room, clapping his hands together with excitement. "Kenna's on her way! I also sent out a message to the other Bennett siblings, inviting them as well. I'm going to grab some pulled pork and buns and pick up some stuff for salads. Ellie, want to experience the legendary Piggly Wiggly? I promise, it's a once-in-a-lifetime adventure."

"The huge cartoon pig on their sign did seem like a can't miss moment." I agreed. The quote 'if you can't beat them, join them' came ringing through my head as I nodded along to my words.

This seemed to please them both. Mom stood up and raced for the backdoor, throwing on shoes while Mitch reached for his keys. Mom returned to my side with a purse in her hands. "You are going to love this. You would not believe the things that they have that most other grocery stores don't even think about carrying. Have you ever seen pig's feet? They have them on the shelves all packaged because people here cook them and eat them."

"That sounds disgusting." I felt my nose curl as I imagined Mitch planning to serve us that for dinner tonight at the barbeque, he was so excited about. Suddenly, I pictured hooves hanging out of a hamburger bun next to potato salad on my plate, and my stomach turned. "Is that something you eat often?"

Mom threaded her arm through mine, leading me toward the front door and out onto the porch where Colton had relocated. He gave me a small smile but mostly kept his head down, eyes focused on the main road as if waiting for something, probably Mason.

Mom walked with me to a nicer truck than the one Colton had driven me here in and helped me up into the back seat. "I haven't eaten it before, but Mitch has. Things like that, mostly the older farmers eat. It comes from a place of not letting anything go to waste. You'd be surprised at some of the things they'll eat."

Instead of getting into the front seat to sit next to Mitch, she climbed into the backseat beside me. "Mitch loves the small diners around here, so we'll go to them often, especially for breakfast. Sheep brains are on the menu, and people order it like it's a side of hash-browns. It's completely normal."

Something resembling Frankenstein's brain popped into my mind, sitting on the middle of a plate with a garnish of basil on top as if it were a delicacy.

"How do you sit near someone eating that? I'd worry it would ruin my appetite." I was slightly afraid my face would stay in a permanent curl if we stayed on this topic.

Mom winked in my direction. "It's all about fooling yourself. Usually, it's cooked up like slightly white scrambled eggs, and I already don't eat scrambled eggs, so it's probably a little easier for me than it would be for others. I'd hate to be the sucker whose meal got mixed up with someone else's."

Mitch hopped into the driver's seat and immediately put the car into reverse, not questioning why Mom had settled in the back with me.

With the windows rolled up, the humidity eased, but it left behind a lingering heaviness. To combat it, Mitch cranked the air conditioner all the way up, sending an arctic blast through the car. Goosebumps prickled along my arms in response.

"Colton's going to stay here and wait for the kids while we hit up the Piggly Wiggly," Mitch said, his attention fixed on the road.

He drove while Mom kept up a steady stream of conversation, pointing out different buildings as we passed. A lot of them were old houses, now repurposed into small businesses—something I hadn't expected. Back home in Vegas, construction was constant, every new shopping center boasting sleek, modern designs, eagerly anticipated by the crowds. But here, there was no rush for the latest chain store. Every shop Mom pointed out had the kind of charm that came with time, history, and the kind of community that held onto its roots.

"We'll have to go there sometime this week. They have some of the most beautiful jewelry, all handmade." A large sign with hand-painted necklaces and bracelets hung at the front. "The woman who owns it grew up with Mitch. That was also the first job Kenna ever had."

"We'll have to add it to our list of places to go." As I spoke, Mitch pulled into the Piggly Wiggly and parked his large truck.

The three of us got out in one smooth motion, and Mitch grabbed a cart, leading the way as we walked into the store. The large sign hung front and center as we passed beneath it, and its eyes seemed to follow me as I moved.

"Ellie, why don't we head to the back and get the meat?" Mom asked. "Then I can show you all the extra items our grocery store has to offer."

It seemed to be a pattern for Mom to link her arm through mine as we walked, as if she was afraid that I might slip away from her after our two years apart. She did it again, steering me gently toward the back of the store. The familiar touch was both comforting and a bit unsettling—like I was a child again, being guided through life.

Mom asked Mitch to add things to our cart—chocolate Pop-Tarts, crunchy peanut butter—my childhood favorites. This, despite my reminder that I tried to eat cleaner these days. But that didn't stop her.

She reached up, brushing her fingers through my hair, lingering just a second too long. "I just want to have them here, just in case you want them," she said, her voice warm, sweet.

I recognized what this was—her way of holding on to a version of me that no longer existed. A quiet refusal to acknowledge that I had changed. That, to her, I was still the kid who curled up on the couch with a Pop-Tart and a jar of peanut butter after a long day.

I let the thought settle without correcting her. "Thanks, Mom," I murmured. If keeping those snacks in the pantry made her feel closer to me, then what was the harm?

"This is it. Look here." Mom gestured excitedly as she pulled me over to the deli at the back. The glass case before us held a disturbing array of fresh meats. I couldn't help but notice the familiar red-and-white checkered design along the bottom of the case, and my mind immediately cataloged it as a link to the past. It was the same pattern from the grocery store down the street from our house growing up. I could almost hear the echo of Olivia and me, skipping over the white squares like a game. Funny how the mind clings to these small details, trying to recreate a sense of normalcy in an environment that felt anything but.

"Brains, feet, tongue, and more," Mom said, her voice filled with a strange hometown pride. "These are all fresh and can be made into sandwiches. And over there, we have the packaged ones in the back, ready to cook."

I couldn't look away from the display. My mind raced to catalog the options—dissecting the familiarity of these foods in this environment, trying to make sense of it all. But it didn't feel like it fit. I wasn't sure if I was more disgusted or fascinated. I clenched my jaw and pushed the thoughts back, unwilling to admit how unsettling it was to be here, seeing things I'd never thought I'd have to analyze.

An older man in a white apron appeared behind the counter, his bright smile almost too wide as he walked toward us. He placed his hands on top of the glass case, leaning in so we could hear him better. "What can I get you? We do samples of anything that looks good."

My mind immediately ran through the possibilities. Samples of brains, feet, or tongue? What would that even taste like? My stomach churned at the thought, but I quickly rationalized that I wouldn't have to eat it.

Nothing looked appetizing, but I couldn't just say that. My brain quickly cycled through several responses—should I politely decline? Should I fake interest? I chose to smile as brightly as possible, focusing on keeping my expression neutral. "Thank you, but I think I'm fine."

The deli worker sat back on his heels, clearly unsure of how to move forward. His hesitation was clear and that made me even more aware of how I must appear in this environment. I quickly shifted my approach, my mind calculating the safest path forward.

"I'm in town visiting, and I haven't seen any food like this before." I watched his face closely as I spoke. "What do you usually sell the most of?"

I phrased it like a simple question, but I was really trying to gauge the situation. The more I observed, the more I realized how out of my element I felt in this small-town grocery store. My brain sifted through these thoughts at lightning speed, but I kept my face carefully composed, maintaining a polite curiosity.

He gave a big smile back to me, leaning his sun-aged arms against the glass, closing the distance between us. His smile was wide, but I couldn't help but notice the wear on his skin, the deep lines that spoke of years spent working under the sun. "A pulled pork sandwich is always a big seller, but I don't have to tell you that Carolina barbeque is always a good seller." His voice was warm, but his grin was a little too eager.

He let out a large, unexpected laugh, and I instinctively took a step back, my brain immediately registering the shift in the dynamic. His skeptical gaze followed, as if he knew I was analyzing his words.

"Or maybe I do. Maybe you should try it?"

His arms shifted again, moving toward the glass, and the moment the lid lifted, I was hit with the sour tang of vinegar. My nose wrinkled in reflex as my mind began categorizing the scent as the famous barbeque that they all spoke so highly about.

I quickly processed my options, weighing my discomfort against the situation. The smell was strong, almost overwhelming, but I didn't want to seem rude. So instead, I kept my expression neutral, pushing my feelings aside.

A strong hand slapped down onto my shoulder in a manner that felt almost parental. I turned slightly, finding Mitch behind me, having completed his rounds through the store. His comforting smile was a contrast to the intensity of the moment, and his hand gave my shoulder a firm squeeze, grounding me. "Hi Don, we'll take some of that lovely pork shoulder you have sitting in there. This girl here is from Vegas for the week, and we're teaching her our southern ways while we have a chance."

I noted how effortlessly he slipped into his southern accent, the way it seemed to fill the air with warmth. The south had its own language, not just in words but in how time seemed to move differently here.

Don, the deli worker, grabbed a container from behind the counter and began filling it with generous portions of the pork shoulder Mitch had asked for. "Vegas? That is far away."

The way he said "far away" made me realize just how different these worlds were. It wasn't just the physical distance—there was an entire way of life in the south that felt worlds apart from the frenetic energy of Vegas.

Mom played with my hair again, a large smile crossing her face as she glanced over to Don. "Very far away, which is why we are soaking it up to have her here this week."

The ease with which she interacted with Don, as if they'd known each other for years, didn't go unnoticed. It wasn't just a small town; it was a community. They lived through the connection.

Don finished loading up the container with the pork and handed it to Mitch, his movements practiced and smooth. "Why don't we send you home with some coleslaw too? Then you can really get the full experience of North Carolina food."

Mitch laughed with his whole body. "Yes, sir! Coleslaw will make this barbecue a real Carolina meal."

I wasn't sure how a scoop of shredded cabbage and mayonnaise could cement this strange grouping of people into a family, but I supposed rituals like these had their own kind of power. Maybe it wasn't really about the food at all—maybe it was about the unspoken understanding, the familiarity in these exchanges. Still, as Don loaded up another container with what looked suspiciously like pre-chewed salad, I struggled to see the appeal.

"Thank you, sir." Mitch took both containers from Don and placed them in our cart before turning his attention back to Mom and me. "Why don't we go find a watermelon to go with our pork sandwiches? Then we can head back home."

The three of us wove through the store in search of watermelons, and I fell into silence as I watched my mother inspect them with practiced ease. Mitch raved about her expert ability to choose the perfect one, going on about ripeness, weight, and the right kind of hollow sound when tapped. I studied the scene, trying to reconcile it with the version of my mother I had known for most of my life—the one who bought pre-cut fruit in neat plastic containers and considered grocery shopping a necessary evil.

Had she always known how to pick a watermelon and simply never had a reason to? Or had she learned this skill only after moving here, slipping so seamlessly into this life that even I hadn't noticed the transformation?

She celebrated after finding the best one, a triumphant grin spreading across her face as if she had won some kind of secret competition.

Mitch steered the cart toward the front, maneuvering through the checkout line with ease, as if the store were an extension of his own home. The woman behind the register greeted them with a familiarity that made it clear she wasn't just an employee—she was another person a part of their world. Within seconds, both Mom and Mitch were eagerly introducing me, their enthusiasm making it impossible to remain an outsider.

The cashier's smile was warm, genuine, and before I could even react, she was stepping around the counter to pull me into a hug. The gesture caught me off guard, my body instinctively stiffening.

Mom explained that they knew the cashier from church, which felt strange considering the last time we had spoken about religion, she had been comfortably agnostic. She had always seemed at ease with the idea that there may or may not be a God, uninterested in the debate enough to lean either way. Now, not only was she attending church, but she was going regularly enough to know the other patrons.

The humidity hit as soon as we stepped outside, thick and suffocating, as if the very air resisted movement. I slowed instinctively, feeling the weight of it, but Mom and Mitch walked forward without hesitation, completely unaffected. I wasn't sure if they had simply adapted to it over time or if it had never bothered them in the first place.

Mitch unlocked the truck and pulled open the back door for Mom and me. We climbed up into the back seat, the cool air still clinging to the upholstery, offering temporary relief.

"There were so many surprises when I first moved out here, especially in the way people spoke. It was like everyone had their own language. I swear, for the first month, Mitch had to translate half of my conversations." She gestured toward the cart stand where Mitch was making his way back to us. "Like this, for example. We always called them grocery carts, but out here, most people call them buggies. I remember the first time Mitch asked me to grab a buggy—I spent way too long looking around, wondering what kind of bug I was supposed to find."

Mitch pulled out of his parking spot with the confidence of a seasoned driver. His hand reached forward to flip on the music, and an old country song came on. His voice immediately started going along with every word, and surprisingly enough, Mom joined in. Her familiar voice found the melody easily, filling the truck cab. As if they were magnets, her hand found mine, and she squeezed it each time her voice got higher as if she was trying to pull me into the song with her. I chose to remain silent and enjoy the drive, watching out the window as hundreds of trees made up the view.

Chapter Three

Mitch pulled the truck into the driveway with the pedal nearly to the floor, probably to give the tires enough traction on the loose gravel. Since we'd left, a shiny blue truck and a yellow Jeep had joined Colton's red one, a silent announcement that my stepsiblings had arrived.

He honked twice, a familiar signal, before he and Mom hopped out without hesitation. I hesitated, my fingers itching to reach for my phone. Just one more attempt to call Olivia. I wanted her voice in my head before I met the stepsiblings—something familiar to ground me before stepping into yet another unknown.

Colton and a younger version of Mitch emerged from the house, summoned by the honk of the horn. Mason crossed the grass-covered front yard with easy confidence, his stride unhurried but sure. When we met face to face, he extended a hand without hesitation. His light blue eyes and blond hair made it clear where Mitch had started before time turned it all into a pleasant shade of gray.

"Ellie, it's nice to meet you. We're all happy to have you here," he said with an ease that suggested he was used to making people feel welcome. "Kenna's inside—she's excited to meet you too. Colt told me all about your drive from Dunn."

"Thanks for taking the time to come out here today for this dinner." I shifted my gaze from Mason to Colton. He quickly took the shopping bags from Mitch. Without missing a beat, Colton offered his arm to my mom, a quiet gesture of care as he helped her up toward the house.

"We should head inside and get this barbecue started." Mason gestured over his shoulder, letting me take the lead even though I was the outsider here. I could hear the rustling of plastic bags as Mitch grabbed bags from the truck. The father and son fell into easy conversation, exchanging brief remarks about the store and Mason's drive, both of which, after a few words, were deemed simply "fine."

Mom had left the front door slightly ajar, uncertainty still hung in the air as I stepped inside. I found Colton talking with a brunette girl in the front room. As soon as she saw me, her face lit up with a bright smile, and she walked across the room toward me. Without hesitation, she pulled me into a tight hug, just like every other woman I'd met so far in Clinton.

Her soft curls framed her face, and bright blue glasses perched on her nose, contrasting with her warm brown eyes. It was easy to see she must have taken after their mother, especially when you compared her to Mitch and Mason. She stood out with her own unique charm.

"Ellie! I'm so glad you're here!" She beamed at me, her energy contagious. "Your mom talks about you all the time, I feel like I already know you!"

Her bright, bubbly personality seemed to fill the room, and I couldn't help but smile back, the corners of my mouth lifting in response to her enthusiasm.

"She talks about you often, too." Our weekly phone calls usually started with work check-ins, then would drift over to Olivia, before moving onto Mitch and his kids. The calls were often just enough to fill up twenty minutes, but it always felt like a roundabout way to share updates on everyone's lives. "So, how's working with your brother?"

She handled the paperwork for the family sheep company while Mason ran the ranch, but beyond that, I never fully understood what their roles were. Mom didn't seem to either, judging by how she'd gloss over the details whenever she mentioned their lives. It wasn't just their lives she couldn't quite grasp, though. She didn't know anything about mine or Olivia's jobs either.

"It's enjoyable," she said with a light smile, her tone easygoing. "I didn't realize how much I knew about the business from all those years of growing up around it. Then suddenly, I was in it, and everything felt natural, which was a huge relief." She spoke as though it were the most comfortable thing in the world—definitely not the response I expected from someone working with sheep and looking this fabulous. "Dad's struggling to let go, though. He pops into the office a few times a week just to see how things are going. Honestly, it bothers Mason more than it bothers me. He hates the thought that Dad's waiting for him to fail. Mason prefers I do the office work since the paperwork was always confusing for him. Handling the animals has always been his thing. Your mom's been a good distraction for Dad. She keeps him busy."

"My dad also has a habit of stepping into my work when it's not needed. That was always difficult," I said, absently twisting the rings on my finger.

Kenna laughed. "Maybe it's just a dad thing."

"Do you live around here?" I asked, trying to shift the conversation away from her work. I figured it was a safer topic to navigate since it was something I could ask questions on. "Colton tried to break down the city when we were driving in, but he didn't point out many personal details."

Kenna led me into the kitchen, still speaking quickly, pausing only to catch her breath before continuing. "I live just outside of town. Some new apartments were built recently, and I share one with my best friend, Addie." She glanced at her watch. "She should be here soon. Dad never leaves Colton or Addie out of anything."

His welcoming nature made more sense now, especially how he seemed to fall into a parental role so easily, even though we had only met today.

We entered the kitchen, where everyone else was already at work. Colton stood by the counter, effortlessly slicing through a large watermelon with a knife that seemed almost too big for the task. Mitch and Mason were visible through the large windows on the back porch, tending to the grill, while my mom washed corn at the sink. The soft chatter between her and Colton was easy and comfortable.

"Jen, do you need help with anything?" Kenna asked, tugging me toward the kitchen sink, ready to nudge my mom aside if it meant having something to do. It was clear that idle hands weren't something these people were accustomed to.

Mom had slipped on an apron over her clothes, and the large chicken print on it was a far cry from the Chanel I had always seen her wear back home. "I just need to grab my pasta salad from the fridge. I made it last night for Mitch, and there's plenty left over."

I didn't remember her ever making a special Italian pasta, so that had to be another part of her new life that I hadn't been privy to.

"Why don't Ellie and I handle this?" Kenna suggested, picking up an ear of corn and peeling back the leaves with a practiced, almost rhythmic motion. Mom smiled softly, rinsing her hands in the clean side of the sink before walking toward the fridge to retrieve something. She moved without much thought, her movements efficient and habitual.

I, on the other hand, was already cataloging everything about this small interaction. Kenna's suggestion had been simple enough, but it was clear she was trying to make herself useful in the kitchen. The way she took charge of the corn so seamlessly made me wonder if this was something they all did often. I filed that thought away, my mind already processing the family dynamics—everyone had their role, even here in the kitchen.

I watched Kenna, noting how she peeled the corn with such precision. It made me realize how much I could learn by paying attention to the little details. The easy flow of conversation between her and Mom was another data point to consider—their rapport was familiar, almost automatic, and it made me wonder about how much history they had together, beyond what I knew.

Mom gave us a wide grin as she passed by, heading toward the back door to join Mitch outside. "Thank you, everyone. I appreciate your help. Many hands make light work, and you're all proving that saying to be true."

I heard Colton's voice from behind me, thanking Mom again for the meal. I noted that his words sounded different from the others. He never included himself in the thanks, almost as if he saw himself as an outsider to the family dynamic, though his actions suggested otherwise. I could tell he didn't quite slot himself into the familial unit as seamlessly as everyone else did, and I filed that observation for later.

I picked up an ear of corn, peeling back the green leaves. The movement was awkward at first—there was a specific way to do it, I could tell. I adjusted my grip, trying to mimic Kenna's smooth motions, but when I exposed the full ear, something caught my eye: a series of long, thin threads wrapped around the kernels, like some organic form of string.

"What about these little strings?" I asked, turning to Kenna.

"They're called corn silks," she explained casually, reaching over and plucking the ear from my hands with a gentleness that didn't surprise me—she was used to handling this task, clearly. "You just pull them off, or we can rinse them under the water. Let me show you."

I watched closely as she turned on the faucet, the steady stream of water hitting the corn with an almost therapeutic rhythm. The silks began to dissolve and disappear, much like she'd said. I analyzed the way they came off in the water—clean, effortless. There was something satisfying about it. I wondered if the process would be as easy on the other ears that I had yet to peel.

She took the brush from the counter, using it to scrub between the grooves of the kernels with methodical precision. She worked without hesitation, making it look simple, even though I knew from experience that it wasn't as easy as it seemed. I couldn't help but take note of the technique. Efficiency. Speed. Even the smallest actions here were well-practiced, like an unspoken system in the kitchen.

Kenna opened her mouth to say something but was immediately interrupted by the sudden swinging open of the front door and a loud greeting. "Hey! Hey! What's up party people?"

An enthusiastic brunette wearing bright pink glasses walked in, carrying a large box of overflowing flowers. The sheer exuberance in her entrance was enough to catch me off guard. She dropped the box onto the table with a dramatic flourish, causing some of the flowers to spill out and scatter across the counter like confetti. It was a move that screamed confidence, but also a lack of concern for the potential mess.

I watched closely as Colton immediately moved his work to the opposite counter, clearly anticipating the intrusion. I half expected him to show some frustration, maybe a roll of his eyes, but instead he greeted her with a wide grin. It was clear he was used to her—and perhaps the disruptions she brought. "Gosh, Addie, did you buy out the entire shop? Maybe you should have left a flower or two for someone else."

There was something about Colton's smile—relaxed, amused— that suggested his patience for the disruption wasn't as thin as I might have expected. It made me wonder how often this kind of chaotic energy appeared in their house and whether he was just accustomed to it. It wasn't a reaction I would have had—my tendency was to maintain control, keep things organized. This situation, with the flowers spilling out of the box, seemed chaotic, but they all handled it with ease.

Addie, on the other hand, didn't seem to mind the mess. She immediately started rearranging the flowers, her hands moving with a practiced speed that suggested this wasn't her first time working in a frenzy. I studied her movements, noticing the way she seemed to move with purpose despite her carefree demeanor. There was a certain efficiency hidden beneath her chaotic actions—she might look like she was just flinging flowers around, but I could tell that this was part of her routine.

I couldn't help but admire the way she fit into this family's dynamic—her bright, loud presence didn't disrupt it. It was more like she was just another puzzle piece clicking into place. I mentally noted that—perhaps being a part of this family meant fitting in with the chaos, not fighting against it. Something I wasn't sure I would ever be comfortable with.

She giggled, pressing her hand lightly against Colton's shoulder before reaching out for the flowers that had spilled from the box. She moved swiftly, tucking them behind everyone in the room's ears. When she got to me, she placed a rose behind my ear, its soft petals brushing my skin as she did.

"You must be Ellie!" Addie exclaimed, her voice bright and warm.

"I'm so glad that you're here! It gives us a good excuse to get together for dinner," she added, her voice full of that infectious enthusiasm.

I smiled politely, my mind briefly analyzing the cultural norms of this family and how these friends blended in.

"Thank you, Addie. It's so nice to meet you," I said, trying to match her enthusiasm. I adjusted the flower behind my ear. It felt a bit out of place, but I didn't want to seem rude by removing it.

Kenna, meanwhile, had already started transferring the corn into a large pot of water on the stove. I followed her lead, moving to assist as much as possible.

"How long do we cook the corn for?" I asked, my voice betraying a little uncertainty. I wasn't familiar with this process, and in a place where things were often casual, I felt the need to adjust to the rhythm quickly.

"About three to five minutes. So, we'll wait to start it when they're almost done outside." Kenna moved through the kitchen with practiced efficiency, pulling salt from the cabinet and butter from the fridge, each motion done without hesitation. It was clear she had done this a thousand times before.

"This is always Mason's favorite part," she added. "Don't be surprised if this is all he wants to eat—well, this and your mom's pasta salad. He's always been a picky eater."

Colton, Kenna, and Addie laughed, the kind of laughter that hinted at an inside joke, one built on years of shared experiences. I noted the ease between them, the effortless camaraderie that I wasn't a part of. It wasn't exclusionary—just natural. A byproduct of history. Still, the realization left a small, hollow feeling in my chest, a quiet acknowledgment that I was an outsider here.

Mom slipped back inside, moving with a quiet purpose. She greeted Addie with a warm familiarity before turning to me, her expression softening. Without a word, she reached for my hand, her fingers wrapping around mine. "Honey, why don't you come outside with me? I want to show you some things."

I followed Mom toward the grill, where Mitch stood in front of it wearing an apron that read, "Don't forget to kiss the cook." Mason stood beside him, chatting easily. Their backyard was an extension of the home renovations—an outdoor kitchen, a pool, a hot tub. Everything was designed for hosting, reinforcing the life Mom had built here.

Beyond the pool, a small fishing boat floated on the surface of a large pond. I shuddered, imagining what might be lurking beneath.

"Come sit with me on these beautiful chairs." Mom pulled me toward a set of white wicker chairs with blue throw pillows, nudging me until I flopped into one. "Can you believe we found these at a flea market?"

"They're great," I said, forcing a smile. It was strange to hear

Mom talk about thrifting like it was second nature. The woman who raised me had been more inclined to buy designer furniture than hunt for deals at secondhand shops.

"Mitch has me thinking about sustainability," she continued, gesturing toward a potted plant near the pool steps. "You wouldn't believe the treasures we've found."

"That's nice," I offered, feeling my interest wane. My eyes drifted past her, through the kitchen window where Kenna and Addie moved in constant motion, prepping the meal without pause. Meanwhile, I was sitting outside discussing home decor.

Mom followed my gaze but misread my distraction as enthusiasm. "Look at that vase on the table," she said, pointing through the window. A large white vase sat in the center. "Five dollars at a flea market. Can you believe it? In the city, that would've been closer to five hundred."

I nodded, but before I had to find another polite response, Kenna and Addie burst onto the porch carrying overflowing plates and bowls, Colton trailing behind with his own hands full. The conversation about patio furniture and thrift store finds dissolved, replaced by the sounds of plates clattering onto the table and Mitch pulling the last of the food from the grill, pride evident in his stance.

Watching him, I was struck by the picture-perfect moment. The all-American man, providing for his family.

Once we were all seated, Mitch and my mom extended their hands, inviting the rest of us to join. "Should we say grace?" he asked, his gaze flicking toward me, gauging my reaction.

Colton, seated beside me, offered his hand. His palm was rough, calloused—evidence of long days working outside. Mom, on the other hand, didn't wait for my consent, simply taking my hand in hers like she had all day.

I rested my hand lightly in Colton's, keeping my grip neutral as Mitch began the prayer. Heads bowed, voices murmured in unison, and I followed along, waiting for the ritual to end. At the solemn "Amen," I quickly withdrew my hands and folded them in my lap.

"So, Ellie, what are some things you want to do while you're here?" Mitch's tone was warm, his presence at the head of the table unmistakably paternal. "Your mom's excited to share our little slice of heaven with you."

I reached for the plate Colton handed me, the scent of vinegar-soaked pork rising as I used the tongs to serve myself a modest portion. "I came to visit my mom and meet everyone. That's what's important to me—anything else is a bonus."

Mitch chuckled, his accent thickening with pride. "Now, get a little more than that. The boys will plow through the plate before it comes back around and trust me—you're going to want seconds."

I gently smiled, reaching back out with the tongs to add a little more meat to my plate to appease him. "Thank you. With how strongly you've sung its praises, I'm excited to try it."

Mitch seemed pleased with the portion now on my plate, allowing me to comfortably pass the dish to Mom. I followed the natural rhythm of the table, mirroring the clockwise motion as each dish made its way around. Colton silently steadied each plate or bowl while I carefully took small portions, my plan forming in case Mitch questioned my servings again—I'd simply say I wanted to make sure I had room for everything on the table.

Thankfully, Kenna had started a conversation with him, which spared me from any more comments about my plate. Mom seemed pleased when I took a generous scoop of the pasta salad she'd made. The Italian dressing she'd poured on it had the same strong vinegar scent as the pulled pork, both of which made my stomach churn.

"So, Ellie, are we going to see you out on the farm tomorrow for some sheep shearing?" Mason glanced at my mom and gave her a playful wink. "What's that saying your mom always repeats? 'Many hands make light work'?"

I'd already had several bites of watermelon by the time he asked, so my mouth was full when I looked up to answer. As I quickly swallowed, all eyes were on me. None of them gave away whether Mason was being serious or not. "Excuse me. What is sheep shearing?"

Mason's face remained unreadable. "It's when we shave the sheep. The wool gets sent off to be made into blankets, clothes, and more. Your mom mentioned the time you took clippers to your sister's head, so I thought you'd be a pro by now and ready to lend a hand."

I couldn't help but cringe at the memory. Olivia and I had been young—seven and three—when I'd taken the clippers to her hair. It wasn't something I was proud of, but it had seemed like the only solution at the time. The gum that I wasn't supposed to have had gotten stuck in her hair while we were playing outside on the playground. I hadn't realized it had fallen out of my mouth until I was halfway across the monkey bars. By then, Olivia had been beneath me, happily playing in the sand, and the gum had dropped right onto her hair.

I knew Mom would be furious if she found out, so I acted fast. I snuck Olivia and me into the house and straight to the kitchen. That's where I found the scissors—sharper than the safety scissors in my schoolbag. I figured they'd work better to cut through her hair, even if I wasn't exactly sure how to do it.

I had successfully gotten the gum out of Olivia's hair and was using the scissors to trim it into an uneven bob when Mom walked in and freaked out at the sight.

She was upset with both of us, but mostly at me—after all, I was the one with the gum and scissors in hand.

It was a story Mom had retold countless times, so I wasn't surprised it had made its way to her new family.

"Yes, Olivia and I had some experience with scissors and at-home haircuts," I said, trying to sound diplomatic. "But I'm not sure I'm ready to do it again." There was no part of me eager to head out tomorrow and cut through thick wool if I didn't have to.

Mom came to my rescue, squeezing my hand. She giggled, probably recalling the chaos of that day. "Oh dear, he's just teasing you. No one expects you to go out there with them."

With Mom's words, everyone else chuckled, signaling they were all in on the joke. Addie spoke up. "If they were serious about taking you out there, I would've pulled you away. Between the two of us, we could've made up a good excuse for you to stay inside and make bouquets with me tomorrow."

Finally, an explanation for the large box of flowers she had walked in with earlier. She'd set it down so quickly, not saying a word, that I hadn't thought to ask about it. But I knew it would linger in my mind when I lay in bed tonight, trying to make sense of my complicated day.

"And why flowers?" I asked, trying to show some interest in my new stepsiblings and their friends.

Addie leaned forward enthusiastically, tucking her long brown hair behind her ear. I braced myself for a long explanation. "I've been working as a dental assistant for the last few years. It's good work. The dentist here in town took me on when he didn't really need two assistants. I think it's because I've made it clear from the start that being an assistant was always going to be a short-term thing."

"Why short-term?" I asked, taking another bite of the pasta salad, crunching through the bell peppers Mom had added.

Addie reached up, taking the flower from her ear and the one from Kenna. She combined them before reaching across the table for the flowers from Colton. Before she could ask, I handed her the one she'd placed on me.

In seconds, she'd turned the four flowers—daisy and roses—into a beautiful little bouquet. "I've always wanted to start my own business —a flower arrangement company, *The Bloom Box*. Right now, it's just a weekend thing, but my goal is for it to become my everything. I have a wedding this Saturday night. The good thing is the dentist's office is closed on Fridays, so I can work on the arrangements then. Thankfully, most weddings are on the weekend, so it takes up the majority of the weekend, but it's worth it."

"This is really beautiful," I said, carefully setting the bouquet in my water cup on the table to keep it from wilting. "You really have a talent for this."

She continued talking about the wedding she was working on for

Saturday, and thankfully, Kenna took over the other half of the conversation, letting me sit back and tackle the massive pile of food still on my plate.

The pulled pork, which Mitch had proudly declared to be a North Carolina staple, was soaked in vinegar. While the smell had been aggressive, the taste was softer although I could still feel it burn down my throat, and instantly, I regretted giving up my water for the bouquet. I tried to clear my throat, but the burn remained.

Then Colton's leg bumped against mine under the table, and he gently nudged his glass of water closer to my plate. He leaned in and whispered, "I haven't drunk from it. You can have it."

I took the glass, lifting it to my lips before I remembered the awful taste of the water from city hall. My stomach churned at the thought, and I instinctively pulled the glass closer, sniffing the contents. There was no rotten scent, which was a small relief. "Does this have that egg taste too?"

Colton's lips twitched upward, clearly amused by my scrunched nose and disgusted expression. "No, Mitch makes sure the water out here is filtered. You should be fine."

I hesitated before taking a sip, mentally comparing the clarity of the water to the foul city hall version. To my relief, it was just normal water—clean and neutral, with no egg taste to complicate things. I gave him a grateful smile before returning to my meal, mentally cataloging the differences between the water and setting a mental reminder to ask whenever offered water.

As I continued eating, I noticed that Colton kept his knees deliberately away from mine, and not once did they cross over again. It was a subtle shift, but the intention was clear: the contact hadn't been accidental.

We continued through dinner, a mix of scattered conversation as one person would bring up a new topic. They were all so gracious, trying to include me, but for the most part, I stayed silent, content to just listen.

It wasn't long before Mason and Mitch shifted to talking about work. The change in tone was obvious, signaling to the rest of us that dinner conversation had wrapped up and the real business was about to begin. Addie and Kenna, reading the signs of their usual routine, got up and started collecting the dishes. I followed suit without thinking, reaching for the plate in front of me before quickly grabbing the one sitting before Mom.

Mom's hand gently covered mine, stopping me from picking up her plate. "Colt, do you mind giving Ellie a tour before it gets any darker? It would be good for her to see around, it's so different from how she grew up in the city."

She kissed the top of my head before rising, taking my plate from my hands in one smooth motion. "The girls don't mind helping me clean up while you're gone. When you get back, we can all finish the night on the porch and watch the sunset."

A walk around the property sounded relaxing after the day I'd had, but it also felt like a trap.

I raised an eyebrow. "I think the walk can wait until later, don't you? I came here to visit with you. I can help put the food away."

She shook her head slightly, a twinkle in her eyes. "Yes, but I'll be here all the time. It's better to go with Colt. He'll show you everything while the girls and I clean up. Then we can meet back up, watch the sunset, or do something else fun."

With one hand on my back and the other on Colton's, Mom guided us toward the back steps leading to the pool. "Take good care of my girl."

Without waiting for a response, she turned and headed back to the table, immediately jumping in to help Kenna and Addie clean up.

Chapter Four

Colton immediately obeyed my mom's request and gestured for me to walk ahead of him down the back porch steps. I tried to think of something to say, mostly to excuse her strange behavior, but words didn't come easily. A few dozen feet down the path, I finally spoke. "I'm sorry she asked you to do this. I don't know why this walk is so important to her."

He flashed a pleasant smile, but it didn't quite reach his eyes. "She just wants you to feel comfortable here."

Instead of walking behind me, Colton moved beside me, his long arms swinging with each step. We stayed mindful of the narrow path, trying not to touch. His boots clomped while my heels sank softly into the grass, forcing me to walk on the balls of my feet to avoid stumbling.

After a few moments of silence, he reached up and adjusted his cap—showing his discomfort. He broke the quiet first. "So, what do you think of Clinton so far?"

I considered it for a beat, weighing my response carefully. "Interesting... That's probably the best word for it."

"Definitely one way to put it." Colton chuckled. "You said you were visiting. Why now? Jenifer's been here for years." He asked, his voice a little unsure.

I paused again, unsure how much I wanted to explain. "Mom's mentioned wanting Olivia and me to visit but never pushed like she has this year. I had some time off, so... I figured it was time."

To say that she was aggressive in her push for me to come visit would be an understatement. It finally reached the point where she threatened to buy a ticket and return to Vegas herself, and that's when I knew she was serious about seeing us. Her soft sobs came through the phone multiple times, and I couldn't ignore them any longer. That's when I caved.

I probably would have come out sooner if I could have convinced Olivia to come with me. I'd always been comfortable with the thought of visiting but was nervous to come by myself. I had no idea what I was walking into, and I hated the idea of doing it alone.

He nodded along, listening intently, clearly with the intention of asking more. "And your sister decided to stay home?"

"She doesn't enjoy the idea of small-town life, but more than that, I think she's still struggling with the idea of our parents not being together anymore. Mom's spur-of-the-moment wedding bothered her far more than it bothered me, which is why she's not here." It was the middle of summer, so the sun was still high in the sky despite the late hour, but I kept an eye on its position, knowing we'd need to turn around soon. "She doesn't remember the fighting. By the time she has any memories of them, their marriage had already sunk into this stony silence. For Olivia, that was a perfectly reasonable place for them to stay."

I could see why he was a good cop—he asked simple questions that somehow forced you to open up more than you usually would. If his questions had been intrusive, I would've caught on and shut down immediately. I wasn't one to share those kinds of details, especially not about my mom, but his questions set me at ease making me more willing to share details than I was used to.

Colton let my words hang between us as we kept walking. We

came up on an old red barn that had clearly been standing on this property for decades. He pushed open the door, gesturing for me to enter first.

"When Mitch's dad built this business, this is where it all started. They had a small house nearby, but it was torn down years ago." He flipped a light switch, illuminating the space as we stepped inside. Walking with me to the center of the room, he continued the tour. "When Mitch took over, he made a lot of changes. He grew the business, and helped a lot of others in the city expand too. My own parents made the leap to grow our farm because Mitch encouraged them to."

He spoke about Mitch with a hero-worship tone, and I could see the high regard he had for family and hard work—values my stepfather shared as well.

"This is just used for storage now. There's a couple of four-wheelers over there, and that truck Mason's been working on for months. He's convinced he can get it running for the car festival next summer." Colton pointed around as he spoke, making a complete circle of the room before gesturing for me to head out. He stayed behind me as we walked down the path toward a large vegetable garden.

"Look right there!" He gently grabbed my arm and pulled me closer to where he was pointing.

I followed his hand to see the faint flickering lights in the air. They reminded me of city lights, flickering as my eyes caught them. "What is that?"

"They are lightning bugs," Colton said, his voice filled with the same awe that echoed in mine, even though I figured he'd probably seen them countless times. "We get them here in the summer. Kids usually catch them in mason jars with holes poked in the lid. Keep 'em for a while, then release them."

"Do you have to go into the forest to find them?" I watched as more tiny insects blinked and vanished in the field.

Colton shrugged, his expression tightening slightly as if recalling a memory. "Not always." He placed a hand on the small of my back to guide me forward. "If you're lucky, they'll get close to the house. You can spot them from the porch. Usually, it happens if you've got a field or pond nearby. They like stagnant water, so as long as the gator, Prius, stays below the water, you'll see 'em."

The mention of an alligator in the pond made my skin crawl. That was confirmation enough that I wouldn't be venturing outside alone during my stay.

Colton kept us moving along, his role as tour guide in full swing. As we passed different landmarks, he explained each one. There was a sort of graveyard of old farming equipment—dumped when newer versions had been purchased. The largest of it all was a red tractor, standing tall beside a massive garden.

"They grow most of their own vegetables out here," he said, walking beside me as we neared the rows of vibrant produce, colors bursting from behind thick green leaves. "Cuts down on costs, and with soil this fertile, it'd be a waste not to use it."

"Do you have a cucumber patch back here? I swear I can smell them. They almost smell rotten." I leaned closer to the garden, but Colt's hand shot out and grabbed my arm, yanking me back behind him.

"Wait!" His grip tightened, and for a split second, it stole my breath away. There was a raw strength in his touch, in his words, that unsettled me—in the best way. "We don't grow any cucumbers here. They're on the other side of the field."

I raised an eyebrow, studying his face. "Then what's the smell coming from?"

"There is an old wives' tale," he said, his voice low and serious. "People say when you smell cucumbers, it means a copperhead is nearby."

His hand closed tightly around mine, pulling me closer to him. My chest pressed against his back as he positioned himself in front of me, protective. Quickly, he unholstered his gun, holding it pointed to the ground, a defensive stance.

"Ellie, watch your step. Look beneath you as you walk back to the path. If you see anything that looks like a branch or something brown, don't touch it. Alert me immediately and stay clear."

I had read about the various snakes to avoid, and copperheads and cottonmouths were at the top of the list. The pit in my stomach deepened. "What if it bites me?"

"We aren't going to let it bite you. We are going to get back to the path and then I am going to get you back to the house."

My strappy heels had already proven to be a stupid footwear choice for the day, but even more so now as I balanced on the toes and tried to be mindful of where I stepped. Colton let me hold tightly onto his arm as I walked toward the gravel path, his left hand remained clasped in mine while his right hand kept his gun trained on the ground.

I was still shaken, my heartbeat racing, but we managed to make it back to the path without incident. When we reached it, Colton didn't let go of my hand. I couldn't blame him; I wasn't sure I'd let go of him either. The fear was still fresh in my chest, and I didn't want to be left alone out here, even if the danger had passed.

"We should probably move a little faster, we don't want to run into any other creatures," Colton suggested, his voice calm but still carrying that undertone of urgency. He placed his gun back into its holster and glanced at me. "Here, get onto my back, and we'll get back to the house faster."

"Get onto your back? I think not." I tried to quicken my pace, now walking on the entire shoe, but the uneven gravel beneath my heels made that more difficult than it should have been.

"Would you just stop?" Colton gripped tighter onto my hand, halting me before I could get too far. "Why are you being stubborn? Get on my back, and we'll be back at the house before you know it."

His tone softened, but there was no mistaking the command in it. I hesitated, feeling a swell of pride in my chest. I wasn't one to easily accept help, and I certainly didn't want to climb on his back like some damsel in distress. But the idea of walking all the way back through this still-churning fear made my resolve crack.

I finally relented and nodded, moving to climb onto his back. He bent slightly to help me, and the moment I was settled, his hands gripped my legs to keep me secure. The contact sent a rush of warmth through me that was more unsettling than comforting. I couldn't help but notice how strong he was, his muscles firm beneath me, and I suddenly felt both small and safe.

As he started moving, his pace quickened effortlessly. I felt the world moving beneath us, the ground passing faster with each step, and it didn't take long before we were back beside the barn. But he didn't stop there. Instead, he kept walking, taking me deeper into the property, as if he had no intention of putting me down yet.

"Were you really going to shoot it?" I asked, my voice still shaky, referring to the gun he'd had pointed toward the ground. "The snake."

Colton glanced over his shoulder at me, his expression unreadable. "If we had to, yeah. I wasn't going to let anything happen to you."

His words carried weight, and it took a moment for me to process them. I knew he meant it. And the way he said it made something in my chest tighten, something I wasn't sure I wanted to acknowledge just yet.

Colton adjusted me on his back and kept walking. "If I could avoid it, I would. They keep the rat and mice population down, plus they feed larger predators that help keep them away from the house."

The alligator in the pond seemed like a big predator, but he didn't seem concerned.

"Why call the alligator Prius?" I asked, eyeing the pond ahead, relieved to be off the ground.

Colton laughed. "The gator showed up about five years ago. None of us had seen it before and left it alone. A property inspector pulled up, snooping around the barn. Mason and I showed up to give him a piece of our mind when Kenna called. She'd just pulled in and saw the gator attacking the Prius. By the time we got there, it had yanked the license plate off. The inspector didn't care about the barn anymore, so we started calling the gator Prius, in honor of it saving the day. Mitch makes sure the pond's stocked with fish now to keep him happy as repayment for saving the day."

He kept me on his back until we reached the back steps, where he knelt down so I could get off safely. I straightened my skirt, offering him a smile. "Thanks for getting me back safely and for saving me from the snake."

Colton grinned, shaking my hand. "This is technically the second time I've saved you today. Is this going to be a habit?"

I could tell he was teasing, but it still caught me off guard, especially considering we'd just met.

Before I could respond, Mom flew through the back door. "How was the walk? Isn't the property gorgeous? Tomorrow, we should throw on suits and lounge by the pool."

The idea of being near the gator in a swimsuit wasn't ideal, but I kept my smile in place. "That sounds great, Mom. I'd love to."

She guided me to the chairs and sat me down beside her. "I was thinking you should extend your trip. Mitch has a friend with a house in the Outer Banks, and we could borrow it for a family getaway. It's stunning out there. I know how much you love the water."

The lack of response from Olivia made Mom's suggestion to stay longer feel even more loaded. "I'm not sure if that's going to be possible. I'd need to talk to my work about the possibility of staying longer."

I had some flexibility with my job, but I wasn't ready to mention that just yet—especially not with Mom pushing me to extend my visit. The dynamics between Mom and I had always been easier with Olivia around. Without Olivia, I was left alone to navigate Mom's expectations, which, as I well knew, could shift at any moment. My gut told me this wasn't just a casual invitation—it was another step in her carefully crafted agenda, a plan I'd been maneuvering around for years.

Colton had slipped inside without a word, leaving me alone with my thoughts. A small part of me envied him, sitting on the couch watching a game with Mason and Mitch. The basset hound, though, didn't seem to care much about any of that, still in the same spot on the rug as he had been earlier. If I hadn't seen his chest rise and fall, I'd have sworn he was a statue.

You'd think I'd be used to Mom's methods by now—the gentle pressure disguised as casual conversation. My mind ticked through the possible outcomes. If I agreed to extend the visit, would it be enough to keep her happy for a while? Or would it just pave the way for more subtle demands later?

"You'll love the Outer Banks," Mom said, suddenly shifting into her tour-guide mode. "It's a fun, laid-back island. The Wright brothers first took flight there. There are beautiful beaches with warm, clear water. You can even take a ferry out to Ocracoke Island. It's where Blackbeard supposedly buried his treasure. People still try to find it."

She wasn't wrong, though—the thought of beaches was nice. And I did like the idea of being near water, something about it always helped me think clearly. But I also knew that if I agreed to this, it would feel less like a vacation and more like a trap wrapped in sunshine. My decision wasn't about the beach or the treasure hunts—it was about how much more of her agenda I was willing to sign up for.

There was little appeal to spending time on an island themed around a pirate, but Mom was so excited that I kept smiling and nodding along. I had learned long ago to play the part, even when the idea felt hollow.

Mom stayed with me on the back porch until late into the night, chatting away long after the game had ended. Colton, Mason, Addie, and Kenna eventually came outside to say goodbye. The girls were quick to offer their support, urging me to reach out if I wanted to hang out or needed anything. Their warmth was genuine, though I wasn't sure how much of it was genuine *interest* in me versus simply extending an invitation to be polite.

The boys were more low-key, offering the same invitation to call if I needed help. I appreciated the sentiment, but after the day I'd had, I wasn't sure I'd be leaning on any of them again, especially after having to rely on Colton twice. I'd made a mental note to handle things on my own.

I finally found the energy to tell Mom how tired I was, and she excitedly told me she'd set up the guest room.

"I worked really hard on it, for you and your sister. I wanted you both to feel at home when you came to visit." She led me up the stairs quickly, her pace making the climb easier since my hands were free— she'd asked the boys to take my bags earlier. My feet were sore from the walk to Dunn and the tour around the property Mom had insisted on. A row of closed doors lined the hall, and she moved with purpose, guiding me to the third one on the left. "It has a bathroom attached. Fresh linens in the closet and soap in the shower," she added, pushing open the door with excitement.

The room before me was decorated with a blue and white comforter on the bed. A small couch with matching cushions sat against the back wall, my purse resting on top of it, and my suitcases were neatly placed on the floor. Gold accents dotted the room, complementing the blue and white theme. I recognized the style from Pinterest under the "Coastal Grandmother" trend, but I didn't think that was the right thing to say.

"Mom, this is beautiful." I picked up a gold shell-shaped ring dish from the counter and held it up, my admiration genuine. "Olivia would love this room."

Olivia would probably call it cliche, but that was a thought I kept to myself.

Mom came in close, kissing my head and pulling me into a tight hug. "I'm so glad you came to visit. My world feels almost whole now that you're here. We just have to work on your sister." She pulled back, her eyes shimmering with unshed tears. "I've wanted to share all of this with you both since the second I got here."

After one last squeeze, she left me to get ready for bed. As soon as the door clicked shut behind her, I grabbed my phone and called Olivia again, but once more, she sent me straight to voicemail. When the beep came, I didn't hesitate.

"Liv, you need to answer. Everything here is so different, and mom is... so different! I don't think you really heard me when I said she's wearing a sweatshirt, an apron, and a ponytail. And she's letting her hair grow out—Mom has gray hair now! Please call me back, or at least text me so I know you're getting my messages."

I tossed my phone aside and went to take a shower, letting the water wash away the dirt and sweat from my walk. But as I stepped out, the humidity immediately hit me again, even with the AC fighting against it. The straps of my heels had left deep indentations on my skin, and I was left with sizable blisters, regretting ever choosing them in the first place.

* * *

I should've known better than to agree to Mom's breakfast plans, especially after she mentioned some eat brains for breakfast. But I really realized how foolish I was when my alarm went off at five in the morning. If I were in Vegas, I'd get up and go for a run, but here, I only had the option of getting dressed and finding Mom.

I quickly threw on a pair of white shorts, a yellow top, and the shortest heels I could find in my bag, wincing as the straps rubbed against the blisters from yesterday. With the heat and humidity, I pulled my hair into a bun and dabbed on just enough makeup to hide the bags under my eyes from the lack of sleep.

Mom was standing in the kitchen with a mug of coffee when I reached the bottom of the stairs. "Do you want some before we leave?" She pointed to the mugs hanging above the coffee maker.

"Mitch will be here in about five minutes to take us to breakfast. You've got time to grab a cup."

I knew there was little chance she had caramel hazelnut creamer in her fridge, especially since the coffee in her own mug looked black. I didn't do coffee any other way. "I'll just wait until the restaurant."

Despite getting the same amount of sleep, her face was bright and happy, with no signs of exhaustion. She was barefaced, dressed in a floral shirt and jeans. The bright pink flip-flops were a surprise, too. She'd never wear something like that back home.

"You look beautiful this morning, Mom."

She squeezed my hand and pulled me closer, her fingers tapping a soft rhythm against my skin. "Honey, thank you. I just pinched my cheeks to bring some color to the surface and threw on some moisturizer. It works wonders." She touched my cheek, her voice softening. "You have no idea what a blessing it is to have you here with me. I feel like the luckiest mother in the world."

We shared a moment of quiet connection until Mitch walked through the door. "Well, look at these two beautiful women standing in my kitchen." His gaze shifted between us, and I couldn't help but notice the difference in his attire from yesterday—pressed dark jeans, a sharp plaid shirt. He had clearly joined Kenna and Mason at work today. "How lucky am I to take the two of you to breakfast?"

Mitch grabbed Mom's purse and held open the front door and truck door for her, his politeness making me feel even more out of place. Mom settled beside me in the backseat, holding onto my hand as if she was afraid that if she let go, I might disappear.

Mitch drove us up to The Waffle House, then jumped out to open the doors for us like the gentleman he was. He walked in like he owned the place, and the woman behind the host stand greeted him with a warm, familiar smile. She was an older woman with bright red hair—so vibrant it could only have come from a box. Her uniform consisted of a blue dress and a white apron around her waist. "Mitch and Jen! It's so wonderful to have you here this bright and happy morning!" She pulled menus from the box behind her. "And you've brought a new person with you today! Who's this cutie?"

Mom pulled me forward, so I was standing between her and Mitch. "This is my daughter, Ellie. She's visiting for the week."

Mom's excitement was contagious, and the woman before us soaked it all in, her smile growing brighter. "Welcome, Ellie! It's so wonderful to meet you!" Her accent was as thick as Mitch's. "Let's head on back to a table. Mitch, Jen, can I start you both off with a cup of coffee?"

They both nodded, and Mom quickly added a cup for me, requesting half-and-half along with any other creamers they had.

The waitress led us to a table in the back. Mitch stopped at every other table, introducing me with a wide smile. It felt like he was going out of his way to bring me into their world, making sure I felt like part of the family. We settled into the booth, and the waitress handed each of us a menu, though I was the only one who bothered to pick mine up. With so few restaurant options around here, I guessed they came often enough to have the menu memorized.

"Take a look. We've got grits and hashbrowns for our value sides," she said before heading off. "I'll be back with your drinks."

I raised my hand before she could leave. "Could I also get a glass of water with lemon?"

She raised an eyebrow, glancing at Mitch for confirmation. He shrugged. "Sure, Hun. But you won't want it once you try the coffee."

As the waitress walked away, Mom leaned in to explain. "Their coffee's the best. There's just something about it."

I had a hard time taking her word for it, considering that before moving to Carolina, Mom's morning ritual involved matcha, not coffee.

The waitress returned quickly, placing three mugs, a large pot of coffee, and a lone glass of water with a single lemon on the plate in front of me. "You're lucky we serve sweet tea, or we wouldn't even keep lemons around here." She handed over a bowl of small creamers. As soon as it landed in Mitch's hands, he passed it over to me, and the weight of guilt settled over me once again.

"This is all we have. If you want something else, you'll have to stop by the Piggly Wiggly next time you're in town. Or maybe run by Walmart and see if they've got anything in stock."

The waitress clearly thought I was being difficult, so I smiled politely, squeezing the lemon into my water and silently promising myself I wouldn't be a problem anymore. I didn't need to make waves —I could just stay in my corner and keep my head down. I wouldn't be surprised if she spat in my food if I kept pushing it.

Mitch and Mom placed their orders with ease, as if he had the menu memorized—probably because they came here so often.

The waitress tapped her pen against her notepad, an exaggerated rhythm that was unmistakably a sign of her impatience. "And what will you be having?"

"I'll take the side house salad, dressing on the side. Thank you." I kept my gaze fixed on the table, as if avoiding eye contact would make my request less of an inconvenience.

As I handed the menu back, Mom leaned forward, grabbing the waitress's arm to stop her from walking away. "I'm so sorry to be a bother, but do you happen to have a straw for her water?"

A white straw was dropped onto the table beside us, and I tried to express my gratitude with a small smile, but the waitress quickly turned and headed back to the kitchen. Mom, meanwhile, had already shifted her attention to Mitch, her head resting on his shoulder. He lowered his head to place a soft kiss on the top of hers, closing his eyes like he wanted to soak in the moment.

Even when my parents liked each other, they never acted this close or genuine. Watching Mitch and Mom together was a different experience—without a word, I could see how much they cared for each other. It made their whirlwind romance make a lot more sense than it had before I got here. The way Mitch looked at her, as if she hung the moon, spoke volumes.

"What are you still doing here? You're usually done with breakfast and back in the office by this time." A voice broke my focus, causing me to jump. I spun around, heart leaping a little when I locked eyes with him.

"Has Mason called you a million times for help this morning? Or is he holding it together? I don't think you've ever been this late to the office in your life."

Colton stood about five feet behind me, his police uniform standing out in contrast to the farmers in overalls and the women in casual clothes. Mitch broke into a wide grin and laughed loudly, drawing the attention of nearby patrons. "We had to let Ellie catch up to the time difference, or we would've been here earlier."

I couldn't imagine getting up any earlier, but from the way my mom nodded, I could tell Mitch wasn't making a joke at my expense. They truly must get up at the crack of dawn, like those farmers in movies. I glanced around the diner, taking in the older men and women, most of them well past retirement age. There were a few younger customers scattered around—mostly high schoolers—and I couldn't help but wonder what they were doing in a diner on a weekday morning.

Colton moved closer, standing beside where I sat, and I could feel the heat radiating off him like the bright summer sun. He gently bumped my shoulder with his fist, and my eyes drifted up to his. The muscles around his jaw tightened, his eyes flickering for a moment before meeting mine. "I imagine you needed to catch up on your sleep after your busy day yesterday."

I nodded, but my heart was racing slightly, the casualness of his touch throwing me off guard. Mom was watching us with narrowed eyes, glancing back and forth between us as though reading some unspoken exchange. "Colton, if I'd known you worked today, I wouldn't have kept you out so late." She gestured to the seat beside me, her hand outstretched eagerly. "Can you sit and eat with us? We'd love to buy you breakfast this morning."

Colton shook his head, the radio crackling in his ear. His eyes went distant for a moment, focusing on the voice coming through his earpiece. As soon as it stopped, he tilted his head toward his shoulder and spoke into the walkie-talkie, his voice a bit gruff. "Officer Bennett responding." After another second, he added, "I can do that. Put the call under my name and I'll be there as soon as I can."

The waitress returned as Colton was still distracted, setting our plates down with a quick pat to Mitch's shoulder. "Let me know if there's anything else you need," she said, though I could see the insincerity in her eyes when she turned to me.

Colton finally looked up, offering us an apologetic glance. "I better get back to work." He bumped my arm once more with his fist, this time lingering a second longer, as if it was a way to hold my attention. "What do you say about hitting up the rodeo with me tonight? I can pick you up around six."

Before I could respond, Mom was practically across the table, grabbing his hand as if she feared he'd pull away the invitation. "That's a perfect plan! She needs to experience a rodeo while she's here. It'll make the trip a success for sure."

I wasn't sure if a rodeo was something I needed to check off my list while I was here, but Mom seemed confident that it was, and Mitch only reinforced her enthusiasm with a nod. "Your mom's right. You need to experience a rodeo at least once before you leave. They're something special."

I could already feel my expression tightening, my attempt at a polite smile probably looking as forced as my enthusiasm. I had no strong opinions about rodeos—I had never been to one—but the combination of horses, loud crowds, and whatever it was cowboys did to prove themselves sounded like an event I could live my entire life without attending.

Still, I nodded along, giving the expected response. "That sounds great. I'm glad I'll get to experience it."

Colton's mouth lifted at one corner, like he could tell I wasn't entirely sincere. The way his eyes held mine made me wonder if I'd failed to hide my reluctance or if he just knew how to read people that well. "Great. I'll pick you up at six."

He flashed bright smiles at both mom and Mitch before heading toward the door. The second he stepped outside, Mom's hand shot across the table, gripping mine like we'd just received life-changing news.

"Ellie! This is so exciting! We have to go shopping and get you something to wear for tonight. A rodeo is always a great excuse to dress up."

Her enthusiasm startled me. I had never once seen her this giddy about shopping when I was growing up. In fact, the last time we had gone shopping together, she had rushed me through the aisles like it was a military operation, already mentally checked out before we made it to the register. But now, here she was, clutching my hand like we were planning the most exciting day.

Mitch nodded, though it was hard to tell if he was agreeing with her or just focused on his food—his fork was already halfway to his mouth.

"I don't think I need a new outfit just to go to the rodeo." I mentally ran through what I had packed. Something had to work. A pair of jean shorts and a plain shirt would do just fine. I'd even managed to get by in my heels so far, despite Colton's insistence they were an accident waiting to happen. "I'm sure I have something in my suitcase that will work."

Mom either didn't hear me or chose to ignore me entirely, her thoughts already racing toward a shopping trip. "We should call the girls. They'd love an excuse to get out of work and go shopping with us."

Her words weren't directed at me anymore. The moment had already moved past me, slipping out of my grasp. I had come here to reconnect with her, but somehow, everything she did made me feel more like an outsider.

Addie seemed completely absorbed in starting her business, and while Kenna might have been able to get away from work, that didn't mean she wanted to.

"I'm not sure that's a good idea. I don't need to buy anything for tonight." I tried once more to reason with Mom, but she was already planning out the details, her excitement carrying her forward as if I hadn't spoken at all.

Across the table, Mitch caught my eye and subtly pointed toward my fork. A silent message: Eat while you can.

Obediently, I picked up my fork and stabbed at my salad. The leaves were dry even after I emptied the entire tiny cup of dressing over them—something I normally wouldn't have done, but the lack of variety in the greens made it necessary. Back home, a house salad was a mixture of romaine, iceberg, and usually some spinach or kale. Here, it was just pale, limp iceberg lettuce that somehow lacked even the satisfying crunch it was supposed to have. It was a small thing, but it felt like yet another reminder of how different everything was here.

Mom went on and on about what a great experience the rodeo was, her excitement steamrolling over any chance I had to protest. I took a page out of Mitch's book, remaining silent except for the occasional "Yes," or "That's so interesting," mostly just to keep the conversation moving in the direction she wanted. It didn't seem to matter whether I was actually engaged—only that I was responding.

Mitch played his part with practiced ease, inserting his own well-timed phrases: "Wonderful," and my personal favorite, "That's great, honey," which he delivered every time with the same even, patient tone. Not too eager, not too dismissive—just the perfect level of detached support that told me this was not his first time playing this game with her.

Chapter Five

Mom went forward with calling Addie and Kenna as soon as we were done with our breakfast and back in the car. She did this even after I insisted that it wasn't necessary. She claimed it was because she needed the female bonding just as desperately as I did, but that seemed like a stretch, especially considering that once Kenna got to the house, Mom suddenly remembered she had errands to run.

She flittered off quickly, leaving the two of us standing alone in the kitchen. Kenna didn't seem thrown off by Mom's strange actions and instead gestured for me to follow her up to the bedroom I was assigned.

I hadn't been in town twenty-four hours, and somehow, Mom had orchestrated an entire evening for me—one that I wasn't sure I wanted.

"So, you're going to the rodeo with Colt?" Kenna asked as she sat on the edge of the bed, watching me closely.

"I guess I am."

"What brought that on?" Quickly, she backtracked, shaking her hand in front of her as if she were erasing the words from the air between us. "Let me explain. We were all going to go tomorrow night. Colt called Mason this morning and suggested that we all go tonight instead. I'm surprised that he's coming to pick you up—that makes it seem more like a date than a casual hangout between a group of people. Addie and I were about to offer to grab you on our way there, that is, if you even wanted to go. You don't seem to be the rodeo type."

We got up to the bedroom, and without prompting, Kenna threw herself onto the made bed, ruffling up the pillows until she found a comfortable position. "Colt isn't exactly the type of guy who does something if he doesn't want to. Don't get me wrong, I could see your mom suggesting that he take you, but I can also assure you that if Colt didn't want to go, he wouldn't."

That did ease my mind—slightly. But it did nothing to answer the real question: why had he asked me in the first place?

"I think he might have a hero complex. He likes to be needed." That might have been a stretch, considering I had only known him for a day, but based on what I did know, it wasn't entirely unfounded.

"Don't we all just want to feel needed?" Kenna didn't wait for a response before pushing herself up from the bed and walking straight over to my luggage like she had a plan. "Are you planning to unpack any of this? If so, now would be a great time. Then we could see everything you have."

I hadn't planned on unpacking. I wasn't planning on staying. Keeping my things in my suitcase made it easier to leave when the week was up. But Kenna seemed set on seeing what I had as options for tonight, so I walked to the closet and retrieved a handful of hangers.

We worked in quiet unison, each opening a suitcase and getting to work. Kenna took it upon herself to hang everything up, and I let her, already deciding that I'd come back later and rearrange them into a system that made sense to me.

When I stepped into the closet, she had already separated my clothes into two piles—one with the items she deemed appropriate for the rodeo, the other... well, everything else. It didn't take much to see that the second pile was significantly larger.

On the left, she had set aside the one pair of denim shorts I brought, along with a light-wash pair of jeans and two plain t-shirts. The right side, however, overflowed with the rest of my wardrobe, including all my shoes, which had been unceremoniously tossed to the floor.

"So, I'll wear these jeans and one of these shirts." I reached for the plain options Kenna had deemed acceptable, a black one and a white one. They weren't particularly exciting, but they would work. "And I can wear my black booties with it."

The black boots had a small wedge—so small that it was basically a flat in comparison to the rest of my shoes.

Kenna seemed to contemplate my words for a moment before clapping her hands together—loudly. It was as if she needed the sound to physically gather her thoughts before voicing them. "Okay. I still have some clothes in my old closet. Let's look in there, and if nothing works, we'll call Addie and have her bring over some options from our apartment. Jen said Colt is coming at six, right?"

I nodded.

She clapped her hands again, as if smashing all her thoughts together. "Then we have plenty of time to put this outfit together and get you all dolled up."

"How much time do you think we need? It's just a rodeo," I muttered under my breath.

Kenna didn't acknowledge my skepticism. In one swift motion, she was out the door, waving me forward like a general leading his troop into battle. Her voice rang out from the hallway. "Come on! We're wasting time."

Following her into her old bedroom felt like stepping into a time capsule. While the guest room I was staying in had been modernized to match the rest of the house, this space had apparently been left untouched.

Pink carpet covered the floor, blending seamlessly into the

equally pink walls, creating a monotone effect that made the entire room feel... overwhelming. Even the bedspread followed the theme, though its bright floral pattern at least attempted to break up the pink-on-pink assault.

I stood frozen in the doorway, struggling to find the right words. "This is very..." I trailed off, my mind supplying only one word: *pink*. It was obvious my mom hadn't yet turned her interior designer skills on this room.

"I know. You decide at nine years old what you want your bedroom to be, and it never really changes, even if you want it to." Kenna gestured to the wall covered in posters of TV stars from our teenage years. Most of the boys were barely clothed, and a few even sported vampire fangs—a nod to the movie everyone was obsessed with when we were younger.

My gaze landed on the wallpaper border along the top of the walls noticing how perfectly it matched the bedspread.

"Mom and Dad told me I could only change the carpet or paint the walls if I did the work myself. Obviously, that wasn't happening, so I made my own small adjustments." She paused, then added, "Mason's room is worse. He still has *Teenage Mutant Ninja Turtles* decals. Donatello is so sun-faded you can't even tell his mask was ever purple."

Kenna walked over to the closet and flung open the doors with a flourish. She'd understated the closet situation. It was overflowing, mostly with large, sparkly prom dresses.

"Sorry about that," Kenna muttered, trying to push some of the dresses back, but the skirts wouldn't cooperate. "Your mom probably told you I did pageants. I keep the dresses here since they take up too much space in our apartment." She looked at them with a soft expression. "It's silly to keep them. I know I don't fit into most anymore, but they were a huge part of my life."

Mom had mentioned the pageant thing but seeing it in person— an entire closet dedicated to these massive, sparkly dresses—was more than I'd expected. It felt like a little girl's dress-up closet.

"That makes sense. If my mom had stayed in Vegas, I'd probably keep some things at her place too." I tried to make it sound light, but it came out a little too sad, like I was fishing for sympathy.

Kenna didn't seem to notice, her attention shifting back to the closet as she rifled through clothes. I quickly redirected, trying to salvage the conversation. "Do you like living with Addie? I've never had a roommate, so that would probably take some getting used to."

Thankfully, she took the bait and jumped on the new topic. Kenna clapped her hands together, eager to share. "It's so much fun! It's like having a sleepover every night." She continued sifting through clothes without pausing. "It's great. It let me leave home but still be in a safe environment. One of my favorite parts is that there's always someone to go places with. We'll hit the farmers' market, go to the gym, or catch a movie together. It just makes life easier to have someone else around."

In some ways, Kenna was describing what it is like to have a sister —something I hadn't experienced since Olivia had yet to return any of my calls or texts since I arrived. The last sign of life I'd gotten from her was a heart in response to my "landed" text.

I knew she was upset that I came, but ignoring me completely was a bit much, especially now that I was out here on my own.

"We could pair something like this with your jeans," Kenna said, pulling out a white top with the smallest puffed sleeves. "What if you wore this? You can borrow boots from Addie or me. Trust me, if you wear those black heels, you'll be miserable by the end of the night. Rodeos mean a lot of walking."

The shirt looked tiny, and given how much smaller both Kenna and Addie were than me, I doubted it would fit. Matching shoe sizes seemed even less likely.

"Try it on while I call Addie," Kenna said, tossing the shirt toward me before pulling her phone out of her pocket. I didn't move to try it on, still holding the shirt awkwardly, so she waved her hand in front of me. "Hurry up! We still have to figure out hair and makeup."

Chapter Six

I could tell the second Colton pulled up. The crunch of his tires against the gravel was the kind of sound that seemed to echo in my head. It wasn't that I needed to be reminded of the time—I could see the clock clearly from where I stood. Five fifty-seven. That gave him exactly three minutes to straighten himself up and walk to the door to begin our night at the rodeo, which was scheduled to start at six. His punctuality was probably a skill honed from his line of work, something reliable and dependable, but tonight, it was only making the whole situation feel more like a timed performance I wasn't ready for.

I stepped closer to the window, pulling the lace curtain aside just enough to see him. He was slow, deliberate, as he stepped out of his truck and adjusted the red flannel blanket across the seat. The action struck me as oddly considerate, a small detail I hadn't expected, but seemed that it was probably just another thing he'd done without thinking about it. People like Colton, I realized, tended to be careful about how they presented themselves. There was a method to every movement, whether he knew it or not.

He wore dark jeans and a green button-up—nothing flashy, but it still looked like he'd made an effort. I found myself wondering if that effort was for me or if it was just a routine of his. Neither of us had called this a date, but standing there watching him approach the door, the idea felt more and more of a possibility. He held his cowboy hat tightly in his hands and fidgeted with it like he was nervous.

Mom, of course, was already at the window, hovering as if she had front-row seats to her own personal drama. "He's here! And he looks so handsome. Aren't you a lucky girl?" She practically bounced down the stairs.

A small part of me contemplated going to my room and hiding under the covers. But, of course, I knew that wasn't an option. Mom would be on me like a hawk the second I even thought about retreating upstairs. So, I stood there, staring at the door, knowing I had to face it, even if I didn't feel prepared.

I glanced down at my outfit: the white top from Addie's closet, paired with her red cowgirl boots and a pair of bootcut jeans from Kenna. The boots definitely looked better than anything I'd packed, according to both of them. Kenna had promised the heat would be bearable once the sun set, and the mosquito and horsefly warnings felt like just another detail in the ongoing narrative of the evening.

Mom made a big show of spraying bug repellent on my exposed arms before tossing a thick jacket over my arm to complete the outfit, as if I needed her permission to be ready. She was taking every opportunity to remind me of the vision she had in her mind—a perfect, seamless evening where everything fell into place.

Addie and Kenna had both been vocal about their support for Colton and me spending time together, so I didn't bother voicing my hesitations. I already knew they wouldn't let me take away from their anticipation of how great this evening would be.. They were invested in the idea of me having a good time, and I could practically hear them telling me to go with the flow. Anything less than that would ruin what they hoped would be a positive experience.

As I reached the door, Mom stopped me, fluffing my hair to revive the curls I'd put in earlier. She reached into her purse and pulled out a lipstick. "Here, put this on your lips," she said, handing me a smooth rose-colored shade. *Juliete's Kiss*—her signature shade since I was a kid. It was the first familiar gesture I'd seen from her all day, and I allowed myself a moment of relief, as if this small act could bring me back to something I recognized. "Put it into your bag. Just in case."

"Are you expecting it to wear off?" I asked with a smile that barely masked my sarcasm, both of us knowing the real reason she suggested I take the lipstick with me. The unspoken implication was clear: Mom was hoping for some romantic spark to occur, something that would imply a need for my makeup to be touched up.

Mom nudged me toward the door, still trying to get me out despite how badly I wanted to stay upstairs and avoid the whole ordeal. "You never know. You'll get hungry for some of that good fair food, and then you'll need a touch-up."

Just as she tugged the door open, Colt raised his hand to knock but stepped back, clearly surprised when we had opened it before he could. "Oh, you're ready?"

His words were half-question, half-confused statement. I hesitated, mentally calculating how best to respond. Was it okay to be this casual about something that felt much bigger than it was? Feeling a little unsure in the borrowed clothes, I spun around, arms outstretched, hoping he'd appreciate the effort I'd put into getting ready. "Does it look okay?"

He gave a quick nod, his smile tight, and immediately shifted his gaze to the floor, as if my asking for his opinion made him uncomfortable. "You look very nice."

"You both look so great!" Mom gushed, her eyes glistening with pride. "I wish I had a good camera; I would pose you two in front of the fireplace for a picture."

The image of my high school prom flashed in my mind. My date, awkward in his tight suit and braces, had stood behind me, grinning uncomfortably as my parent's snapped photos in front of the fireplace. The memory still had a way of making my stomach twist. That had been awkward enough, but this? With Colton and I essentially strangers, the idea of a posed photo felt like a level of discomfort I wasn't ready for. It seemed like something you only did when you were already comfortable in a situation, not when you were still trying to figure out what the whole evening even meant.

"That's okay, I imagine Colton is excited for us to get there." I grabbed my handbag and pressed it into Colton's chest, gently nudging him toward the stairs. "There's just so much to see—the booths, the vendors, not to mention all the food we can try. It's probably best if we get going."

Colton gave me a confused look. "We don't have any time constraints. We could take a picture if she really wants one."

Mom's hopeful expression flickered between us, but I quickly shut it down with a shake of my head. "Don't encourage her. If you give her an inch, she'll never stop." I muttered the last part under my breath, continuing to push him toward the stairs. Over my shoulder, I called back to Mom, "We'll be back late. You don't need to wait up."

We made our way down the path to the truck. As always, Colton opened the door for me like a gentleman and helped me into the cab. "We could've taken the picture. I wouldn't have minded."

I had time to form a response as he walked around to the other side of the truck. The bench seat felt different today, the center console now occupying the space that had once been open. For some reason, that small change in the layout made me feel more comfortable. The truck shifted slightly when he got in, and the engine roared to life.

"I appreciate that," I said, choosing my words carefully, "but I know how it would go. She gets a little excited and then goes overboard." My mind shifted, finally landing on the topic I'd been working through all day. "So, the rodeo... what brought on this outing?"

Colton pulled out of the driveway, his hand resting on the headrest behind me as he maneuvered, using the back window to guide himself. His proximity made the cab feel smaller, and I could feel the heat from his body and catch a faint whiff of his cologne.

As he centered the truck on the road, he glanced at me, and this time, the look was different—more intense than the shy, reserved glance he'd given me earlier at the house. "You and Jen keep saying you're only here for a week. So, I figured we'd make it count. And I bet you've never experienced a rodeo before."

He placed his hand on the center console between us, and the small space between us seemed to shrink even more. I noticed that unlike last time, he didn't reach for the radio. There was something deliberate about it, as if he wanted me to be aware of him. I didn't know why, but I could feel the tension in the air.

"I decided that if you're going to experience a rodeo, you need to do it right," he continued. "That wouldn't happen if Mitch and Jen took you. Mitch would have you sitting in his box seats, all cushioned and comfortable. To truly experience the rodeo, you need to get into the nitty-gritty."

I had no idea what "getting into it" meant, but I kept my smile polite, the words rolling off my tongue without much thought. "Kenna said they were joining us. Is Mason picking them up?"

Colton nodded, his eyes still fixed on the road, but his hand remained between us. For a moment, I couldn't look away. His tan fingers, relaxed and confident, rested on the console. I had the sudden urge to reach out and touch him, but I pushed the thought aside, opting instead to look straight ahead at the road. It felt like the safer choice.

"Yeah, he's picking them up at their apartment. I wanted to get there early so we could talk to some of the riders before they do their thing. I also figured we could grab dinner at the fairgrounds before the rodeo starts. Maybe even play a fair game or two if you're up for it."

With each word, it felt more and more like a date. I tried not to focus on that. "We get to meet the riders? I thought they'd be too busy getting ready for their competition."

"Some will be," he replied, his tone casual. "But not many people get to go backstage. We've been given a VIP pass."

I tried to gauge what that meant, but he didn't give anything away. His eyes stayed focused on the road ahead, leaving me to wonder about the implications.

The rest of our drive was silent, but it wasn't the awkward kind of silence from earlier. This time, there was a charged stillness in the air, like static electricity that I didn't know how to handle.

Colton bypassed the parking attendants, heading straight for the large arena. As we neared the back of the building, dozens of horse trailers and large trucks came into view. He pulled up beside one of the largest trailers, the front emblazoned with a cute pink logo. Colton put the truck in park and flashed me a grin that seemed almost boyish, his excitement palpable. "Are you ready for this?"

"As ready as I'll ever be," I muttered, grabbing my purse and the jacket Mom had insisted I bring. Colton rushed over to my side and helped me out of the truck.

We walked toward the gate, and instead of presenting tickets, Colton got us through with nothing more than a nod to the security guard.

"Don't we need to pay?" I asked, a bit surprised by the ease with which we were being let in.

Colton chuckled softly, his green eyes twinkling with that same mysterious glimmer I hadn't yet figured out. "Nope. We're on the VIP side of the fence. I'll show you why."

As he reached down for my hand, it felt more natural than I'd expected—almost as if it were the most normal thing in the world. Though I could've easily followed him through the crowd on my own, his hand seemed to be his way of guiding me through. I gripped it tighter, the warmth of his skin spreading up my arm and sending an unexpected jolt of energy through my body. Wherever we touched, there was a sizzle—something I couldn't ignore, even if I tried.

We passed a few small booths, mostly for rodeo maintenance—

things like a water station and first aid—but Colton passed both without hesitation, as if he had a specific destination in mind.

"Do you know someone who works back here?" I asked, glancing around at the bustle of the crowd.

Again, Colton stayed tight-lipped. "Just wait. We're almost there." He seemed to enjoy leaving me in suspense as we dodged and weaved through the busy crowd of cowboys and cowgirls, each one with a clear sense of purpose.

He gave a single nod to many of the people we passed, a simple but obvious greeting that seemed to hold some kind of unspoken power. Not once were we stopped, despite neither of us looking like we belonged. Everyone else was either dressed in their work-worn clothes or their finest attire, including bedazzled buttons and embroidered designs on their shirts. It was easy to tell who was here to work and who was here to compete.

"Are those chaps?" I asked, astonished, as a man in maroon chaps walked past us. "I thought those were only worn in commercials or old Western cartoons."

Colton laughed at my reaction, pausing his quick pace to look at the man who was walking past us. I had completely stopped and was staring in surprise. "Nope. Most of the people who bull ride wear them—or those who compete in bareback riding," he explained, glancing around to make sure we were still heading in the right direction. "Come on, we're almost there."

He pushed past people with ease, stopping only when we reached a small trailer with the same logo as the one that we parked next to outside the arena. Colton pushed open the door with the same enthusiasm Kenna showed when rummaging through her bedroom closet. "Hey, Paisley, are you here?"

A tall, slender brunette popped out from behind a partition—likely placed there for moments like this when people might throw the door open unexpectedly. "Hey! Oh, my goodness, you brought someone with you!" She rushed over to me with a smile that mirrored Colton's, though her eyes betrayed her surprise at seeing him with someone beside him. She bounded down the stairs, stopping right in front of us. Enthusiastically, she reached for my free hand and shook it, her sly smile telling me she had noticed where our hands were still intertwined. "I'm Paisley!"

"It's nice to meet you, Paisley. I'm Ellie." I tried to match her energy, but her sunshine-like enthusiasm made it difficult. "Are you part of the rodeo? Those are some great pants." I gestured to her outfit—a black shirt with bedazzled trim and pants that had a glittering stripe running down the sides.

Paisley shook her head and gave me a playful, confused look. "No, this is just my casual look."

Colton rolled his eyes, clearly unimpressed with his sister's sense of humor. "She's messing with you. Paisley is a barrel racer. She's competing, which is a big reason we came."

Apparently, my face betrayed my confusion, because Paisley jumped in to explain. "Barrel racing is a rodeo event where a horse and rider race around a cloverleaf pattern of barrels, trying to make it through the fastest time." She gestured to her outfit, running her hand down the side of her pants in a theatrical manner. "The outfit's meant to make me stand out. If they don't get too dirty tonight, you're more than welcome to borrow them whenever you want."

I tried to picture the image Paisley was using to explain her event, but without any real success. The two of them continued talking as if I weren't there. Wisely, I stood quietly and took in their words, mentally sorting through the conversation.

"So, the rodeo? Feels very high school for a date," Paisley teased her brother, the sparkle in her eyes deepening. "Did you make sure to get good seats?"

High school for a date, I thought, raising an eyebrow. Was Colton really that predictable? Or was it simply his way of testing the waters, to see if this could become more than just a casual encounter? I couldn't quite pin it down.

Colton shrugged, not letting his sister get under his skin. "We only managed to grab some last minute because we originally had tickets for tomorrow." His eyes drifted from one side of the field to the other, scanning the crowd. I noticed how he subtly angled his body, ensuring Paisley and I were shielded from whatever he was watching.

He's hyper-aware of his surroundings, I mused, mentally making a note. It was an odd contrast to his laid-back demeanor. Why would he need to be so alert here?

"There you are!" Addie shouted as she jogged over, beaming from the inside out. Her feet kicked up a cloud of dust, and I saw she had traded her scrubs for a pair of jeans, boots, and a flannel shirt. Behind her were Mason and Kenna, both dressed similarly in a casual style that contrasted with the way they had dressed me earlier.

The group of three reached us, and Paisley greeted them enthusiastically.

I'm the odd one out again, I thought, but this time the feeling was less uncomfortable.

"Have you been here long?" Kenna asked, as Mason and Colton exchanged silent nods of greeting. I shook my head, and that was enough for her to keep talking. "We have some time before the rodeo starts. I vote we get some food."

"Food sounds great." I jumped in with my support, mostly because it gave us a chance to walk around. The way Colton kept scanning the area around us made me uneasy. *What is he looking for?* I wondered, glancing at him again, my curiosity spiking.

The group all agreed to explore, except for Paisley, who had to stay behind and prepare for her event. We said our goodbyes to her and started walking toward the rest of the fair. Addie quickly took on the role of my personal tour guide. "This is the backside of the rodeo. We go through the gate, and that's where the fairgrounds are. We can check out the booths and all the different vendors. They sell everything from makeup to clothes. My favorite booths are the ones with the different foods. I always suggest getting a little of a lot so you can try different things."

As she spoke, I observed the way the others moved. Mason led the group, with Kenna at his side. Addie walked alone, and Colton stayed by me. His hand hovered just above my back whenever someone got too close, a protective gesture I couldn't decide if I appreciated or found a little overbearing.

Is he doing this because he feels obligated? My mind ran through the possibilities. It wasn't the first time I'd noticed him looking out for me, but the feeling of being watched was something I wasn't used to, especially from someone I barely knew.

"What would you like to eat?" Colton leaned in so I could hear him over the music blaring from nearby booths. A jewelry booth played a popular song, and the sound was almost deafening.

"What do you recommend?" I asked, trying to focus. I knew the classic fair food—corn dogs, kettle corn, funnel cakes—but around us were large signs offering unfamiliar options. Cinnamon rolls, fried cheese curds, turkey legs? There were so many choices, many promising something I'd never tasted.

"It feels overwhelming to pick anything on my own," I admitted. My mind instinctively categorized the food options: safe or adventurous. I wasn't sure which route to take.

Colton pointed to a booth a few feet away. "Why don't we start with a corndog, then we can grab something else later. Gives you time to work up an appetite for cotton candy or kettle corn."

I wasn't sure how much else I'd be hungry for, considering how massive the corndogs looked in the hands of people around us, but I agreed and let him lead me toward the booth.

The girls and Mason headed off to a different booth, planning to meet us at the picnic tables later.

Colton helped guide me into the line, positioning himself behind me—a protective move, as if he was setting me up in the safest position.

"So, why did you become a cop?" I asked, trying to make conversation. "It seems like you'd be a farmer or rancher like your father and brother. Not that you're not a great cop." My words stumbled, especially as I noticed Colton surveying the area around us, his eyes scanning for anything unusual. He probably didn't want anyone overhearing this conversation. "I admit, I haven't met many people who've chosen that profession, but you seem to have all the qualities we associate with it, like those we see on TV. And you haven't stopped watching the people around us—like you're waiting for something to happen." Obviously, he had keen observation skills, but I had also known his loyalty.

Colton let his usual flat expression slip into a smile as his eyes shifted from surveying the crowd to meeting mine. "My grandpa was an officer. He loved it. Always talked about how honorable it was. So, when it came time to figure out what I was going to do, it felt like the only option."

He took a small step closer, his gaze still focused on me. "What about you? What made you choose your profession?"

His question mirrored mine, but I could tell there was more to it —something he'd probably wanted to ask since we first met, when we talked about Paisley's degree, and I'd casually mentioned mine.

"I've always noticed patterns," I explained. "They stand out to me, almost like they're trying to make themselves known. It's a useful skill when it comes to statistics—understanding how things work and adjust with different variables."

It wasn't so much a conscious choice; it was more like the profession found me, especially since it was a career path like my dad's. He'd pushed me in that direction, and at eighteen, it just made sense.

Colton's hand hovered at the small of my back as we moved forward in the line, keeping me shielded from the crowd. We stepped up to the window, where a woman with bright lime-green hair and several facial piercings leaned out. "What are you going to have, Hun?"

I hadn't even looked at the menu, since I had been so focused on Colton. I gave him a quick, uncertain glance. "Just order me whatever you're getting."

He nodded and ordered two corndogs, lemonade, and a couple sides of honey, then guided me to the side of the line. "We're number two fifteen. They'll call it out over the speaker."

"Why honey?" I was happy to try anything, but honey didn't sound like it would improve the corndog or the lemonade.

Colton stepped away for a moment to grab napkins and lids for our lemonades. "They're famous for this. You pour honey on the corndog. Paisley showed me, though she saw it on their Instagram when they announced they'd be here."

It sounded... strange. Sweet on savory? But I didn't argue, instead taking the food and drink from Colton when our number was called. I plastered a smile on my face as he led us to a picnic table near the back of the field. Mason, Kenna, and Addie were still getting their food at the taco booth, and I could spot their figures in the crowd, moving between the other booths and the smell of sizzling food.

"So... you really pour honey on the corndog?" I asked, looking at the massive corndog in one hand and the small packet of honey in the other.

Colton opened the packet with practiced ease, his fingers quick and sure. "Yeah, just a little, though. It's sweeter than you'd expect. If you don't like it, you can have mine, or Mason can grab you a taco."

I hesitated, studying the corndog like it was a science experiment I wasn't sure I was ready to conduct. I hadn't expected this from the fair—funnel cakes, sure. Corn dogs, of course. But honey on a corndog? I bit into it slowly, the warm batter and the tang of honey mingling on my tongue.

Colton watched me, his eyes not missing a detail. The kind of focused attention he always seemed to give—like he was studying a problem or trying to figure me out.

I chewed, trying to pinpoint what I thought. It wasn't horrible, but the sweetness clashed with the savory in an unsettling way. "It's... interesting." I said, trying to soften my reaction with a smile, but I didn't think it quite hit the mark. "Not my favorite, though."

He grinned, clearly amused by my reaction. "You don't have to keep eating it if you don't like it."

Mason, Kenna, and Addie arrived at the table just as Colton set the honey back down. Kenna wrinkled her nose as she caught sight of the corndog. "Eww, did you really try it with honey? Paisley has tried to get me to do that, but I just can't do sweet meat. Especially on a corndog. They're supposed to be savory, not sweet."

I couldn't help but chuckle at Kenna's dramatic flair. Her reaction was the opposite of my internal analysis, where I couldn't help but wonder if the sweet-and-savory combination could work with the right balance of flavors. But it wasn't the right moment to dive into that, especially not with this group.

I had to admit, though, Kenna had a point. The sweetness of the honey was off-putting, and I wasn't sure it belonged on a corndog.

"Do you want a taco?" Mason asked, pushing a full plate of tacos toward me. "I'm willing to make a trade or even share."

I shook my head, finishing off the rest of the corndog without the honey. Colton, on the other hand, was clearly unfazed. He continued with his corndog and honey combination.

I wondered if he was really enjoying it or just trying to be polite, but I didn't ask. I had a feeling he wasn't the type to complain about things that weren't to his taste.

We all finished our food, and it wasn't long before Addie, full of golden retriever energy, took over as the group's unofficial leader. I could feel her knee bouncing beneath the table, restless as usual. Without warning, she jumped up from the table, her enthusiasm commanding attention.

"There are games to be played—why are we still sitting around here?" she exclaimed, practically vibrating with excitement.

With that, the rest of us stood up, slipping back into our usual positions. Colton settled beside me as we walked toward the game booths.

"What do you want to play?" Colton asked, his voice a little softer than before, as if he were genuinely curious. I could tell he didn't mind tagging along for whatever game we ended up at, but I wondered if he was simply enjoying being with the group—or with me.

"How about that basketball game over there?" I pointed to a large basketball hoop surrounded by a small group of teenage boys.

"You want to see my mad skills?" Addie asked as she sprinted toward the hoop, her voice filled with playful challenge. Kenna and Mason followed quickly behind, exchanging a few quick words with the teenager working the game before they paid for a couple of balls. Within moments, both girls sunk a ball into the hoop, their competitive spirits clearly in full swing.

Colton and I approached the group, but we stayed a few feet away, content to observe rather than participate. He leaned in slightly, his voice low so only I could hear. "I wouldn't guess basketball to be your thing."

"It's not." I nodded toward Kenna. "I saw the basketball statue in her room." I was still trying to piece things together—little details like that were starting to reveal more about these people, even if they didn't talk about it openly.

He chuckled softly, bringing his lemonade to his lips for a quick sip. "Look at you, with your power of observation."

I tried to focus back on the game, but my mind couldn't stop running. They're all trying really hard to make sure I'm comfortable here. Probably my mom's idea. It was sweet, but it made me feel like a project, and I wasn't sure how I felt about that. I appreciated their kindness, but there was a thin line between being considerate and making me feel like an outsider who desperately needed to be included.

If I decide to stay longer, this kind of attention could build resentment. They meant well, but the constant need to ensure I was happy was almost overwhelming. At some point, I needed to show them I could stand on my own—without the extra care and the fawning.

"So, you plan on staying longer?" Colton pushed, just a little. If I wasn't mistaken, there was a glimmer of hope in his eyes—small, but unmistakable.

I shrugged, keeping my gaze on the basketball hoop. The hope in his eyes was dangerous, especially paired with the way he was acting tonight. It made me feel like I could be coaxed into staying longer which felt like too much to think about tonight.

"I'm trying to keep my mom happy."

It wasn't an answer, but it was enough to keep him from asking more. At least for now. I wasn't opposed to staying longer—at least, not in theory—but I wasn't about to admit that to him. Not yet.

I had promised her a week, and that was all I was willing to give when I agreed, even though I could feel her desperation. She'd been dropping enough hints, making it obvious she was hoping for more. Hoping that I'd see this place and staying as what I was missing in my life.

But I wasn't ready to make any changes to the original plan. Not when I knew that staying might only lead to more questions, I wasn't ready to answer.

Chapter Seven

"Are you ready for this?" Colton leaned close to my ear; his voice barely audible over the roar of the crowd. The arena was far louder than I'd expected, and conversation was only possible if we shouted into each other's ears. "I can guarantee you've never seen anything like this before."

I glanced at the man Colton called a rodeo cowboy, and I had to agree. His outfit was like nothing I had ever seen. Bright checkered chaps covered worn blue jeans, and his shirt— colorful and oversized —featured a giant beer logo. Even his hat was unconventional, a bright pink one adorned with glitter and the remnants of a feathered boa. It almost looked like a decoration left over from a bachelorette party.

I leaned in closer, trying to catch every word over the noise. "You're going to have to explain as we go. I have no clue what's going on."

Colton pointed out toward the arena, where I saw a handful of kids standing nervously by a group of sheep. "The first event is called Mutton Bustin'. Parents put their kids on the backs of sheep and send them out into the arena."

I raised an eyebrow. "That seems like a liability waiting to happen." My mind immediately calculated every possible worst-case scenario. Sprained ankles, concussions, or worse.

Colton chuckled and quickly shook his head, stepping even closer to make sure I could hear him. "I've been coming to the rodeo since I was a kid. I've never seen anyone get hurt from Mutton Bustin'. Brendan, Mason, and I all did it when we were younger. You have to wear a vest and a helmet, which helps avoid injuries. Sheep are docile. Most kids fall off within the first three seconds after the gate opens, so it's more of a show than a dangerous event."

While that did ease some of the tension, I still couldn't shake the thought of kids being launched off wooly animals at high speeds. I could already picture the chaos. My mind raced through the physics of it all—sheep darting left, kids losing balance—and I couldn't shake the image of something going wrong. "Brendan put Oakley in it this year. She's wearing a sparkly top so we can spot her."

"I'm not sure how I feel about this," I muttered, my unease refusing to loosen its grip.

The announcer stepped forward with the rodeo cowboy, signaling the start of the event. In an instant, the gate swung open. Just as Colton had predicted, the kids charged out, only to fall off their sheep even faster than I expected. We caught a glimpse of Oakley, her face set in determination, before her sheep veered too sharply to the right and sent her tumbling into the dirt.

A small, mousy-looking boy emerged as the winner, crowned the "king" of Mutton Bustin'. Colton leaned over to explain, "Kids like him are usually the underdogs. Their size makes it harder to balance on the sheep, but sometimes that works to their advantage."

The crowd cheered vigorously, the excitement for the next event buzzing in the air. For most, this meant they were one step closer to the bull riding—the real spectacle of the evening.

"Paisley's event is next," Colton said, his tone shifting as his eyes locked on the gate. "There are ten other girls in her division, and one of them is the best in the state. Paisley's been trying to beat her for the last four rodeos without success." His voice softened as he leaned forward, looking for his sister in the crowd, the shift in his expression telling me just how much he cared.

I could tell this wasn't just another competition to him. "Our parents are down there with her. Brendan's probably down there too, considering Oakley just went out."

I watched his face, trying to read him. He was so invested in the outcome, and I couldn't help but wonder how much this race meant to him too. I wasn't sure if I was imagining it, but it seemed like there was something deeper beneath his excitement—an edge of something personal.

"Do you want to go join them?" I asked, trying to be supportive. If he went, I'd be left alone, and that wasn't something I was looking forward to.

Kenna, Addie, and Mason had bought their tickets separately, so they were sitting on the opposite side of the arena. From where we sat, I could see them and wave.

Colton snapped his attention back to me, as though remembering I was still there. "No, there are too many people down there. And I wouldn't want to leave you alone."

"So, did you do any other rodeo events?" I asked, shifting the conversation to a conversation topic we could build on.

"I did a little team roping with Mason when we were younger," he said casually, his tone like it didn't mean much to him. "But the people who qualify for the rodeo really dedicate a lot of time and energy to it. That's not something either one of us could do."

We'd seen the kids doing their Mutton Bustin', the men riding bareback and team roping. Colton had explained that the next big events were the barrel racing for women and bull riding for the men.

Before we had entered the arena, Colton had grabbed us both water bottles and a large bag of kettle corn, swearing that was the only way to watch a rodeo. He tore open the bag and offered it to me. "Here, try some. There's nothing better, especially when it's warm like this. Though I'll probably say the same thing when we hit up the caramel apple booth before we leave."

Grateful, I took a handful, remembering how it was freshly made right in front of us. The warm, sweet flavor hit my tongue. "That's good. I don't think I've ever had kettle corn before."

"Watch this!" Colton pointed to a rodeo cowboy who was setting up three barrels in the dirt. One man was poised to ride atop the barrels, while another pushed them. His feet moved quickly across the barrel without slipping once.

His excitement was contagious, and I couldn't help but grin. My gaze shifted to the gate where the girls were lined up on their horses. A mix of emotions played across their faces—anticipation, excitement, and nerves. In front of us, a family sat with two young girls, both dressed in knee-high cowgirl boots and matching pink hats. They bounced enthusiastically in their seats as they watched the events unfold.

I couldn't help but notice the way the younger girl's eyes never left the arena, the intensity with which she watched every movement, her small body leaning forward as though trying to dissect each action before it even happened.

The first two girls made it through the event without a problem, both pushing their horses to run faster. Colton pointed out the camera and the timer attached to it. "The goal is to be as close to fifteen seconds as possible. A fast time is usually about fifteen and a half seconds. The two girls who just went have set the bar high, so that will make it tough for Paisley."

I couldn't help but run through the data in my head—calculating the angles, timing, speed. Colton leaned forward, his hands flying to his lips as if in silent prayer. "Paisley's up next."

I could see his sister on her horse at the front of the gate, ready to go, her face set with determination. I found myself observing her posture—her legs positioned just so, her back straight, her gaze locked ahead.

Across the arena, I spotted Kenna, Addie, and Mason, all with anxious expressions, as if they were right there with Paisley, competing alongside her.

Paisley shot off the line in a flash, and I heard Colton suck in a sharp breath as he watched. She flew around the first barrel, turning her horse quickly to make the second, then bolted to the third. The coordination between her and the horse was almost poetic—every stride perfectly timed, a beautiful balance of speed and control.

As soon as she cleared the last barrel, I saw her heels dig into the horse's sides, urging it to push harder toward the finish.

"Fifteen oh five!" Colton shouted, raising a fist into the air as she crossed the timer. "Wahoo! That a girl!"

Relief and pride filled Colton's voice, and I could see it mirrored on the faces of Kenna, Addie, and Mason. The entire arena erupted in cheers as Paisley claimed the top spot.

One of the young girls in front of us cheered louder than the others before turning to her mom. "That girl has a white hat! Next year, I want to buy a white hat too." She paused; her lips pursed as she thought carefully about her next request. "I want pants with glitter down the sides. I think they'd look good for my school pictures."

Colton's chest puffed out a little as the pride on his face took on a new layer. Hearing a little girl wanting to look like his sister made the moment feel even more special.

"She did so great!" I could see why people loved this. There was something undeniably thrilling about the environment. Every single person around us was locked into the action, fully immersed in the excitement. The shared energy was tangible. "You must be so proud of her."

That was an understatement. Colton was practically glowing, a smile that was so wide even he noticed it. He tried to pull his lips into a flatter expression, raising a hand to nervously tug at his bottom lip, but his happiness was stronger than any attempt to calm it. His smile wouldn't be tamed.

"You have no idea," he said, his voice thick with pride. "She's been working at this since she was little." He nodded toward the girls in front of us, their eyes still glued to the arena, their energy contagious. "Paisley was just like them once, watching a barrel race and telling our dad that she was going to be one of them someday. Then when she got home, she handed him her piggy bank, and said she wanted to use the money to buy her own horse."

I couldn't help but consider the logistics behind the story—the determination, the practicality of making her dreams happen. It wasn't just about the sport; it was the kind of focused dedication that propelled people forward. That type of drive, fueled by her own sense of agency, was something I could admire.

Still, it was strange to think how far a child's dream could go with just a few small but significant steps. A piggy bank, a horse, and now, here she was—one of the top competitors at the rodeo.

"Must've taken a lot of guts for her to do that," I said, my voice quieter now, considering not just her actions but the mindset it took to pursue something like this. "I'm so impressed that she chased her dreams."

Colton's smile softened as he thought about his sister, his eyes distant for a moment. "She's never been one for dreams. As soon as she wants something, it's all about executing the plan. I've never seen anyone go after anything the way Paisley does. Once she decides, nothing can get in her way."

I stared at him, letting his words sink in. For Paisley, it wasn't about dreaming big or long-term aspirations—it was about getting things done. Where I would have analyzed the steps and the variables in play, Paisley just dove in.

I couldn't deny the power of that approach. Sometimes, executing the plan without hesitation was all it took. But it also made me wonder—what did that mean for someone like me, who always needed to understand the "why" before acting? Did my need for analysis slow me down, or was it the thing that protected me?

The thought lingered, but I pushed it aside as I focused back on Colton's words. He was proud of her, and that pride was genuine. In a world where execution sometimes overshadowed thought, it was clear Paisley had mastered both.

* * *

Colton kept his hand behind my back as we walked toward his truck, the hum of excited people creating a buzzing sound all around us. Rodeo participants were loading up their trailers with animals and gear, their voices blending with the general chaos.

We had celebrated loudly as the last two bull riders topped the charts, truly proving that they sometimes leave the best for last. A huge rush of noise filled the air as everyone cheered, and a man a few feet down from us even threw off his shirt and pounded his chest in celebration.

"Are you hungry? We could stop and get something to eat before I take you home." Colton spoke to me, but kept his eyes ahead, nodding occasionally at other men as they passed by. "You didn't eat much before the rodeo."

"What are my options?" I asked, a slight challenge in my tone. I could've asked him to take me home, but I enjoyed being with him. Colton Bennett had a calm steadiness that made everyone around him feel at ease.

A small smile tugged at his lips, a silent acknowledgment that my answer had pleased him, even though he'd left the question open-ended. "Well, I could take you somewhere simple like McDonald's, but you don't seem like the simple type."

No one in Clinton had been shy about their opinions, especially when it came to my style. Even the girls had commented on how little I'd packed, as though I couldn't blend into their world. "I can be simple when needed."

"If you say so." A mischievous smile flashed across his face. "Have you ever had a cheddar bo?"

"What the heck is a cheddar bo?" I laughed, the absurdity of the question catching me off guard. Colton clearly thought I was anything but simple—and I couldn't help but wonder what exactly he meant by "cheddar bo."

He helped me into his truck, then quickly ran around to the other side to get in. As soon as he sat down, he cranked up the heater since the night had started to cool. "The restaurant's called Bojangles. Most people go there for their biscuits and gravy, but my family's partial to their cheddar bo biscuits."

Colton threw the truck in reverse, using my headrest for leverage as he leaned back to check his blind spot, just like he had earlier. Once we were lined up with the other trucks to leave the arena, he resumed our conversation. I couldn't help but smile at how he needed silence when he was focusing. "It's a buttery biscuit with cheddar cheese broiled in. Most people put a little butter or honey on it, but those of us who live on the wild side throw a little grape jelly on it."

"Grape jelly?" I tried to suppress my disgust, but from the look on his face, I could tell my nose had scrunched up a little too much to hide my distaste. "Listen, I'm willing to try anything once, but cheddar cheese and grape jelly together sounds... well, disgusting."

His hand rested between us on the armrest, and I watched his thumb tap out a rhythm I couldn't hear, as if he were playing an invisible beat. "Trust me, there's nothing better. Angels will sing the first time you taste it."

Colton reached over and cranked up the music, humming along softly as the words flew from the speakers, like he was completely alone in the truck.

Instead of going through the drive thru like I expected, he slid the truck into a tight spot between two other cars.

He looked like a kid, all eager energy, as he helped me out of the truck. Inside, the tables were packed, and the line at the counter had a few people waiting. "Do you want anything else?"

I glanced at the menu, while the biscuits were calling my name, I was also a little nervous that the gross sounding combination was really going to taste like it sounded. "Maybe some fries and a water?"

He pointed to a seat by the window. "Why don't you take a seat, and I'll grab the food?"

I followed his direction, then watched how many people stopped to talk to him while he stood in line. I'd kept my phone tucked away all night, trying not to be rude, but now that Colton was at the counter, I pulled it from my pocket.

There was a text from Kenna, asking if we were having fun, time-stamped before the end of the rodeo. Another from my mom, reminding me that the door would be unlocked when I came home. A thumbs-up emoji from my sister, which basically felt like a proof of life—my earlier text to her had been a plea for her to come and a reminder that mom missed her.

My favorite was the text from Addie: a photo of Colton and me smiling at each other. His hat was low on his head, and both of our cheeks were flushed from the heat and the sun.

Without really thinking, I saved the photo to my phone, then quickly turned it off and slipped it back into my pocket.

Colton's arrival was announced with a drumroll on the edge of the table as he sat down across from me with a grin. He was clearly proud of what he had foraged for our evening snack. Before him on the tray sat four tinfoil-covered biscuits, beside them a handful of small containers filled with grape jelly. Our two water glasses and my small container of fries looked almost silly beside what he considered the masterpiece of our meal.

"Do you want me to make it up for you?" Colton asked. With a nod, I watched as he reached for one of the biscuits and a container of jelly. He peeled back the top, revealing the deep purple shade of the jelly inside.

"If you don't like it, that's okay. I'm happy to get you something else off their menu. We can even go somewhere else if this isn't your cup of tea. I know you don't usually eat like this," he added.

I snatched up the fries and my water, grinning. "You already did get me something else as a just-in-case."

He finished smothering the cheddar cheese in grape jelly before presenting it to me with a wide, expectant smile. "Now, I expect you to be honest with me."

I held up my hand, giving him a flat, serious look, even though I was fighting a giggle. "Scout's honor."

I took a bite of the buttery, fluffy biscuit, sinking my teeth into the cheddar cheese and grape jelly. The sweet and bittersweet combination was strange, but surprisingly good.

"You were right. That is good." I paused, considering the angel-singing comment. It still seemed a little dramatic, but I let him have his moment. "This was truly better than I was expecting."

Colton pumped a fist into the air, drawing a few curious glances from nearby tables. "That's what I'm talking about!" He quickly fixed up a biscuit for himself and started eating. "Trust me, I get why you had reservations. Cheddar cheese and grape jelly seem like they'd be disgusting together, but for some reason, it really works."

At one point, his eyes rolled back in enjoyment, exaggerated just to make me laugh.

"It does call into question the first person to try this and why they decided to give it a go," I said, taking another small bite, still surprised by how much I liked it.

Without me having to ask, he grabbed my second biscuit, slathering on a thick layer of grape jelly before handing it over to me with a proud grin. "I should've warned you I was going to change your life today."

I couldn't help but smile at his cocky expression, so sure of himself.

He continued eating for a second, clearly savoring the biscuit. After swallowing a large bite and taking a long sip of his water, he spoke. "I imagine you've been to a lot of nice dinners, but there aren't many good places to stop for a drink out here other than the bar or Applebee's. I just wanted to take you out for something new."

He wasn't wrong. Back in Vegas, going out for a casual drink was everyone's first move, and if they did anything else, it was probably to go out for a nice dinner. I couldn't picture Colton Bennett doing either of those things as part of his dating routine.

"So, the rodeo was your opening move?" I wasn't sure why I was pushing him, but something in me felt like if I pressed just a little more, I'd get the answer I truly wanted.

Colton, however, seemed prepared for that. He brushed past my comment, moving onto something else before I could collect myself. "Yeah, bringing a small part of myself into your world felt like the way to go. Not to mention, you aren't very forthcoming with information about yourself. And anything your mom said... well, it didn't quite line up with the woman before me."

"I'm different than how she described?" The question felt almost like a joke, considering the woman I kept running into was far from the posh, put-together version of my mom I grew up with.

"Very." He reached for a fry casually, the action so effortless, so natural, that it almost seemed like we always shared food. My eyes followed his every move—there was something about how he didn't try to draw attention to his actions, but still made everything seem significant. It was strange. "We usually remember the version of others that we knew the most. It makes sense why she made you seem younger than you are. When I realized you were the daughter she always spoke of, I was honestly surprised that you weren't a teenager."

I pursed my lips and gave him a glance over, taking him in—eyes scanning, the way I would any new variable to understand it. Colt, in all his simplicity, seemed to have layers I hadn't considered. "Interesting observation." I let my body relax into the booth just a little, feeling the protective shell around me shrink. But the words had already slipped out before I could stop them. "Is that why it feels like a slap in the face every time I see her?

There it was—my vulnerability, slipping through despite my best efforts to analyze and compartmentalize. Colton's gaze softened, and a sympathetic expression crossed his face that made me feel like a child again.

"None of us have ever talked about the day when Jen got here," he said after a pause, the words slowly forming like he was giving them careful thought. "Mitch called Mason and Kenna on his way home from that cruise, telling them that he'd met the love of his life, and they were going to meet her. She came home with him and never left. It was fine. Their mom had been gone for long enough that the idea of their dad being in love again didn't feel strange. The shock was how different she was." His eyes drifted, a soft chuckle escaping as he recalled a moment that I would never be part of. "She walked up that first day in white pants and a pink shirt. Heels, tall ones, very similar to the ones you wore that first day we met."

The way Colton spoke made me realize how often I'd been comparing myself to my mother. It wasn't just about how she looked—it was everything else that felt out of sync. "Yeah," I muttered, the sadness creeping into my voice before I could stop it. "She used to look a lot like me."

I wanted to avoid going deeper, but something in his expression kept me there. His words about my mom didn't change the ache inside. And maybe it wasn't the pain of the comparison—it was the realization that what I had once admired in her, the control, the way she held everything together, wasn't something I had the ability to do anymore. Not with the woman I see now when I look at my mom.

Suddenly, knowing that no one would ever look at the two of us and say the words "you look just like your mom" again, left me feeling really lost. Growing up, looking like my mom had always been the one constant. It was the reassurance I needed when everything else around me changed. Whenever I questioned whether I was pretty, I could just look at her and remember all the times people had fawned over her, telling her how young she looked, asking if she was my sister. She always smiled and graciously thanked them, and if I was around, she'd run her hand through my hair, smiling gently before saying, "I'll never be as beautiful as my girl," as if I was the one who carried all the beauty for our family.

His hand suddenly covered mine across the table, warm and

grounding. The roughness of his skin was a quiet reminder that, in this moment, I didn't have to be strong for anyone. "I can still see the resemblance between you two," Colton said softly, his voice steady. "And I think one day you'll see it again, too."

* * *

The two of us sat in complete silence, the soft hum of the radio the only noise between us. The tension from the restaurant still lingered, thick and unspoken. Colton had made it obvious he saw this as a date. And while I hadn't encouraged it, I hadn't exactly discouraged it either—especially as the night went on. There was something about him that was just easy to be around, and I couldn't tell if that was a good thing or a very, very dangerous thing.

We pulled into the driveway, but neither of us moved to get out of the truck. He cut the engine and turned to face me. His gaze was steady and intense, like he had been waiting for this moment.

"Ellie, we've known each other for just over twenty-four hours, but you haven't left my mind since the moment I walked into the city building and saw you sitting there with your million bags and your ridiculous high heels." His voice was calm, but there was a certainty in his words that made my stomach tighten.

"That's very nice," I said carefully, reaching for the door handle but making no real effort to leave. "But I think we're getting ahead of ourselves here." My voice stayed level, but my pulse had picked up, my mind already constructing a dozen logical explanations for why he was saying this. "I think I'm just new and shiny."

He smiled slightly and pressed on. "I don't think we're getting ahead of ourselves. I had a really great time tonight, and I'd love to go out with you again."

My mind, unhelpful as ever, instantly constructed an entire sequence of possible futures. I saw him pulling up to the house for another date, that same beat-up truck and faded hat a constant in my life. I imagined easy conversation, laughter, the kind of natural rhythm that made it feel like we'd known each other longer than just a day. And if I stayed—if I let myself want this—there was a version of my life where it worked.

I realized my hands were clenched tightly in my lap, my nails pressing into my skin. Slowly, I released them, feeling the prickling return of circulation as I started fidgeting with my rings and bracelet, grounding myself back into reality. "I'm not going to be here very long." The words felt solid, like something I could hold onto. "It's not worth it when I'll be gone next week. We don't want to get attached if this isn't going anywhere."

Colton didn't argue. He just looked at me, steady and certain, his voice softer this time. "What if I want any second that I can get with you?"

As silly as it was, I knew that—even if I didn't have all the answers, even if I couldn't calculate the outcome—I was starting to want the exact same thing.

Chapter Eight

The morning after the rodeo, I still wasn't completely convinced it hadn't all been a fever dream—until I saw the photo Addie had sent staring back at me.

Colton and I, heads close together, grinning like we had no idea the rest of the world existed. Anyone looking at this picture could see it—I was happy. Ridiculously happy. Happier than I had expected to be when I boarded the plane to come here.

Then my phone lit up with a message from my assistant, trying to schedule a meeting after my returned flight.

The sight of it sent a tight, twisting sensation through my stomach. I had planned this trip expecting a week to feel long, assuming I'd be eager to leave before the seven days were up. Logically, nothing had changed—Vegas was still home, my job still waiting—but none of those facts settled the unease creeping in. The math didn't add up.

Shoving the thought aside, I hurried through getting ready and headed downstairs.

Mom sat at the kitchen table, her hair in a messy bun and glasses perched on her nose. I stopped short. I had never seen her wear either before.

Her eyes lifted from the newspaper, immediately locking with mine. "Hi, honey. How was last night?"

"Good." I went straight for the coffee pot, inhaling the scent of dark roast, hoping it would help shake the lingering fog in my head. "Do you have any creamer?"

Mom shook her head. "We don't. I usually only drink coffee when we go out for breakfast, and Mitch likes his black." She pursed her lips, thinking. Then she got up and rummaged through the cabinet, emerging with a small container. "We have hot chocolate packets. You could make a mocha?"

I hesitated before taking the packet, stirring the powder into my mug. The first sip was sharp and bitter, the coffee overpowering the chocolate. I swallowed it down anyway, suppressing a grimace.

I grabbed some milk from the fridge and poured it in, hoping it would soften the taste before joining Mom at the table. An assortment of muffins sat in the center of the table, perfectly arranged like something out of a magazine.

She moved quickly, setting one on a plate in front of me. "I made your favorite—blueberry muffins. They're still warm from the oven."

I didn't have the heart to tell her that it was Olivia who loved blueberry muffins. I had always preferred chocolate. But that was back when Mom wasn't around much, so it made sense that she wouldn't remember. If I had to guess, the nanny who handled our muffin fix had probably worked for my parents the same year Mom disappeared for a six-month "spa retreat" that somehow resulted in a mommy makeover and a new set of boobs. She had been absent a lot through the years, but that one was especially memorable.

"Thank you for making them for me." I pulled the top off the muffin, breaking it into small pieces as I ate. "This is great."

Knowing she had put time and effort into making something she thought I loved, I forced a smile and swallowed each bite, despite how much I hated the taste of cooked fruit.

Mom wrapped her hands around her cup, keeping it close to her face trying to hide her smile. "How was the rodeo?" She tried to sound casual, but I caught the slight change in her voice. She was pushing—gently, carefully—but pushing nonetheless. "Did you have a good time with Colt? Kenna texted Mitch when she and Addie got home and said everyone had a great time. I'm sorry we were asleep when you got back. I didn't even realize we had fallen asleep until we woke up this morning. Isn't it funny how that works? The harder you try to stay awake, the more likely you are to fall asleep."

Her words tumbled out quickly, filling the space like she was trying to keep me from having too much time to think before answering.

I thought back to last night—the way Colton had shared exactly what he wanted, like there was no other options to consider. "Yeah, I had a great time. I'm sorry we stayed out so late. He took me to Bojangles after the rodeo to try a cheddar bo."

Mom suddenly perked up, leaning forward in her chair so quickly that a few strands of hair fell loose, framing her face. Her green eyes sparkled with excitement. "What did you think? Did he have you try it with grape jelly? Isn't it the weirdest thing you've ever eaten?"

"They were delicious." I tried to keep my voice neutral, but I could already feel the grin tugging at my lips. "He was really excited to share them with me."

Mom caught my expression, and her own smile deepened like she'd just uncovered a secret. Not wanting to give her too much time to analyze me, I pivoted. "What do you want to do today? I'd love to spend time together—unless you already have plans with Mitch."

That seemed to be exactly what she was hoping for. Her excitement bubbled over, her words tumbling out almost too fast to process. "I was really hoping you'd say that!" If possible, her eyes shone even brighter. "I talked to the girls about going out shopping today if you're up for it. What do you think? Or we could just do something like get pedicures, like old times?"

I hesitated for half a second, not because I didn't want to spend time with her, but because "old times" had never been quite as picture-perfect as she made them sound. Still, the hopeful look on her face was hard to ignore. "That all sounds great. How about I run upstairs and finish getting ready? You can call Kenna and Addie and see what they want to do—shopping or pedicures."

She agreed, and I headed upstairs. As soon as I stepped into my room, I spotted my phone on the bed, abandoned in my rush to join Mom for breakfast.

Two notifications waited for me.

Olivia: Okay, fine. You win.

Olivia's message was vague, frustratingly so, considering she hadn't bothered to respond to any of my messages all week.

And one waiting from Colton—which surprised me, considering I hadn't given him my number. That meant he'd asked someone else for it. I could only imagine how that had gone. Kenna and Addie would have given him a hard time just for fun, and Mom? She would have woken me up too excited and needing to discuss the previous night if he had asked her.

Colton: I had a great time last night. I'd like to take you out again.

If I was being honest with myself, I wanted to see him right now. That thought hit hard, knocking me slightly off balance. Probably a good thing he had his own life and a job that would keep him busy — forced patience might be the only kind I had.

I quickly typed out a response, forcing myself to keep it casual despite the way my heart was racing.

Ellie: I would love that. What do you want to do?

Colton: Now that's a surprise. Be ready for anything.

I stared at the message a second longer than I needed to, willing myself not to read into it, before tossing my phone onto the bed and racing to get ready.

Downstairs, Mom was back in the kitchen, putting away the muffins. She had changed into a nice blouse and a pair of shorts, the casual elegance of someone who never seemed to misstep.

She glanced up as I walked in, a knowing smile tugging at her lips. "That's a good look on you. But your feet will be killing you by the end of this."

I had kept my outfits simple, sticking to minimal jewelry—just my signature small pendant necklace. Kenna had generously offered up anything leftover in her closet and dresser, so I'd borrowed a pair of blue jeans and a plain shirt. Shoes, however, were limited to whatever I had packed. Addie was the one I matched sizes with, and her old red boots didn't exactly scream "shopping day." So, I settled for the most sensible option I had: a pair of wedge sandals.

Glancing down at Mom's feet, I couldn't help but giggle. Her plain pink flip-flops were no more practical than my own choice. I shrugged, slinging my purse over my shoulder as I headed for the door. "Looks like we're both going with what's comfortable. Besides, these were my only real option."

Mom was right behind me, tossing her bag over her shoulder before giving me a gentle push through the open door. "Don't you worry. Before we meet the girls, we'll swing by Walmart."

* * *

While we did stop at Walmart like she insisted, I managed to escape without flip-flops—despite her repeated claims that everyone should own a pair and her offer to buy them for me. I was pretty sure I got away with it because Addie and Kenna texted, they were too busy to join us which distracted her from the need to make sure I had flip-flops.

Mom may have mixed up my breakfast order with my sister's, but she did remember that I loved chocolate-covered pretzels, tossing a bag into the cart along with some cheap dish towels she claimed would make great gifts for people at her church.

As we wandered through the aisles, I watched her—the easy way she moved through life, unbothered and unapologetic. There was a calmness to her, a peace that felt almost foreign compared to the whirlwind of my life in Vegas. Back there, my days vanished in a blur of meetings, emails, and rushed meals.

Mom glanced over our cart, comparing it to her handwritten shopping list—because of course she used paper instead of a list on her phone. "Mitch has been talking about everyone coming over for dinner tomorrow. Would that be, okay?"

I frowned. "Of course. Why are you asking me?" She gave nothing away, so I kept going. "Kenna mentioned these dinners were a weekly thing. I'm sure they'll be happy to keep their normal routine."

That first night featured a special welcome dinner in my honor, but it wasn't lost on me that my presence here had thrown a wrench into their lives since it threw off their normal routine—and it would likely continue to do so, especially now that I was considering a longer stay.

Mom and Mitch were thrilled to have me, that much was obvious. But would they still feel that way if I stayed?

"Great!" Mom beamed, already pulling out her phone. "I'll check with everyone and see what time works."

Her fingers flew across the screen, reminding me of the days when she'd book Botox and waxing appointments with ease.

At the checkout, we joined the shortest line, though it was still three people deep. I traced my fingers across the counter, stalling trying to find my words before blurting out, "Mom, what would you think if I stayed a little longer?"

She froze; eyes suddenly shiny with unshed tears. "You want to stay?"

I immediately realized how easy it would be to get her hopes up—

and that was the last thing I wanted to do. "Just a little longer," I hedged. "A week feels short, and it's going by so fast. Maybe we could take it week by week? I've got PTO saved up... maybe I could stay through the summer."

Mom hesitated. "Will your dad be okay with that?"

It was the first time she'd mentioned him, and the way she said "dad"—tight-lipped, almost like an insult—made her feelings clear. I couldn't blame her. Their divorce had been ugly, and he'd never been the warmest presence in my life.

"I haven't told him yet," I admitted. "But I'm an adult. I can make my own decisions."

Even to my own ears, it sounded weak.

Telling Dad I wasn't coming back anytime soon wasn't a conversation I wanted to have. He hadn't been happy about this visit, accusing me of "running away" just like Mom had. As if visiting my mother was some reckless, career-ending decision—unlike his frequent business trips to Cabo, which conveniently involved more drinking than actual work.

We shuffled forward in line, and as Mom greeted the cashier, something shifted in her attitude. It was subtle, the way her tone softened, but I noticed.

"How are you today?" she asked, her voice warm and sincere. "Isn't it beautiful out?"

The woman in the bright blue Walmart vest barely looked up, moving the items across the scanner with steady hands. "I wouldn't know. Came in before the sun was up."

Mom didn't miss a beat. "Oh, well, you'll love it when you get out of here. The sun's shining, and it's the perfect kind of warm. It'll feel like a whole new day when you step outside."

I watched the cashier's frown waver, then disappear. The change was almost imperceptible at first—just a slight shift in her posture, her eyes softening—but it was there. The power of a simple kind word. It made me wonder how much of what we said, or didn't say, affected people's day without us even realizing it.

The cashier's voice softened. "Only thirty minutes left on my shift," she admitted, scanning faster now with a renewed attitude. "I can't wait to go see it."

Mom grinned. "I hope the rest of your day is wonderful."

I didn't say it out loud, but I thought, if I had said that I would have overthought how it would be received. The cashier's change in mood was instant. No second-guessing, no analysis, just a simple exchange that shifted her outlook. I wasn't sure I could ever be that spontaneous.

By the time we left, the woman's bad mood had lifted, and she even waved as we walked away.

Back at the car, I turned to Mom. "I've never seen you do that before."

She pulled onto the road with a small shrug, not fully focused on my words. "Do what?"

"Completely change someone's attitude in three sentences."

She smiled. "Sometimes the world just needs a little kindness. If I can sprinkle some sunshine, why wouldn't I?"

I couldn't help but wonder if I could try that more often. Maybe it was easier than I thought—just offering a little bit of kindness without worrying about how it would land. But then again, it felt like everything in my life needed to be meticulously thought through, and I wasn't sure if I could let go of that just yet.

I watched her, the ease of her words settling in my chest. My mother had always been someone I thought I understood. I'd observed her throughout my life, cataloging her every move, dissecting her decisions in my mind. But maybe—just maybe—this visit would help me understand more completely. It felt like there was more to her, some layer I hadn't fully seen before.

Mom turned on the radio, and the music filled the silence between us. She smiled and waved at each person we passed as if they were old friends. I couldn't help but notice how effortlessly she interacted with everyone, how easily she found warmth in even the most mundane exchanges. I wondered if I could learn to be that comfortable in my own skin. The thought seemed foreign, almost impossible for my analytical brain to imagine.

Kenna's yellow jeep sat in the parking lot waiting for us, and Mom pulled her car in beside it. "I'm so glad that Kenna was able to join us after all," she said. "I know it's a little late in life, but she's quite excited to have a sister. Sure, she has Addie—and that's great—but you know as well as I do that the bond between sisters is something truly special."

The idea of us being considered sisters made me chuckle quietly. We were adults, living on opposite sides of the country, and the notion that Kenna and I might naturally form a sisterly bond seemed almost laughable. And yet, I could see why Mom and Mitch kept pushing for our families to come together. They longed to create a blended family connection

"Welcome in. Pick your color, and I'll be right with you," the woman at the front desk said, motioning toward the towering wall of polish. The sharp smell of acetone hit us as we fully stepped into the salon, growing stronger when the door swung shut behind us. It almost felt suffocating, but I ignored it, knowing it would fade once we got settled.

Underneath the display, Kenna sat in one of the waiting chairs, phone pressed to her ear. She looked up as we walked in, flashing a warm smile before pointing to her phone and mouthing, *Mason*, so we'd know who she was talking to.

Mom let out a soft sigh. "Those kids are always so busy. Mitch knows it's time for him to retire, but he can't just step away. He doesn't want them to feel like he's abandoning them."

I watched her as she drifted toward the red section of the color wall, plucking a sophisticated burgundy shade—nothing too flashy. Meanwhile, I wandered in the opposite direction, my eyes scanning rows of soft neutrals and pastels. White had always been my go-to, but today something about the lighter greens caught my attention. I couldn't quite explain why, but they felt calm, muted—almost like they belonged in a quieter, more peaceful life. My fingers hovered over a particular green bottle, the exact shade of Colton's eyes.

"I don't think Mitch will ever really retire," I said absently, still staring at the polish options in my hand. "He loves what he does too much. You can see it when he talks about work."

It wasn't a judgment; it was just an observation. People don't retire easily when they find purpose in what they do. Mitch's reluctance to step away from work was a pattern I'd seen in others—my father included. Work was both an anchor and an escape, a source of control when everything else felt uncertain. It wasn't about money, not for Mitch. It was about avoiding that empty space when there's nothing left to occupy your time.

Mom smiled, a knowing softness in her expression. "He does. But it's more than that. He's proud of what he's built. Growing something from the ground up and passing it on to his kids—there's no better feeling for a Carolina man."

The woman at the counter approached, her voice warm as she greeted us. "Ladies, thanks for coming in today. I have seats ready for you."

We followed her to a row of plush chairs, settling in just as three technicians emerged from the back, their aprons freshly tied. As we handed over our chosen colors, they got to work without missing a beat.

Kenna finally ended her call, setting her phone down with a sheepish smile. "Hey, sorry about that! Mason had a few questions, and, well... it turned into a lot more than I expected."

She glanced at our nails, eyes scanning the bottles we had chosen before raising an eyebrow. "Jen sticking with her classic color, huh?"

Mom laughed, shrugging lightly. "Why mess with perfection?"

Kenna smirked. "Fair enough." Her gaze shifted to the bottle I'd handed over. "Ellie, I got to say, that color— it reminds me of a pale Frankenstein."

A knot of unease twisted in my stomach. Kenna's comment hit harder than it should have, and I instantly regretted my choice. The sage green, which I'd been so excited about moments ago, suddenly felt like the wrong choice.

"Well, I guess the foliage around us was kind of the inspiration. I usually go for white, so... even this pale of a green is a stretch for me."

I could feel my mind already turning over the implications of that comment—was it too daring? Was the color too much? I hadn't realized that something as simple as choosing a nail color could trigger such self-doubt. It was just a shade, right? But I couldn't shake the thought that maybe I was trying too hard to be different.

Kenna shook her head, reaching out and grabbing my hand, as if to stop me from second-guessing. "Hey, I'm not ragging on Frankenstein. I like it. Besides, white's boring."

Mom adjusted the settings on her chair, the soft hum of the massage function filling the air as she leaned back into the plush leather. She sighed in contentment, letting the woman at her feet pamper her. This moment, with my mom at peace, there was also something about this newer, warmer version of her—the one I was getting to know—that I found myself enjoying more.

Kenna's fingers flew across her phone screen again, her attention still anchored to the buzz of work. "Sorry, more from Mason," she muttered, her eyes glued to the device as if pulling away was impossible.

I felt the need to pull my own phone out of my purse, finding something to do while my companions seemed lost in their worlds. But I fought the urge, reminded by the harsh reality that the only people I regularly texted were my sister and dad—neither of whom I wanted to talk to right now.

The technician seemed to notice my internal struggle and nodded toward the magazine rack behind her. "Want something to read? We've got a few new ones."

Gratefully, I grabbed a gossip magazine, flipping through pages of celebrity gossip and fashion "dos and don'ts," trying to lose myself in the fluff. A week ago, I would've been fully immersed—judging actresses in tight dresses, scrutinizing the shoes they paired with them, or analyzing their makeup choices. But instead, my thoughts kept drifting back to Colton and the way he'd openly shared his thoughts. The unanswered questions still lingered in my mind—he'd said he enjoyed being with me and wanted to keep seeing me, but the ambiguity of his words left me unsettled.

I flipped another page, but the words blurred together, my mind still trapped in its cycle of overthinking. The quiet hum of the salon filled the air, but I couldn't shake the noisy thought that something was missing—like I was standing on the edge of a decision I wasn't quite ready to make. I had a great time with Colton. I liked him, but there was the nagging question in my mind if he liked me as much as I liked him.

"Ellie," Mom's voice cut through my thoughts again, softer this time. "Are you okay?"

I glanced up, meeting her eyes, and instantly, I knew she wasn't asking about my nails or the magazine anymore. There was something else there, a quiet concern that made me hesitate. Was she sensing my unease?

"Yeah," I said, though it felt like a lie as the words left my mouth. "I'm just thinking."

Kenna, still distracted by her phone, didn't even seem to notice. She was too focused on Mason's texts, her thumb moving across the screen with practiced speed.

Mom leaned in slightly, her voice low. "You know I'm here if you want to talk."

Her offer felt like a lifeline, but I wasn't sure I wanted to drag her into the mess of my own thoughts. She had enough going on in her own life. And besides, what would I even say? That I didn't know what I was doing here? That I didn't know if staying longer was the right choice? That I couldn't stop thinking about a guy who seemed to disappear as quickly as he appeared?

"Thanks, Mom," I said, forcing a smile. "I just need some time to figure it out."

She gave me a knowing look, the kind she'd always given when she knew I wasn't being fully honest, but she didn't push. Instead, she reached for her own phone, clearly content to let the silence fill the space between us.

I glanced down at the bottle of sage green polish again, the color still too reminiscent of Colton's eyes. Maybe it was foolish to get so attached to something so small, but I couldn't help it. The more I thought about him, the harder it was to separate my feelings from the reality of a life here.

The nail technician continued her work, and I let my mind drift again, knowing I wasn't any closer to an answer. I could stay in this moment for as long as I needed to, but sooner or later, I'd have to decide what came next.

The technician quickly finished up my nails, and I watched as she carefully applied a topcoat, sealing the color in place. I closed the magazine and glanced at my phone, but no new texts had come through from Colton, and I felt a strange mix of relief and disappointment. The silence between us felt heavier now, like I was waiting for something I couldn't name.

Mom was already standing, tapping her foot lightly as she adjusted her purse on her shoulder. "All done, sweetie. You like the color?" Her question felt less like an observation and more like she was making sure I was okay.

I nodded absently; my toes still cold from the polish and the basin of water. "Yeah. It's different, but I think I'll get used to it."

"You don't have to keep it if you don't like it," she said gently. "But if you do, I'm glad you're trying something new. Sometimes, a little change is a good thing."

I smiled, a little more genuine this time. Maybe staying here, for a while at least, was what I needed. I could figure out the rest of it later.

Kenna finally finished with her phone, slipping it into her purse with a soft sigh. "I'm so sorry. I thought I could sneak away, but work just followed me. Always does," she said with a playful roll of her eyes. She stood up and came over to join Mom and me at the front.

"Addie and I were thinking about doing a girls' night tonight. What do you think?"

"That sounds really nice," I said, my voice a little lighter than it had been all day. "I think it'll be good to just chill tonight."

Kenna smiled brightly; her excitement practically infectious. "Perfect! We'll set it up. Just a simple, relaxing evening—no work, no distractions. Just us." She turned to Mom, her grin widening. "What about you? You in?"

Mom laughed, adjusting her sunglasses on top of her head with a playful wink. "I might be getting up there in age, but don't you worry. I can still hang with the best of you. Count me in."

I glanced between the two of them, taking a moment to consider the idea. A girls' night—nothing to worry about, no heavy discussions, just an easy evening.

As we headed to the car, my phone buzzed in my hand, and for a split second, my heart skipped. I didn't need to look at the name. I knew it was him.

I hesitated, thumb hovering over the screen. Should I read it? Or should I wait? I'd spent enough time overthinking. Maybe it was time to let things unfold, instead of trying to control them.

Mom was already in the car, and I slid into the passenger seat beside her, slipping my phone into my purse without looking at it. Colton could wait, I decided. For now, I was just going to enjoy the moment.

We pulled away from the salon, the sun warm on my face, and the day stretched out before us—peaceful and free of expectation.

Chapter Nine

Quietly, I slipped into the house, easing the door shut behind me. It let out a high-pitched squeak, and I winced, freezing in place.

The old hound dog on the rug barely stirred. He cracked one eye open, regarded me with mild disinterest, then let out an exaggerated sigh and flopped his head back down. Clearly, he wasn't kept around for security.

Another late night with Colton. Ever since he'd dropped me off after the rodeo, we'd been seeing each other as often as we could. Only four days had passed, but it felt like a whirlwind of a million adventures.

This morning had been no different. I'd jolted awake to the unmistakable roar of an engine outside my window—Colton, arriving on a four-wheeler like some small-town Paul Revere. The noise sent my heart hammering, and I'd scrambled out of bed, rushing to the window in alarm that the noise would wake the whole house. But Mom and Mitch were already up, their room empty, the bed neatly made. I had come here to spend time with my mom, yet somehow, I'd managed to be gone for most of my trip so far. Still, there was something comforting about their early wakeups, especially since I was constantly coming and going at all hours.

Colton's unpredictable work schedule meant he was gone at odd times, so we had to steal whatever moments we could. And when I wasn't with him, Kenna and Addie were quick to pull me into their world—inviting me over to their apartment for movies, late-night talks, and impromptu girls' nights. They seemed thrilled to have me around, and I had to admit, I liked feeling included.

By the time I finished brushing my teeth and dragging a brush through my hair, Colton was already seated at the kitchen table, looking right at home. A cup of coffee sat in front of him, a newspaper spread open in his hands. He was dressed in another pair of worn jeans and a faded Cabela's T-shirt, his signature baseball cap resting on the table instead of his head. I could only guess he left it off out of some deep-seated instinct to be the perfect Southern gentleman.

As soon as I stepped into the kitchen, his face lit up with a warm smile. "Morning. How'd you sleep?"

His voice carried a teasing edge, and I caught the glint of amusement in his eyes. He knew full well he'd dropped me off at one in the morning, and now, barely five hours later, I was stumbling into the kitchen.

I grabbed a mug and poured myself a cup of the freshly brewed coffee, reaching for the hazelnut creamer Mom had picked up for me. I added a generous amount, sweetening the dark, bitter blend Mitch preferred.

I'd watched Mitch drink it straight from the pot, cup after cup, never once flinching at the sharp taste. I was not surprised to find that Colton drank his in the same way. And a small part of me wondered if it was because he admired Mitch so much. As a kid, he'd probably watched his every move, mirroring him until their habits became indistinguishable.

I took a sip of my own coffee, the sweetness balancing the bitterness in a way that made it just right. It was a small thing, but I'd always been particular about my coffee—finding the right balance, adjusting the ratios until it was just how I liked it. The same way I analyzed patterns in people, looking for consistencies, for connections. My brain had to find patterns, break them down, try to make sense of them. By doing that, I could usually read people, map out their habits, predict their next moves. But with Colton, there were contradictions and maybe that's why I felt so unsettled by him. He was predictable in some ways—his work ethic, his loyalty—but in others, I couldn't quite pin him down. And for someone like me, that was both frustrating and intriguing.

Mom walked into the kitchen, her eyes immediately landing on me as she came in for a tight hug. "I'm surprised you're up. You got in late last night."

Her voice was warm, but the moment she turned and saw Colton sitting at the table, her movements hitched. A slight pause, just long enough for me to notice, before she raised an eyebrow in his direction. "Did you stay here?"

Colton reacted before I could, shaking his head so fast it was almost comical. A faint blush dusted his cheeks, and he jumped to his feet like a man who had just been caught somewhere he didn't belong. "No, ma'am. I dropped her off late last night and came to pick her up early this morning." He stepped closer, the blush furthering how awkward this conversation was for him to have. "Just trying to spend as much time with her as possible before she decides to leave."

There it was again—*before she decides to leave.* The words settled between us, unspoken meaning hanging in the air. He hadn't outright asked me to stay longer, but he'd hinted at it more than once the last few days, and the weight of that expectation pressed against me.

Mom didn't comment on the shift in energy, just offered a knowing smile. "I'm glad the two of you are getting along."

Colton wiggled his eyebrows at me, his expression playful, and I laughed despite myself. I knew that look—he did it often. A joke forming in his mind, something teasing, maybe even slightly inappropriate, but instead of saying it out loud, he'd just grinned and shook his head. It was a pattern, a little tell of his that I'd started to recognize.

I narrowed my eyes at him, trying not to laugh at his reaction. "Cool that thought right now."

Colton's grin widened, and he took a slow sip of his coffee, deliberately avoiding any eye contact.

Mom watched our exchange with a knowing smile before gesturing toward the back porch. Through the window, I could see Mitch settled into the couch out there, two large glasses of sweet tea—one undoubtedly waiting for her. She'd always had a way of making the smallest routines feel sacred, and something about the sight of them sitting out there together, made my chest ache with something I wasn't ready to name.

"I need to go check on Mitch," she said, but then hesitated, her gaze drifting back to me. Without thinking, her fingers brushed through my hair, an old habit she seemed to fall into when she was lost in thought. "Just check in throughout the day if possible. I just want to know that you're okay."

There was something in her tone—something careful, almost hesitant. It wasn't a demand, just a quiet request, but I heard what she wasn't saying. *You've been gone a lot. You're slipping through my fingers again.*

Before I could respond, Colton's voice broke through the moment, effortlessly light. "Don't worry, Miss Jen, I'll keep her safe and out of trouble. I'm taking your girl on an adventure today—out on the four-wheeler."

Mom hummed, unimpressed. "That's exactly what worries me."

I rolled my eyes, but before I could protest, my mind wandered back to last night. The rain had started while we were out at dinner—our *first* official date, at least according to Colton. He kept insisting that the rodeo didn't count, that it had only been a test to see if I wanted to be seen with him.

I'd laughed at the time, but now, thinking back on it, I wondered if there had been some truth hidden under the teasing. If maybe, despite all his confidence, Colton had been waiting for me to prove something to him, too.

Yesterday, I'd woken up to a call from him—far too early for someone who'd barely slept. He'd wasted no time, skipping right past pleasantries to announce that he'd had a great time and wanted to take me to breakfast *before I had a chance to change my mind.* I'd barely managed a groggy response before he added, "Be ready in thirty. I'll be there."

It had been easy to say yes. Too easy. I hadn't even tried to argue that this—whatever *this* was—wasn't a good idea. That I wasn't built for whirlwind romances or stolen moments before sunrise. That I wasn't like him.

He'd shown up right on time, looking way too awake for how early it was, and taken me straight to the same diner where Mom and Mitch had brought me the day before. Still, he insisted that *wasn't* a date either. "Breakfast doesn't count," he'd said, lifting an eyebrow at me over his coffee. "You can't charm someone when they're still only halfway awake."

It had become a pattern—him casually inviting me along, finding excuses to spend time together, each outing toeing the line of something more without ever crossing it. Until last night. That was different. He'd shown up at my front door with a bouquet of flowers, both of us dressed up, both of us fully acknowledging what this was. There had been no excuses, no loopholes. We were dating.

Well, kind of.

Mom's voice pulled me back to the present. She gave me a long, skeptical look, one eyebrow raised. "You are going on a four-wheeler?"

It was a fair question. Up until this week, the idea of me willingly climbing onto one would've been laughable. And yet, here I was, drinking coffee early in the morning, about to do exactly that.

I hadn't really thought he was being serious last night when he'd suggested this for today's activity. Which, in hindsight, was the only reason I'd smiled and agreed to go. I'd assumed it was just one of those offhanded suggestions people make but never follow through on —like saying we *should* go skydiving someday or *ought* to take a road trip to nowhere.

But Colton had called my bluff. And now, standing here in my pajamas, I was faced with the undeniable truth: he wasn't joking. The four-wheeler idled outside. He'd shown up with no other ride in sight. If I wanted to go anywhere with him today, I'd have to climb onto that thing and hold on for dear life.

"Yeah, Colton is really excited about sharing it with me," I said, stalling. I glanced down at my sleepwear and grimaced. "I don't exactly have anything to wear for it, though. We might need to go another day—after I have a chance to go shopping for something."

Colton's lips curved into a slow, knowing smile. "Figured you'd say that." He gestured toward the front door, where a small camo duffle bag sat on the floor. "Paisley packed some of her old riding gear for you. Should be everything you need."

Hesitantly, I walked over and unzipped the bag. A sea of camo greeted me. Jackets, pants, even gloves—all blending together in one indistinguishable camo mass. I shot him a look. "You really did think of everything, didn't you?"

He just grinned.

With a sigh, I grabbed the strap, slinging the bag over my shoulder. If nothing else, this was a commitment to whatever chaos the day held. Clutching my coffee like a lifeline, I started up the stairs to change, already running through a mental list of possible scenarios— mud, speed, potential bruises. I wasn't opposed to adventure, exactly, but I preferred to *prepare* for it. And right now, I was stepping straight into Colton's world without any real sense of control.

Still, despite myself, there was a tiny flicker of curiosity beneath the hesitation. Maybe—just maybe—letting go for a little while wouldn't be the worst thing in the world.

Pulling out the camo pants, shirt, jacket, and boots, I almost felt like a character in one of those survival shows I'd always scoffed at. Thankfully, everything fit better than the clothes I'd borrowed from

Kenna and Addie—everything slid on easily, and the boots actually fit my feet.

Still, the bulky fabric of the pants made every movement feel exaggerated, and I almost waddled down the stairs toward them. Mitch and Mom were back at the table with Colton now, all of them with coffee mugs in hand. As I approached the kitchen, the conversation fell quiet.

With each step I took, the pants made a swooshing noise, signaling my arrival. All three of them turned to face me, clearly waiting for me to make my entrance.

"That's a good look on you." Colton grinned, stepping closer to offer me a hand down the small step into the kitchen, clearly noticing how hard it was for me to bend my knee in these pants. "Although, you do look like if Barbie had an endorsement from Cabela's."

"Ha ha, very funny," I shot back, my voice dripping with sarcasm as I moved further into the room. "Do I really need to wear all of this? It's too hot and humid outside. There's no way I'll survive in this gear."

As I voiced the complaint, I found myself wondering how much of this was Colton's idea of fun versus him just *wanting* me to be part of whatever world he'd so effortlessly built around himself. There was something strangely comforting about the chaos that swirled around him, even if I wasn't always prepared to dive headfirst into it.

All three of them nodded their heads enthusiastically. "When you're on the back of one of those things, it can get really cold," Mitch spoke up, an experienced look crossing his face as he recalled a memory of his own four-wheeling days.

Quickly followed by my mom, who added, "It's safer if you're covered up. If you get too close to a tree, they can cut your arm or your leg."

"And don't forget about the ticks," Mitch chimed in with a grimace, his face contorting in disgust. "Those nasty little things can ruin your day in a heartbeat."

I shuddered at the thought, but before I could protest further, Colton must have seen the "rescue me" look in my eyes. With a swift, reassuring move, he took my hand, pulling me toward the door. "Well, Mitch, Jen, I promise I won't keep her out too late," he said, his voice light but firm, "We'll both have our phones on if you need anything."

I gave a small, relieved smile. There was something about Colton's presence that made everything feel just a little easier to face, even if I had no idea what I was about to get into.

Silently, I thought *Maybe don't need anything.* Because, truth be told, I didn't want anyone interrupting our day together—especially with the excitement in Colton's eyes. When I first met him with his weathered baseball cap and his worn-down truck, I knew Colton Bennett was a country boy through and through, so none of this—the four-wheeler, the adventure—was really a surprise. But what *was* surprising was that I actually wanted to go. With him. And that realization made me pause for a second.

Colton's hand was warm in mine as I carefully stepped down the stairs, my legs not quite used to the weight of the gear. He moved beside me, steadying me with an ease that made me feel a little less clumsy. We reached the four-wheeler, and he helped me swing my leg up and over the large vehicle, his touch firm and considerate. I was starting to get used to the way he seemed to anticipate every move I made.

His hands brushed lightly against my hair as he placed a helmet on my head, adjusting the strap beneath my chin until it was tight but comfortable. "You only need this stuff for when we're going through the trees," he explained, his voice warm and easy. "When we get back to my place, you can lose the extra layers, and we'll just ride around my property."

He climbed onto the four-wheeler in front of me, his movements fluid, like he'd done this a hundred times before. As he reached back, he grabbed my hands and pulled them around his torso, urging me to settle in close. "Keep your arms here," he said, his voice steady but reassuring. "And when we make a turn, lean into it with me—otherwise, we might tip over."

I could feel the beat of his heart through his shirt, his muscles shifting as he prepared to take off. The thought of it—riding through the trees, leaning into turns with him—made a flutter of excitement stir inside me. Maybe this wasn't going to be as bad as I had thought.

I tightened my grip around him as the four-wheeler roared to life beneath us, its engine growling to life with a powerful hum. Colton expertly backed out of the driveway, and I could feel the rumble of the wheels against the dirt as we shot down the back roads. As we approached a stop sign, his hand would reach back to rub against my knee, or the hand still wrapped tightly around his waist. Each touch, even so brief, seemed to spark an unexpected warmth inside me.

We took a few turns, venturing further from the small town, winding our way toward the woods, until the scenery shifted. On one side of the dirt road, rows and rows of cotton stretched out, soft and white against the green landscape, while the other side was lined with tall stocks of corn, their rustling leaves whispering in the breeze.

As we broke through a small clearing, the trees emerged—lush and dense, their rich green canopies almost suffocating in their thickness. The feeling of being surrounded by so much nature, by so many trees, was exhilarating, but there was a part of me that felt a twinge of nervousness. The four-wheeler fit snugly between the trunks, but with how close the branches reached out, I couldn't shake the feeling that one wrong turn and we'd be in danger of getting trapped.

Colton slowed, adjusting his speed as he turned just enough to speak to me, his voice carrying back through the wind. "Don't forget to duck around the branches, some of them hang a little low."

The way his voice, steady and sure, cut through the rush of wind, grounded me. Even if I couldn't control everything around us, I trusted that he could navigate this terrain like second nature. My heart raced with the thrill of it, the air fresh with the scent of dirt and greenery. The only thing left for me to do was to keep my arms wrapped tightly around him, lean when he leaned, and trust that we'd make it through the woods unscathed.

"You brought me to the woods; do I need to be worried about us running into a bear?" I hesitantly looked around, feeling the invisible eyes of at least one or two wild creatures lurking in the shadows. In the back of my mind, I could practically hear the thudding of a bear's paws as it paced nearby. I thought about my google search I had made before I came here, more horrifying images of dangerous wildlife I could now practically see hiding behind every tree. If there had been a snake in the garden, I knew there were probably a few hundred wild animals out here too, but bears weren't the only thing I was worried about encountering. I had read enough to know North Carolina's forests were also home to spiders the size of my hand and alligators that could lurk in the most unlikely places.

The worst part was that every terrifying thing I had googled appeared in shades of brown and grey, blending into the surroundings so well that it was impossible to tell where the threat might be hiding.

Colton shot me a radiant smile, his eyes sparkling with the joy of being out here in the woods, completely at home. "We're making enough noise that any wildlife will probably make themselves scarce before we even get close. But if anything pops up, I'll take care of it."

I couldn't decide if his confident grin put me at ease or made my anxiety spike. Did he *really* think this was safe? But before I could fully process it, Colton turned back to face forward, roaring the four-wheeler to life as we barreled deeper into the woods.

I had barely registered the sudden acceleration when it hit me. He hadn't answered my question—no mention of whether we were about to run into a bear. Great. I wasn't sure if I was relieved or even more on edge now, but one thing was for sure: I was holding on to him a lot tighter than I had before.

* * *

We had spent a few hours out on the four-wheeler before Colton decided it was time to return to civilization, a decision I was extremely grateful for. I had been having fun once I convinced myself that we could probably outrun anything in the woods on the four-wheeler, and that if Colton said he'd handle something, I could trust him to do just that. But I was mostly relieved that we were heading back, because the steady vibration of the wheeler had caused my legs to grow strangely numb, and I wasn't sure how much longer I could hold on without feeling like my limbs were going to fall off.

As we neared his house, I realized we hadn't yet been there, even though we'd spent so much time together since the rodeo. Instead, we'd gone on dates, and I found myself curiously wondering what his place might look like. From what he'd said, it was a small three-bedroom house about fifteen minutes away from my mom's, but he hadn't elaborated much on the details. He'd mentioned that it had belonged to his brother before his family moved into their childhood home, so I had no real expectations—just the fact that Colton had a house at all seemed to speak to a settled, steady kind of life. He parked the four-wheeler between his truck and police car, the grass around them looking uncut but still well-kept.

When we walked up to the house, I blinked in surprise. The exterior was a dull brown, but there, smack in the middle, was a bright yellow door that practically screamed for attention, the kind of color you'd see on a childhood lemonade stand. It stuck out like a sore thumb against the otherwise muted tones of the house.

As Colton unlocked the door, I couldn't help but comment, "That's a bold statement piece." My eyes lingered on the large brass doorknocker shaped like a bird, its detailed feathers making it look almost too fancy for the otherwise laid-back exterior. The wicker wreath of fake flowers tied around the knocker made it all the more... unexpected. It was very feminine in a way that seemed out of place.

He looked up at the bird and the wreath above the door, then shrugged. "Oh yeah, Paisley added them. Said the place looked too much like a bachelor pad, so I let her add some things."

Bachelor pad seemed generous—more like a hotel room, honestly. The walls were bare except for a few duck decoys near the stone fireplace. The leather couch faced a big flat screen, but there wasn't much else.

"It's a slow work in progress, making it my own," Colton said with a playful grin.

I raised an eyebrow. "A work in progress, huh? With that yellow front door and bird knocker, it looks like you've already moved in and put a unique spin on it."

He laughed, unbothered. "You want something to drink? I'll get lunch started." He dropped his shoes and headed toward the back of the house.

I followed into the kitchen, noting the shift in atmosphere. The living room had been dark and heavy, but the kitchen was bright, with huge windows letting in the sun.

I smirked. "I didn't expect you to have a bench with a pillow cover."

A yellow-and-pink floral pillow sat on a built-in bench under the window. Not something Colton would've picked out himself.

He dug through the fridge. "Some of its leftover from when Brendan and his wife, Lucy, lived here. My mom occasionally shows up with thrift store finds, convinced they'll change my life."

Colton returned with sandwich makings and two water bottles. "How about a sandwich? We could try Smithfield barbecue for dinner. Get the crew together or we could go on a date?"

I moved to help him set things on the counter. "Am I going to love Smithfield as much as I loved the cheddar bo? Will I have to pick a favorite?"

He grinned, opening containers for the sandwiches. "No contest. It's like comparing Johnny Cash to Dolly Parton—both amazing in their own way, no need to compare." He nudged me toward the barstools. "Now take a seat. I'm about to blow your mind with the best sandwich ever."

Colton quickly assembled the sandwich, layering mayo, mustard, turkey, and cheese on the bread. He slid over to the pantry, returned with a bag of chips, and ripped it open with a flourish, adding nacho cheese chips to my sandwich.

"Chips in the sandwich?" I asked, skeptical. My nose curled in disgust despite my effort to hide it. "That can't possibly be good."

He slid the plate toward me, gesturing as he stepped back. "Trust me, I felt that same way originally. Lucy came up with this when she was pregnant with one of the girls. Everyone thought it was awful, but I tried it to make her feel better. It's better than you'd think. The chips add a nice crunch."

Back home in Vegas, I would've eaten a kale salad or grabbed a green smoothie for lunch, working through the hour to stay ahead of everything. I never would've thought to throw chips on a sandwich—too many calories, too much guilt.

I hesitated, eyeing the sandwich for a second before taking a bite. The crunch was surprisingly satisfying. I swallowed, a little surprised by how much I liked it. "Okay, that's good. Not something I'd ever tried on my own."

Colton grinned, already preparing a second sandwich for himself. He sat down beside me at the counter, unwrapping it with the kind of focus usually reserved for a long-lost treasure. "See? That's what I'm saying. There's just something about the crunch that makes it so addictive." He practically inhaled the first few bites, as if he'd never seen food before in his life.

I couldn't help but laugh at the way he savored his sandwich. "You really get into your food," I said, amusement dancing in my voice.

"Hey," he said between bites, voice muffled, "life's too short not to enjoy the little things." He paused, wiping his mouth with the back of his hand.

"So, what's your plan after this?" I asked, taking another bite, trying not to overthink the question. The quiet around us felt different. In Vegas, everything was rush and noise, constant movement.

But out here, in the wide-open space, everything felt slower, more... thoughtful. Maybe too thoughtful.

Colton shrugged, playing it off. "Yeah? Are you bored already?" He raised an eyebrow, half-teasing, half-curious.

I quickly shook my head. "No, I'm just trying to figure out our day." His idea of a date at the Smithfield restaurant was starting to sound intriguing, especially with how highly everyone had spoken of it. Even more so now that he was comparing it to Dolly Parton level of good. "We've got quite a bit of time before we will want to eat again, so I'm just trying to figure out what we want to do next."

I took another bite of my sandwich, silently trying to match his speed. He was flying through his, barely pausing as we spoke.

Then he dropped it, as casually as if we were talking about the weather: "I mean, we could be having sex. That would be a great way to fill our time."

The dry bread caught in the back of my throat, and I immediately pounded my fist against my chest to dislodge it. Once I was able to clear my throat, I grabbed my water, taking a quick swig. "Colton! You can't just say things like that. We haven't even kissed yet!"

He leaned in close, his face inches from mine. The warmth of his breath brushed across my cheeks, deepening the flush I knew was already there. "Oh, I'm very aware of that," he said, his voice low and teasing. "Don't worry, I plan on rectifying that... very soon."

"Yeah?" I tucked my tongue into my cheek, leaning into his warmth and the strong smell of his sweat from our four-wheeler adventure. "How soon?"

I was expecting him to say something just as flirty as he had done before, instead his hands came up to my neck, cradling it gently as his lips crashed into mine with an intensity I was not prepared for.

Colton kissed me like he'd been holding back for too long, like he was making up for lost time. His hands, rough and warm, held me steady as he deepened the kiss, his fingers brushing against the sensitive skin at the nape of my neck. The sensation sent a shiver down my spine, my fingers instinctively gripping the front of his shirt, pulling him closer.

The faint taste of salt and the lingering flavor from the chips mixed with the scent of him—earthy, a little like sun-warmed leather and sweat, all of it intoxicating. My heart pounded so hard I was sure he could feel it through my skin.

Colton slowed just enough to tease, his lips barely brushing against mine before diving back in, as if he needed to memorize every part of this moment. His fingers slid into my hair, tilting my head so he could kiss me deeper, and I let him. I gave into the way he made the world around us disappear.

When we finally broke apart, his forehead rested against mine, both of us breathing hard. His grip on my hair loosened, his thumb stroking absently along my skin like he wasn't quite ready to let go.

"Soon enough for you?" he murmured, his voice husky, edged with amusement.

I swallowed, barely able to think past the way my lips still tingled. "Yeah. That worked."

His slow, satisfied grin was the last thing I saw before he pulled me in again for another kiss.

Chapter Ten

Just like every time before, Colton opened the truck door and offered his hand to help me down. But this time, when my feet hit the ground, he didn't let go. Instead, he shifted, draping his arm over my shoulders and pulling me close, his warmth settling against my side.

Our kiss had unlocked a new kind of closeness, and since then, he hadn't let go of me once. His hands always had to be touching me—holding mine, resting against me in some way—especially when we rode in the truck. Before, he had always left space between us, careful to avoid even the chance of brushing against each other. But today, he pulled me over, settling me in the middle of the bench seat, our fingers tightly intertwined.

"Ellie Monae," he said, his voice softer now, more certain. "Do you know how much I've enjoyed being with you this past week? And how happy I am that you decided to stay through the summer?"

The decision hadn't come easily. I'd spent the last two nights lying awake, running through every reason I should leave—work, obligations, the life I had waiting for me. But when the thought of going back made my stomach twist, I knew. I couldn't leave.

So, I cashed in the rest of my PTO, sent my sister a long text explaining my decision, and waited for a response that never came. Left on read. Again. And suddenly, I found myself wondering just how deep a grudge she was willing to hold. It was no secret she wanted nothing to do with Clinton, but I did—and that had to count for something.

Colton's fingers traced an easy, absentminded pattern along my shoulder, his touch pulling me back to the present. To him. To the way he was looking at me now—like I was something worth holding onto.

"You have no idea how glad I am about it, either," I admitted, tilting my head up to meet his gaze.

Eventually, I pulled away, murmuring something about getting some rest. The past week had been a whirlwind, and between the long rides, late-night conversations, and Colton's effortless ability to get under my skin in the best way, exhaustion had finally caught up with me.

By the time I made it inside my mom's house, it was quiet—the kind of stillness that comes with living out in the country. It was three in the morning, and I knew Mitch would be getting up soon to start his day, so I tried to be as quiet as possible. As usual, the hound dog raised his head to acknowledge me before going right back to snoring.

I trudged upstairs, kicking off my boots at the door to my bedroom before flipping on the light.

I barely registered the shape on my bed at first. Just a pile of blankets and a multitude of pillows. My body was already in motion, ready to collapse onto the mattress—

Then I heard it. A soft, steady snore coming from the weft of dark hair against my pillow. The owner of the hair had just the back of their head sticking out from the large mass of pillows and blankets.

Colton's words from earlier sprang to mind: *"If it was a snake, it would've bit you."*

I froze. Oh. A sharp chill going down my spine.

"Mom!" I whisper-shouted, stepping back into the hall and

making a beeline for the master bedroom. "Mom! I think there's someone in my bed!"

I could hear a rustling of her waking up and it was a few seconds before Mom opened her bedroom door, her head full of bright pink Velcro rollers. She blinked at me, clearly still half-asleep. "Ellie, what is going on?"

I pointed toward my bedroom door, my voice rising now that I was no longer alone. "There is someone in my bed."

Before Mom could respond, the figure emerged from my room, and a startled shriek escaped my lips.

"Oh, shut up," Olivia's voice cut through the moment as she stepped fully into the light. She crossed her arms, unimpressed. "Why are you freaking out?"

"You're here?" I closed the space between us and pulled her into a tight hug. "What made you change your mind?"

She pushed me off, never one for physical contact. "Well, I had a sister leaving me desperate voicemails and a few begging texts, which got me thinking about coming. But the text from Mom—the one informing me that you decided to stick around for the summer and that you're dating a cowboy? Yeah, that's what finally did it."

Her text—*Fine, you win*—suddenly made a lot more sense.

I searched her face. "So, you're saying Mom gossiping about my love life is what finally got you here?"

Olivia smirked. "More like the sheer *shock* of it. You? Dating a *cowboy*? What happened to the Ellie who swore she'd never be caught dead in a place like this?"

I rolled my eyes, but the comment cut deep because I had been asking myself that question all week long. "Things change."

She raised an eyebrow. "Clearly." Her gaze flicked over me, and something softened in her expression—just for a second, before she shook it off. "I figured I should see this disaster firsthand. Make sure you haven't completely lost your mind."

"Wow. Your love is overwhelming."

"You *did* wake me up in the middle of the night with a scream," she shot back, rubbing her eyes. "I thought you were the rational one."

"I *am* rational," I said, crossing my arms. "But maybe next time, you could announce your presence instead of breaking into my bed like some kind of fairy tale villain."

Olivia snorted. "Please. If I were a villain, I'd have taken the whole bed. I left one side open for you."

"So... are you really staying?"

She hesitated, then shrugged. "For a little while." A cheeky grin spread across her face. "Figured you shouldn't get to have all the fun."

Mom, still standing in the doorway of the bedroom, sighed and reached up to adjust one of her Velcro rollers. "Well, since neither of you are being quiet, I suppose I should put on some coffee. Mitch will be wanting to get up soon to start his day."

Olivia yawned, stretching her arms above her head. "Yes, please. I drove for hours to get here. I need caffeine if I'm not going to be getting any more sleep."

I frowned. "Wait. You drove?"

Olivia shrugged like it was no big deal, but my stomach twisted. That wasn't like her. Sure, she'd always been impulsive, but she valued her time too much for a spontaneous, cross-state road trip which only pointed to how intense I had been with my calls.

I studied her, the way she leaned against the wall, arms crossed over her chest like a shield which was usually more my speed than hers. "Liv... is everything okay?"

Her expression flickered—just for a second—before she forced out a laugh. "I'm fine. Just needed to see for myself what kind of cowboy spell you're under."

Liar.

But I would let it slide, for now.

Instead, I hooked my arm around hers, steering her toward the kitchen. "Come on, then. You can continue to judge my life choices over coffee."

She smirked. "Oh, I fully intend to."

We made our way back to the kitchen, and Mom flicked on the coffee pot. Within seconds, the rich, bitter aroma filled the room. I grabbed the creamer from the fridge—she would never willingly choose hazelnut, but after one sip of Mitch's coffee, I knew she'd be reaching for anything to cut the bitterness.

"So, you drove here?" I pressed, not ready to let the conversation drop.

We settled at the kitchen table while Mom rustled through the cupboard, emerging with the blueberry muffins she'd baked a few days ago. She set them between us before hurrying into the pantry, pulling out more food and stacking it on the counter beside her.

"Oh, blueberry! My favorite!" Olivia reached over and immediately tore into the muffins. "The only option I had was Dulles International Airport on this short of notice, so I had to pick up a rental car to make it here."

"That's so far. Why didn't you just wait and fly out later?"

Olivia huffed, then jabbed a finger in my direction. "Oh no, you *do not* get to come at me for that." She leaned in, eyes narrowed. "Not when *you* were the one sending cryptic texts and leaving desperate voicemails about how 'everything is different here.'"

I opened my mouth to argue, but she cut me off, mimicking my voice in a dramatic whisper so that Mom wasn't overhearing us. "You need to get here. Mom is wearing a sweatshirt and a ponytail!" She let her voice raise just a little to further her point and the dramatics. "No Botox! Mom is *without Botox!*"

"'Liv, you don't understand. It's just different. I can't explain it, but I needed to talk to you." I huffed and gestured toward Mom, who was still in the back of the kitchen. She was pulling out the items to make Mitch's breakfast. "You see that, right? She has turned into a Stepford wife."

Olivia dropped the act, her voice returning to normal as she studied Mom. "I'll admit, it's weird. I never would've expected her to wear something like that or be so casual about it." She paused, her brow furrowing. "But she *does* seem happy."

I sighed, rubbing my temples. Okay, maybe I *had* been a little dramatic when I called. But it had been a *huge* shock that first day—to walk up and see her looking *like that*, acting so... different without a warning. Now, though? Now, I was used to it. More than that, I welcomed it.

She was warmer now. More open. More like a mother.

"I'm sorry I freaked out and woke you up, but you really shouldn't have been in my bed without warning," I said, crossing my arms.

Olivia shrugged, completely unbothered. "I figured one of us should use it. And since you were off with Colton, it was mine for the taking."

I huffed out a laugh, but my gaze kept drifting back to Olivia. She was always so easygoing, yet something felt off—the way she avoided eye contact, how she kept picking at the edges of the muffin wrapper, her untouched coffee sitting on the table.

"So, how's work?" I asked, leaning back in my chair. I was fishing, but most of Olivia's stress usually came from our dad. The two of them were so different that their unsupervised time together often ended with her calling me in tears and him calling in a state of overwhelming frustration.

She had opened her boutique, *The Velvet Hanger*, a few years ago and was now in the middle of an expansion. Just before I left, Dad had toured two new properties with her, helping her weigh her options.

"Dad is helping me find a new property, and he's steamrolling over me like always."

I could only imagine. The last time they went property shopping, it had been a disaster—three months of radio silence, both too pissed to be the first to break. Dad had finally extended his version of an olive branch by buying a property himself and leaving the building plans on Olivia's porch, as if that was a compromise. It wasn't the one she wanted, of course, but by then, she had accepted it mostly to keep the peace since she knew how badly it bothered me.

"He's acting like it's his project," Olivia went on, crossing her arms. "I swear, if he pulls another stunt like last time—" She stopped, shaking her head.

Mom came up and joined us at the table, joining our conversation. "What happened this time?"

She scoffed. "We walked through a few places, and I had a favorite—perfect location, lots of natural light, enough space to expand—so of course, he hates it. He thinks it's too modern, too trendy. And instead of just saying that, he suddenly has a dozen reasons why it's 'not a smart investment.'" She made air quotes. "Then, today, I find out he's already talking to the realtor about a totally different property, one I never even considered."

That sounded like Dad.

I smirked. "Do you think he will leave the plans on your porch again?"

She groaned. "It wouldn't surprise me at all."

The two of them were too alike for their own good. Where I took after Mom, Olivia was all Dad—opinionated, stubborn, and convinced she knew best. A small part of me was convinced that was why they clashed so much. They saw too much of themselves in each other.

"You know he's not trying to sabotage you, right?" I spoke up in his defense. "In his own way, he is helping."

She exhaled, rubbing her temple. "Yeah, I know. Doesn't make it any less infuriating."

I didn't envy her. Convincing Dad to back off was a battle she'd fought her whole life, and as much as I loved them both, I had no intention of getting in the middle of this round especially now that I was finding such peace out here.

I nudged her foot under the table. "So, how's *The Velvet Hanger* going?"

She sighed, leaning back in her chair. "Good. Stressful, but good. Expanding was supposed to make things easier, but between Dad and the logistics, I'm starting to wonder if it's even worth it."

I tilted my head. "You don't mean that."

She hesitated, then shook her head. "No, I don't. I just—I've worked so hard for this, you know? I want it to be perfect."

I did know. Olivia had poured everything into that boutique, building it from the ground up, and now she was finally at the point where she could grow it into something bigger. Of course, she wanted to get it right.

Her smile faltered just a bit before she masked it with another yawn. "You know. Life is always busy. You know how it is when you are working with Dad. Never a dull moment."

I knew that tone. She was dodging the same way I was stalling—neither of us good at hard nor awkward conversations, a trait we'd both inherited from our parents.

"If you want to stay awake for more than five minutes, you're going to need a second cup. Drink this while I brew more." Mom jumped up from the table and grabbed the coffee pot from the machine and brought it to the table, so that we could refill our cups when we were done.

Olivia accepted the coffee with a grateful nod but didn't take a sip right away. Instead, she let out a sigh—one that felt heavier than usual.

I waited, knowing that she would be more willing to open up if I gave her space.

"I didn't expect you to be this far into the cowboy thing. I thought you only dated corporate guys?" Olivia's voice was light, but there was something beneath it—curiosity, maybe even hesitation—like she was testing the waters.

I frowned. "It's just for the summer. Nothing permanent." The words felt hollow the second they left my mouth.

"Right." She dragged out the word just enough to make me wonder if she believed me – I didn't believe myself either.

Mom, sensing the shift in mood, cleared her throat. "Well, I'm glad you two are talking again. I'm going to check on Mitch." She stood, taking her coffee with her, leaving me alone with Olivia.

I hesitated for a second, then leaned forward. "Liv, is everything okay?"

She met my gaze briefly before looking away, her lips pressing into a thin line. "Everything's fine." The words were too smooth, too calm.

A beat of silence stretched between us.

"Liv," I tried again, gentler this time.

She exhaled slowly, her fingers tracing the rim of her mug. "I just needed a change of scenery, that's all."

I wasn't convinced especially as her fingers tapped against the side of her mug, restless, like she had something she wanted to say but wasn't sure how.

"You sure?" I pressed, lowering my voice. "Because you don't seem fine."

She exhaled sharply through her nose, shaking her head slightly. "It's just... a lot. The expansion, managing everything on my own. I thought I had things under control, but it turns out business expansions come with a ridiculous amount of stress." She let out a dry laugh, but it didn't reach her eyes.

There it was.

I frowned, studying her carefully. Olivia didn't complain—at least, not unless things were really bad.

"Why didn't you say something?" My mind raced, already cycling through solutions, trying to figure out how to fix this. And the biggest one and the last thing that I wanted to do was going home, slipping back into my role as the buffer between her and Dad.

But the thought of leaving, of giving up what I'd found here, settled like a weight in my chest.

For the first time, I wasn't willing to do it.

She lifted a shoulder. "Because it's my problem to figure out."

"Liv." My chest tightened. I leaned back, dragging a hand through the ends of my hair. "You know that you can always talk to me. I'm here for you."

She didn't have an answer for that and honestly, neither did I.

* * *

Witnessing Kenna and Addie meet Olivia felt like watching my two lives blend into one.

Kenna, always quick with a smile, was the first to pull her into a tight hug. "It's so good to finally meet you, Olivia," she said, her voice light and welcoming.

Addie, not far behind, gave her own version of a soft but genuine smile. "I've heard a lot of good things about you," she added, her tone warm and sincere. "Your mom talks about you all the time."

Olivia blinked, momentarily taken aback by the warmth of their gestures—it wasn't just polite courtesy. Kenna's relaxed confidence and Addie's gentle encouragement were entirely genuine.

She hesitated for a moment, her usual reserve making her wary, but then she smiled back. "It's nice to meet you both," she said, her voice a little softer than usual as she shook Kenna's hand, then Addie's.

Kenna flashed a grin, giving her a light, almost teasing nudge. "I bet this is all really different from Vegas."

Olivia chuckled softly, a hesitant sound that warmed her eyes. "I didn't know what to expect, honestly. But this... this is nice." She glanced around as if taking it all in, the wide-open space, the comfortable warmth of the porch, the distant hum of crickets filling the silence between words.

Addie nodded, her expression thoughtful as she stepped back slightly, studying Olivia. "I'm glad you think so. We were so happy to hear from your mom that you were coming. I bet it was a great surprise for Ellie."

Liv smirked before turning back to Addie. "I can see why she's stayed. Ellie seems like she's really found her place here." Her voice softened slightly, something unspoken lingering beneath the words. "And I can't let her have all the fun."

Addie gave a knowing smile. "Well, if you stick around long enough, you might just start to see what she sees in this place."

"And fun your sister is having," Mitch chimed in, stepping onto the porch. He was back in his apron, fully in command of the barbecue. "Did she tell you all about our grand adventure to the Piggly Wiggly?"

For most people, a comment like that might have been a not-so-subtle nod to my relationship with Colton. But Mitch was being completely sincere—because, in his mind, a trip to the local grocery store truly counted as an adventure.

Olivia's arrival had perfectly coincided with Mom's big dinner—a joint meal with Colton's family. The timing felt like something out of a sitcom, and I wasn't entirely sure if that was a good thing.

It was one of those evenings where everything felt a little too coordinated, and I couldn't shake the sense of pressure building in my chest. I'd always been nervous about meeting new people, but now, with Colton in the picture, the anxiety felt like it had multiplied tenfold. His family was so important to him, and I had no idea how they'd take to me.

His parents and siblings were all set to come tonight, and while I'd had the chance to meet Paisley before, everyone else was a mystery. Colton had told me a few stories—some funny, some heartwarming—but that didn't give me a clear picture of what to expect.

What if I didn't fit in? What if I said the wrong thing? My mind spiraled, imagining all the ways the evening could go wrong.

Olivia, on the other hand, seemed calm—*even* excited. She left Addie and Kenna on the back porch and slipped into the kitchen, chatting with Mom about dinner preparations. I slipped back into the house and into the front room, lingered by the window, my eyes darting nervously to the driveway. Colton had promised it would be fine, that everything would go smoothly, but his reassurance didn't do much to quiet the flutter of butterflies in my stomach.

I wanted to make a good impression. I *needed* to.

My dating history was sparse, and meeting the parents? That had been even rarer. In fact, according to a survey I once read, about 70% of couples say meeting each other's parents is a major milestone in the relationship—and for a good reason. Apparently, relationships that survive the "meeting the parents" phase are more likely to last, but how did that change when both parties already knew that the relationship had a predetermined end date.

Somehow, the thought of meeting Colton's parents felt like we were stepping into something bigger—making whatever we had into something more serious. And that made me uneasy, unsure of whether we were ready for that step.

I glanced at my phone again, looking for some kind of distraction or even a message from him saying that they had to cancel, but there was nothing. Just me, my racing thoughts, and the growing sense of pressure as the minutes ticked by.

"Why are you so nervous?" Mason was walking through the front room toward the kitchen when he saw me and stopped, interrupting my inner turmoil of thoughts.

I looked up, forcing a smile, though it probably didn't reach my eyes. "I'm fine," I muttered, shaking my head as if trying to convince myself more than him.

Mason didn't buy it. "You're anything but fine. You've been pacing back and forth like you've got ants in your pants. You shouldn't be this jittery over meeting someone's parents."

"Yeah, you're right. Something about this is different," I muttered, running a hand through my hair and leaning against the armrest of the couch. "I don't know why I'm freaking out."

"Because this is the first time, you're not just meeting someone's parents for the sake of being polite. This time, it's real. You're seeing what Colton's life is like outside of you two. It's like... you're stepping into his world."

I hadn't realized it until Mason said it, but he was right. This wasn't just a meet-and-greet to be polite. This felt like an introduction to a whole new world, a new chapter. One where everything— my relationship with Colton, our future—was suddenly being judged and scrutinized by the people who had shaped him.

"You've got this," Mason added, his voice softer now, giving me that reassuring half-smile I had seen him use on his sister to calm her down when she got anxious. "Just be yourself. Colton likes you for a reason, and if his parents don't see that, that's their problem, not yours."

I nodded slowly, feeling a little calmer than I had a few minutes ago. Maybe Mason was right. The pressure I'd been putting on myself was all in my head. I needed to stop trying to control everything and just let things unfold.

"Thanks, Mason," I said, the words coming easier now. "I appreciate it."

"Anytime," he grinned. "Now, when they get here, just walk in and show them the real you. I'm sure they'll love you."

His words lingered in the air, and I felt a small weight lift off my chest. It wasn't the reassurance I thought I needed, but maybe that's exactly what it was—just a little reminder that I didn't have to be perfect.

With a deep breath, I stood up. Maybe, just maybe, it wouldn't be as bad as I'd built it up to be.

Chapter Eleven

I had assumed Colton had modeled himself after Mitch—his mannerisms, the way he carried himself—but watching his father, Thomas Bennett, I was starting to think that was just how these southern men were. There was an ease to them, a quiet confidence that didn't demand attention but still made itself known.

Thomas and Roseanne pulled up in a large white truck, its tires crunching over the gravel driveway. The moment the truck came to a stop, Thomas was already moving, slipping out of the driver's seat with practiced efficiency. Without hesitation, he rounded the front of the truck and opened the passenger door, offering a hand to his wife. There was no fanfare to the gesture—just muscle memory, as if helping Roseanne down was as natural to him as breathing. She accepted with a small, familiar smile, the kind exchanged between two people who had spent a lifetime together.

Thomas looked every bit the hardworking farmer, though today, he was dressed for company. He wore a neatly pressed plaid button-down, the sleeves rolled up to his forearms, revealing skin darkened and weathered by years in the sun. His jeans were clean, the fabric stiff enough to suggest they hadn't yet seen a full day's work. Deep wrinkles lined his face, the kind that came from a life spent outdoors, but what stood out the most were the smile lines—dozens of them, stretching from the corners of his eyes to his cheeks, as if laughter had carved its place there over the years.

The front door banged open just seconds after he closed the car door behind him. Colt's two nieces came flying inside, their high-pitched shrieks cutting through the warm afternoon air. "Papa!" they screamed in unison, their tiny boots pounding against the wooden floor as they ran toward him at full speed.

Thomas barely had time to brace himself before they collided with his legs, wrapping their small arms around him as tightly as they could. Instead of staggering, he dropped into an easy crouch, sweeping both girls up into his arms.

"Well now, what's all this fuss about?" he drawled, his accent thick with affection for his grandchildren. "Y'all act like you haven't seen me in years."

One of the girls giggled, tucking her face against his shoulder. "Mommy said you were coming today!"

"That right?" Thomas glanced up at Roseanne with a knowing smile before turning back to the girls. "Guess I better make sure I brought something special for my favorite little ladies, then."

Their eyes widened with delight, their excitement bubbling over as they wiggled in his arms, already begging to know what he had for them.

I watched the scene unfold, a grandpa pulling a small handful of chocolates from his pocket and handing one to each of his grandbabies. A warm feeling spread through my chest as I saw how effortless it all was—the way Thomas carried himself, the way he interacted with his family. It was clear where Colton had learned how to be such a good man.

Roseanne was just as beautiful as I had imagined—graceful, poised, and every bit the classic Southern belle Colton spoke so highly of. Even in her sixties, there was a timelessness to her beauty, the kind that came from confidence and a life well-lived rather than from vanity. Her silver-streaked brunette hair fell in soft waves, framing a face lined with years of laughter and wisdom. She had that kind of warmth that made a person feel welcome before she even said a word, her honey-brown eyes radiating quiet kindness.

She wore a crisp, button-up blouse tucked neatly into a flowing skirt, the fabric swishing with every step she took. A string of pearls rested against her collarbone—simple, elegant, the kind of accessory that never went out of style. And despite the heat, not a single bead of sweat touched her skin, as if southern women like her had mastered the art of staying cool through sheer will alone.

There was something about her presence, the way she held herself, that made it easy to see why Colton admired her so much. She wasn't just beautiful—she was the kind of woman who made a house feel like a home, who carried love in the way she spoke, the way she moved, the way she looked at her family like they were the best thing in the world.

It took Roseanne no time at all to cross the room, her steps sure and graceful, before she reached for me, pulling me into a tight hug. Her embrace was firm yet gentle, carrying the soft scent of lavender and a hint of vanilla. Her skin was impossibly soft, warm in a way that felt both comforting and familiar, as if she had known me far longer than just this moment.

After a long moment she finally pulled back, keeping her hands on my arms as she gave me an approving once-over, her honey-brown eyes full of warmth that matched her son. A slow smile spread across her lips. "Colton didn't do you justice when he talked about you, sweetheart. You're even prettier in person."

I felt my face heat at the compliment, Colton silently snuck in the house, greeting those behind us warmly and his eyes caught mine as I spoke to his mom. "Thank you so much."

She gave my arms a reassuring squeeze. "I can already tell you're special. Heaven knows it takes a strong woman to keep up with a Bennett man, but I have a feeling you're up for the challenge."

A flurry of butterflies took flight in my stomach. The weight of her gaze wasn't intimidating—it was knowing, like she had seen enough love stories unfold to recognize when one was just beginning.

Before the moment could stretch too long, Roseanne looped her arm through mine, the gesture effortless, as if we were already old friends. "Now, I hope Mitch has made sure you've felt right at home, sugar," she said, guiding me toward the kitchen, moving through my mother's house as if it were her own. "But if there is anything you need, just let me know and I will take care of it for you."

Colton chuckled as he finally joined me, shaking his head. "Mama, she's fine."

"Hush, boy," Roseanne chided playfully, waving him off. "I'm just taking care of your girl."

Your girl.

The words settled over me like a warm breeze, unexpected but not unwelcome. I glanced at Colton, half-expecting him to correct her, but he just smiled, letting it slide.

I couldn't help but return the smile, letting the warmth of her welcome surround me. Something told me that once Roseanne Bennett decided you were family, there was no going back—and for the first time in a long time, I wasn't sure I'd ever want to.

Roseanne and I had barely made it into the kitchen where Olivia sat at the table playing on her phone when the front door swung open again, ushering in Brendan and Lucy, with a beaming Paisley in tow. The youngest Bennett sibling slipped through the back of the crowd, disappearing upstairs to join Addie and Kenna with a familiarity that made it clear she felt at home.

While my eyes instinctively followed Paisley for a moment—the only other person I really knew—it was Brendan and Lucy who held my attention. Brendan and Colton looked remarkably alike, though their resemblance had its distinctions. One favored their father, the other their mother, but it was Lucy who stole my focus.

When people talked about pregnant women having a glow, they must have had Lucy in mind. The late afternoon sunlight caught her auburn hair as she stepped into the kitchen, creating a halo-like effect around her. But it wasn't just the light that made her radiant—it was something in the way she carried herself, a quiet, effortless joy that seemed to shine from within. Her belly sat big and round beneath a flowing maxi dress, the fabric draping over her bump with soft elegance.

I had never imagined being pregnant. But something about the sight of Lucy, the way she carried the weight of impending motherhood so naturally, so beautifully, made me press a hand against my own flat stomach. The thought was fleeting, barely formed, but it lingered in the back of my mind like a whisper I wasn't ready to acknowledge.

She approached us with a warm smile, balancing a large container of decorated cupcakes. Half of them looked professionally crafted—perfect swirls of frosting and delicate sugar details—while the other half bore the unmistakable touch of tiny, eager hands. A few smudged sprinkles and uneven icing lines pointed to the patience of a mother who let her children create alongside her, imperfections and all.

Brendan stepped up beside her, his presence as steady as the easy grin on his face. His hand rested at the small of Lucy's back, a silent gesture of support—one that didn't seem necessary but was there, just in case.

Before I could get too caught up in my own thoughts, Roseanne patted my arm lightly. "Come on, sugar, let's get the food before these people start circling like vultures."

She grabbed a few plates of food from the counter and started to reach for the cupcakes Lucy was holding, but her daughter-in-law shook her head with a laugh. "I've got them. If Brendan's going to hover, he might as well make himself useful and grab the plates."

Brendan rolled his eyes but didn't argue, disappearing into the kitchen with Colton following close behind.

The warm, inviting energy of the house shifted as we followed them outside. The smells of roasted chicken and fresh-baked bread filled the air, wrapping around me like a comforting embrace. My mom was already moving between the grill and the table, humming under her breath as she arranged dishes. It was the kind of effortless coordination that only came with experience of hosting large family dinners.

"Ellie, sweetheart, could you grab the silverware?" Mom asked, glancing over her shoulder. "And Brendan will you let the girls know that we are all ready to eat?"

I nodded, stepping toward the drawer, only to find myself side by side with Colton as he reached for the same thing. Our hands brushed, and for a second, the rest of the room faded.

"Are you feeling okay?" he asked under his breath, his voice just low enough that only I could hear. "You seemed to have dazed out there for a second."

I hesitated, my fingers curling around a stack of forks. "Yeah," I said, but even to my own ears, it wasn't entirely convincing.

Colton's eyes searched mine, his easy confidence flickering with something softer. Something knowing. He didn't push, didn't press, just held my gaze a second longer than necessary before gently taking the silverware from my hand. His fingers brushed mine, brief but steady, and an unfamiliar warmth settled in my chest. He noticed—really noticed—when I wasn't okay, and I wasn't sure what to do with that.

Across the room, Roseanne was helping Lucy get settled, fussing over her that she shouldn't be on her feet all day. The sight sent a pang through my chest, but I shook it off, focusing on setting the table instead.

As I placed a fork beside each plate, I couldn't ignore the question settling deep in my bones. What if I could belong here? The thought was dangerous, tempting in a way I hadn't expected. Because once you start wanting something, it's that much harder to let it go. And I was really starting to enjoy the thought of staying here with Colton.

Once everyone gathered around the table, Colton made a point of pulling out my chair for me, ensuring I sat beside him, with Olivia on my other side. The simple gesture made me feel like I belonged, a little anchor in the whirlwind of family and noise.

Dinner settled into a comfortable rhythm, filled with easy conversation and the familiar clatter of silverware against plates. The Bennett siblings were a lively bunch—quick with a joke, never short on a story, and more than happy to fill any silence with laughter. Being with his siblings seemed to help Colton relax.

It was easy to get swept up in their energy. I found myself laughing as the warmth of their hospitality made me feel at ease, despite my initial nerves. As the meal went on, I realized just how natural it felt to be here. How, maybe for the first time, I could see what it would be like to be part of a family like this.

I had spent most of the meal observing, taking in the way Roseanne doted on her boys, the way Thomas and Mitch were the quiet anchor of their families, and how seamlessly Lucy fit into the fold. It was... nice. Easy. A world away from the more formal, reserved dinners I had grown up with.

And then, in a flash, the attention turned to me.

"So, Ellie," Paisley said, leaning forward with a curious glint in her eye. "What's your plan after the summer? Us girls were talking about going on a trip in the fall, and we could always use a fourth, or a fifth if you want to join Olivia."

I swallowed a bite of cornbread, suddenly hyper-aware of how many eyes were on me. "I, um—" I started, but before I could gather my thoughts, Brendan flashed a grin, a mischievous glimmer in his eyes.

"Careful, Paisley," Brendan teased, leaning toward her. "That question might send Colton into a crisis." The eldest Bennett brother reached over to nudge Colton's shoulder, a playful challenge in his gesture.

Colton shot him a look, his lips twitching into a half-smile. "Real funny, Brendan."

A chuckle rippled through the table, but I was still stuck on the question, on how uncertain my answer was. The thing was, I *didn't* have a plan. Not a real one, anyway.

"I'm still figuring that out," I admitted, forcing a small smile. "I was supposed to be heading back to Vegas soon, but I don't know when that will happen now."

There was a quiet moment after I said it, like my words had weight I hadn't even realized. That was the truth. I had come here thinking this summer was just a temporary escape, but now, with Colton, with the ease of being with a family, I wasn't so sure anymore.

"Well, lucky for you, figuring things out as we go along is something we're real familiar with," Roseanne said warmly. "Just means you've got options."

The way she said it made it sound less terrifying and more like an opportunity, something wide open rather than something uncertain. I exhaled, feeling a small bit better living in the unknown.

Conversation picked up again, flowing away from me, and I took the chance to sneak a glance at Colton. He was already looking at me, his green eyes soft, knowing how uncomfortable questions of my staying made me. He reached under the table, his fingers brushing against my knee—a small touch, but one that sent warmth through me.

As the meal wound down, I followed Roseanne into the kitchen, feeling like I needed to move, to do *something* with all the emotions swirling inside me. She handed me a dishtowel without question.

"That wasn't so bad, was it?" she asked, amusement flickering across her face.

I let out a breathy laugh. "I survived."

"You did more than that, sugar." She gave my arm a gentle pat. "You belong here more than you realize."

I didn't know what to say to that, so I just kept drying the plate in my hands, my chest tightening with something I wasn't ready to name. Because I was starting to think she was right.

The hum of conversation from the back porch drifted softly into the kitchen as Roseanne and I worked side by side, clearing away the remnants of dinner. The laughter of the others carried a gentle warmth, a comforting counterpoint that helped ease the tension I still couldn't quite shake off.

Roseanne hummed softly as she gracefully loaded the dishes into the sink. Her presence, calm and steady, had an almost soothing effect on me. We didn't speak much, but the quiet companionship of working together in the kitchen felt right.

The sound of the kitchen door creaked open, and I turned to see my mom step in, very hesitantly as she watched Roseanne and I bonding.

"Need any help?" she asked, glancing around the room with a practiced eye, taking in the disarray we were tackling.

Roseanne smiled warmly, teasing my mom. "Always room for an extra hand, darling, especially when it's your kitchen."

"I'm glad you could join us, Roseanne," Mom said, folding the towel in her hand. "It's nice to have another mom around this house full of young people."

Roseanne's smile softened. "It's my pleasure. I've always enjoyed a good family gathering. I love when we all get the opportunity to come together."

As they talked, I couldn't help but notice how effortlessly they'd slipped into this easy rapport, making the kitchen feel warm. It was obvious how quickly they must have become friends once Mom came here.

The evening had settled into a calm quiet, the sounds of the bustling family fading into the background as they all went into the family room. The men threw on the football game.

Colton and I had slipped outside to the backyard, away from the noise and laughter, to enjoy a few moments of peace. The warm glow from the pool's lights cast soft reflections on the water, making the whole area feel like it was bathed in a dreamlike haze.

We sat side by side near the edge of the pool, the night air still and comfortable around us. Colton had a relaxed smile, his arm casually draped over the back of my chair, his gaze steady on the horizon.

"I think that was the best family dinner I've ever been to," I said, my voice quieter than usual, though the words were true. There was something about tonight that had felt different—a kind of warmth that made everything seem like it fit together, even with all the noise and chaos. With the entire Bennett family there it made it feel even warmer than my first night, or maybe it was how comfortable I was starting to feel with everyone.

He glanced over at me, his eyes reflecting the same contentment. "Yeah? I'm glad you felt that way," he said with a slight grin. "My family sometimes can be... a lot, so I'm glad you have enjoyed spending time with them."

I chuckled softly. "They're a lot of fun." I let the peacefulness of the moment sink in, feeling the weight of meeting his family finally ease off my shoulders. "And you... you looked so relaxed with them. It's nice to see you like that."

Colton looked over at me, his gaze softening. "It's different with them," he said. "It's easy to be myself around my family." He shrugged lightly, as if the idea of his family being his comfort zone was something simple, even though when it came to my family it was the opposite.

I nodded, taking a moment to soak in the view of the stars above and the faint ripples in the pool. "I can see that," I said, looking back at him. "It's so nice to see you that way. I had only seen you act that relaxed when we are alone."

He let out a quiet laugh, his voice low and warm. "Guess I just feel that comfortable around you too."

For a moment, we sat there in comfortable silence, just watching the gentle movement of the water, the night wrapping itself around us. There was something so natural about being with him like this— just the two of us, no pretenses, no pressure.

"You know," Colton said after a few beats, his voice quieter, "I don't think I ever really appreciated how good it feels to be surrounded by family. Not until tonight, getting to share it with you."

I glanced at him, catching the sincerity in his words, and I felt my chest tighten with something soft. "I get that," I said, leaning slightly closer. "I didn't know what I was missing until now."

He turned his head to meet my gaze, a tenderness in his expression that made my heart beat a little faster. "I'm glad you're here. It feels complete to have you here." he said quietly. His words felt like a promise, something that settled deep inside me and wrapped around my heart.

I smiled, the warmth of his words enough to make me feel like everything was exactly where it needed to be. "I was just thinking the same thing."

I felt my heart pick up its pace, the space between us suddenly feeling smaller. Colton's gaze never wavered, his eyes soft and steady on mine, and I could feel the weight of the moment settling over us, wrapping around us like the warmth of the evening air.

Without thinking, I leaned in just slightly, the pull between us undeniable. Colton's hand, which had been resting casually on the back of my chair, shifted, his fingers brushing lightly against my arm causing a rush of goosebumps to come down my skin. The touch sent a ripple of warmth through me, and I found myself closing the distance.

He didn't hesitate, his hand moving to cup my cheek gently just as he did the first time we kissed. The contact of his touch was sending a spark through my skin. Slowly, he leaned forward, his breath warm against my lips. My heart skipped a beat as I met him halfway, the anticipation was slowly building between us.

When our lips finally met, it was soft and gentle at first, but as the kiss deepened, the sparks between us grew stronger, more urgent.

His other hand slid around to the back of my neck, pulling me closer as if he couldn't get enough of me. His lips pressed against mine deeper than before, even going as far as to nibble across my bottom lip.

Slowly he pulled the smallest bit away and the warmth of his breath only furthered the heated tension between us as he moved his lips against mine.

The world around us seemed to fade, the only sound the soft splash of the water against the pool's edge and the beating of our hearts in sync. It was a kiss that held everything—everything we had been feeling, everything we hadn't said yet.

And when we finally pulled away, both of us a little breathless, I couldn't help but smile. His forehead rested against mine, and I felt his smile against my lips.

"I've wanted to do that all night," Colton murmured, his voice rough with emotion.

I laughed softly, the sound a little shaky. "Me too."

He pulled me into a tighter embrace, and for the first time all night, I felt completely, utterly at home—like this, with him, in this moment. And for a while, everything was perfect—the night, the quiet, and the feeling that we were both exactly where we were supposed to be.

Chapter Twelve

With Olivia's support Mom finally got her way and we were on our way to the beach. The drive to the Outer Banks felt like an endless stretch of road, the promise of the beach on the horizon and the salty air just barely teasing the edge of my senses.

The van Mitch had borrowed was packed with chatter as we made our way down the winding roads. With Mason, Kenna, Addie, Colton, Olivia, and I all piled in the back of the van, it truly felt like we were kids again on a summer vacation. The sound of laughter and the hum of the engine filled the space as we bumped along the road, and for a brief moment, I was transported to the idea that we could always live like this and enjoy simpler times. Mom and Mitch sat in the front seat, Mitch driving while Mom would randomly turn around and flash us a wide smile, her eyes gleaming with the same kind of joy that seemed to ripple through the whole group.

Mom had talked in great detail about the beach house; a family friend owned it and had allowed the Richen and the Bennett families to visit every summer since they were all kids, so they were all very comfortable there. Olivia and I were both excited about the opportunity to visit a place that was filled with so many memories.

Addie had taken charge of the music, cranking up a playlist of beach tunes that made the whole atmosphere feel like one endless road trip to freedom. Kenna was in the back with Mason, the two of them arguing good-naturedly over who could make the best sandcastle when we got to the beach. Olivia and I shared a seat, occasionally catching each other's eye and exchanging glances—about what, I wasn't entirely sure, but in that moment, we were both content.

The windows were down, and the warm summer air rushed in, mingling with the sound of Colton's low laugh from the backseat from where he sat right behind me. Every now and then, I'd glance back at him and find his gaze meeting mine, a fleeting connection that made my heart beat a little faster, even though I still wasn't sure where we stood now that we had a budding relationship. But that didn't seem to matter right now. All that mattered was this—a van full of people, headed to the beach, the promise of a few carefree days ahead.

As the road stretched on for what felt like forever, I sank back into my seat, feeling a quiet sense of belonging—surrounded by people who were starting to feel like family just like Mom had wanted. And for the first time in a long while, I allowed myself to believe that maybe, just maybe, this summer could give me the clarity I'd been looking for when I had decided to come visit Mom.

When we finally pulled into the beach house, a two-story place with huge windows that faced the ocean, the sound of the waves was more soothing than I expected. The house was everything I imagined —a perfect place to escape. As soon as the door of the van opened, the scent of salt and sand hit me harder than it had before, and I took a deep breath.

Olivia and I carried our bags up to the room that we'd be sharing, which was tucked in the back of the house. I could already feel my shoulders easing at the sight of the ocean stretching out before me. It was nothing like the city skyline I was used to, but something about it made my chest feel lighter.

"This place is incredible," Olivia said, setting her bag by the bunk beds and flopping down onto the bottom bunk with a carefree attitude that I was envious of. "I'm really glad you decided to come visit Mom and that you were annoying enough for me to feel the need to come join you."

I gave her a smile, trying to ignore the feeling of being pulled between my life now and the one waiting for me back home. "I think I'm going to love being here just as much as I enjoying being with Mom in Clinton." I said, my voice quiet, but sincere.

The rest of our day passed in a haze of sun and sand, the ocean pulling me in as I dipped my toes into the water, feeling the cool rush of waves as they crashed against my feet. It was a small moment of peace, standing there in the shifting tide, watching the water stretch out into the horizon. I could have stayed like that for hours, but I knew I couldn't get too comfortable—I was still in jean shorts and a tank top, with no swimsuit available. Olivia and I had decided to hit up *Sunsations* in the morning to grab the beachwear we'd didn't think to bring when we had packed for North Carolina.

Mitch and Mom had left to go to the grocery store to stock up for the week since our beach house had a large kitchen, we had planned to cook most of our meals. The boys had gone off on a long walk, Colton and Mason in search of surfboards to rent, the idea of riding waves calling to them. Addie and Kenna had wandered off as well, determined to get ice cream from a little shop they'd frequented when they were kids. The beach was a place of memories for them, and they were eager to relive some of those moments once more.

That left Olivia and me alone by the water, the salty air swirling around us, mixing with the sound of seagulls calling overhead. For a moment, it was just us, the waves, and the faint hum of distant laughter from the groups surrounding us. It felt right—comfortable, even, in a way I hadn't expected. I'd always associated the beach, sunburns and sand between my toes. But today felt different, probably since this was my first family vacation to the beach.

"Hey, after we get our swimsuits tomorrow, we should hit the beach hard," Olivia said. "I think I need a good tan to really feel like I'm on vacation."

I laughed, nodding. "That sounds like a great plan."

As the sun began to dip lower in the sky, painting the water in shades of pink and orange, I felt a sense of peace settle over me, but I was worried it was the kind of peace that felt fleeting. I let myself enjoy the quiet moments by the sea with my sister beside me.

We had spent another hour out on the beach, letting the salt air tangle in our hair and the last warmth of the sun soak into our skin. When the evening started to roll around, we finally made our way back up to the house, where Mom and Mitch had already started dinner. The scent of grilled seafood and butter filled the air, mixing with the crisp ocean breeze that drifted in through the open windows. One by one, everyone gathered, settling into the easy rhythm of family dinner, just the way Mom loved.

Laughter echoed around the table, the sound of forks scraping against plates and glasses clinking together filling the space. It felt familiar in a way that made my chest ache—like something I hadn't realized I'd missed until it was right in front of me. Mom thrived in moments like these, where everyone was together, where the world felt a little smaller and a little kinder.

After dinner, as conversation lulled and people started peeling away from the table, I volunteered to clean up. I needed a moment to myself, to process the warmth in my chest and the weight of the thoughts still unsettled in my mind. The sound of running water and the distant crash of waves outside filled the kitchen as I worked, helped me to think.

The view from the kitchen window was breathtaking, the ocean stretching out endlessly, the sun sinking lower on the horizon, turning the water into liquid gold. It was peaceful in a way I hadn't expected, like the world was slowing down just for me.

That was when Colton walked in.

I felt him before I saw him—the shift in energy, the way the air in the room seemed to change. Then he leaned against the doorway, his signature half-smile playing at his lips, his eyes holding that unreadable glint that always made my heart flutter. His hands rested on the doorframe, his biceps flexing slightly with the movement, and I hated how easily my stomach flipped at the sight.

"Do you always volunteer to do the dishes?" he asked, his voice warm, teasing.

I smirked, rinsing off a plate before setting it in the drying rack. "Only when I need an excuse to be alone. This is a lot of people in a small house, and I am lucky enough to share a room with my sister all week. I know I will be lacking some alone time."

Colton hummed, pushing off the doorframe and walking toward me. "Lucky me, then since I wanted some alone time with you."

I rolled my eyes, but my lips twitched at the edges, the action betraying the amusement I felt. He stopped beside me, reaching for a towel, and started drying the dishes without another word. It was effortless, the way he fit into the space next to me, like he'd done it a hundred times before.

We worked in comfortable silence for a few moments, the tension between us simmering beneath the surface, present but not suffocating. It was in the way his shoulder brushed mine, the way his fingers lingered just a little too long when I passed him a plate and the energy between us tingled with electricity.

Eventually, he broke the silence. "You seemed happy today. Not many people take a long care ride like that in such stride."

I paused for half a second before nodding, focusing on the dish in my hands. "Yeah. I enjoyed the ride. It was fun to see that side of everyone."

"Good," he murmured, and when I glanced up at him, there was something softer in his expression, something I wasn't sure I was ready to name.

Everyone else was in the family room, the low hum of a movie drifting through the house, broken up by occasional laughter and the rustling of snack bags. The plan was to go ghost crab hunting as soon as the sun fully set, something that Addie had insisted was a must-do while we were here.

Colton must have sensed my thoughts drifting because he set down the towel and turned to face me fully. "Come with me," he said suddenly.

I raised a brow, a giggle flying from my lips when I took in the mysterious look on his face. "Where?"

Our destination was the front porch where two sturdy beach chairs sat. He had grabbed two bottles of water from the cooler on the way out, handing me one as we stepped onto the deck. The wood was still warm from the day's sun, the air thick with the salty scent of the ocean.

Colton gestured for me to sit before sinking into the chair beside me. He stretched his legs out, resting his arms on the sides, tilting his head back to look up at the night sky as it slowly turned from day to night.

"I used to come out here when I was younger," he said after a moment, his voice quieter now, like he didn't want to disturb the peaceful hum of the waves. "Whenever we stayed at the beach, I'd sneak out onto the deck after everyone went to bed and just listen while watching the stars. Think about everything and nothing at the same time."

I turned my gaze upward, taking in the vast sky above us. The stars were clearer here, unhindered by city lights, spread across the darkness like a beautiful array of scattered diamonds.

"What'd you think about?" I asked softly, wrapping my fingers around the cool plastic of the water bottle.

Colton shrugged, his lips quirking up in a small, almost self-conscious smile. "Depends on the summer. Sometimes it was what I wanted to do with my life. Sometimes it was just dumb stuff, like what it'd be like to live in a lighthouse or if fish ever got sick of swimming."

I laughed, shaking my head. "And now?"

He turned his head to look at me, his expression thoughtful, serious. "Now, I'm thinking about how you fit into my world. How much I have enjoyed spending the time with you this summer."

A lump formed in my throat, the weight of his words pressing into me, making it hard to breathe. I wanted to say something; to tell him I was thinking about the same thing—about how easy it felt being here with him, how natural. But I also knew that thoughts and reality were two very different things.

So instead, I reached over, lacing my fingers with his. He squeezed my hand in response, neither of us saying anything else as we sat in the comfortable silence.

It had been a few short minutes when the door opened and Mason's goofy grin appearing. "Are you ready for some ghost crab hunting?"

* * *

"Come on," Colton said as he hopped down the steps into the sand, looking back as I hesitated to join him. "I know you've never been ghost crab hunting, but you can't possibly be this scared. I won't let them get you."

I crossed my arms, eyeing him skeptically as I stepped onto the cool sand, much more aware of where I placed each foot compared to when Olivia and I had run out earlier. "I can totally be this scared. They have freaky little eyes."

Colton smirked, teasing. "Depends on how fast you can move when they start running at you."

That made me pause. "Wait. They run?"

"Oh, yeah. And they're fast." He reached into his pocket, pulling out his phone and flipping on the flashlight. "But that's what makes it fun."

Before I could argue that my definition of fun didn't involve being chased by tiny sand creatures, the rest of our group spilled out onto the beach, flashlights in hand, buzzing with excitement.

He chuckled, reaching for my hand as we walked toward the shoreline where the others were already starting to spread out, their flashlights sweeping across the sand. Every so often, someone would let out a laugh or a startled yelp, confirming that the ghost crabs were, in fact, very real and very fast.

"Okay, city girl," Colton said, coming to a stop and pointing his flashlight at a tiny white crab skittering across the sand. "There's your first one."

I squinted at the small creature, watching as it froze under the light, its beady eyes locking onto us before it suddenly darted sideways – heading toward me. I jumped, instinctively tightening my grip on Colton's hand.

He laughed. "You're jumpier than I thought you would be."

"I don't like things that move unpredictably," I muttered, earning an even bigger grin from him. "I would rather be prepared."

"Well, that just makes this more fun." He let go of my hand and crouched down, holding his flashlight steady as he reached out with his other hand.

My eyes widened. "You're not seriously going to—"
Before I could finish, Colton scooped up the crab, holding it gently between his fingers as he stood. "See? Harmless."

I took a cautious step back, eyeing the creature as its legs wriggled in the air. "That's debatable."

"Want to hold it?" he offered, his smirk deepening when I immediately shook my head.

"Absolutely not." I tucked my hands in my back pockets, as if that would further my point.

Colton chuckled, lowering the crab back to the sand and watching as it scurried away. He looked back at me, his expression softer now, less teasing. "I think that you will be surprised at how much fun this is. I promise, I won't let it pinch you."

I hesitated, glancing around at the others. Addie and Kenna were laughing as Mason tried to catch one, and Olivia was crouched down, pointing out a smaller one nearby as Mom and Mitch stood beside her, a loving look gracing both of their faces. It wasn't scary to any of them—it was fun. Maybe I was missing out.

With a deep breath, I nodded. "Fine. But if it so much as twitches, I'm done."

Colton grinned. "That's my girl."

Mason had disappeared the moment we stepped inside in pursuit of a shower, and we had only been back at the house for a few moments when Mom and Mitch announced they were heading to bed. Addie and Kenna also called it a night, already set on waking up early to hit the beach. Olivia followed the others, tossing a sarcastic comment over her shoulder about claiming the bottom bunk since she was going to bed first—so I'd just have to deal with it.

I barely heard her. My focus was elsewhere—on the quiet settling over the house, on the way the warm glow of the kitchen lights cast soft shadows across Colton's face as he leaned against the counter. On the fact that, for the first time all day, it was truly just going to be the two of us.

Colton stretched, rolling his shoulders before shoving his hands into his pockets. "Well," he said, drawing out the word as his gaze flicked toward me, "guess that means we got the place to ourselves."

My stomach flipped at the way he said it—casual, teasing, but laced with something deeper, something that sent a slow heat curling through me.

"Guess so," I murmured, suddenly hyperaware of every inch of space between us and how many steps it would take before we were face to face.

He fully pushed off the counter, stepping closer, his fingers brushing mine like he wasn't sure if I'd pull away. I didn't.

"You want to do something a little crazy?" His voice was low, rough around the edges.

I raised a brow. "Like what?"

A smirk tugged at the corner of his lips. "Do you trust me?"

I huffed out a laugh. "That depends."

He didn't elaborate, just tugged me toward the sliding glass door that led to the back porch. We stepped onto the deck, and Colton released my hand just long enough to pull off his shirt, tossing it onto one of the chairs.

I blinked; my mouth suddenly dry. "Um—"

"Relax, Ellie," he said, grinning as he backed toward the steps that led to the pool. "I'm not suggesting anything scandalous. Just figured we could go for a swim."

I glanced toward the small in ground pool the house provided us with. "We don't have swimsuits."

His grin widened. "So?"

I narrowed my eyes. "So, some of us didn't grow up in the middle of nowhere, swimming in ponds and rivers and whatever else you small-town boys do. Some of us are dignified, only swimming at the rec center where a swimsuit is required."

"Then it's about time you experienced it." He held out his hand. "C'mon, city girl. Live a little."

I hesitated, the logical part of me screaming that this was a terrible idea. That the water was too cold and that it was reckless and impulsive and completely out of character for me.

But then Colton gave me that look—the one that made my heart stutter in my chest, the one that made me want to throw caution to the wind just to see what it felt like.

So, before I could talk myself out of it, I reached for the hem of my shirt and pulled it over my head, leaving me in my sports bra and shorts.

Colton's gaze darkened, but he didn't say anything, just grabbed my hand and led me toward the water.

We stepped down onto the first step and the water wrapped

around my ankles, stealing my breath with its cool touch, but I didn't back away. Not this time.

Colton squeezed my fingers. "Ready?"

I exhaled, letting the tension drain from my shoulders. Then I nodded.

And together, we went deeper into the water.

Chapter Thirteen

Sunsations was exactly what I expected—a brightly lit beach store crammed with racks of swimsuits, overpriced sunscreen, and enough souvenir t-shirts to last a lifetime. The smell of coconut-scented suntan lotion filled the air, mixing with the faint scent of salt and plastic floaties.

Olivia and I had barely stepped inside before she made a beeline for the swimsuit section, already shifting through a rack of bikinis with practiced ease.

"You're going to try on everything, right?" she asked, not even looking at me as she tossed a neon pink top over her shoulder and started to create a pile in her arms.

I sighed, running my fingers along the edge of a black two-piece that seemed like the safest option. "Define 'everything.'"

Olivia finally looked up, giving me a knowing smirk. "Everything that makes you look hot."

I rolled my eyes. "So, your definition of everything."

"Obviously." She grabbed a deep red bikini and held it up in front of me as if she could picture me in it. Without hesitation she threw it into the pile. "Oh, this would look amazing on you."

I barely had time to protest before she shoved it into my hands, already moving to another rack. "Liv, I haven't worn a bikini in forever—"

"Then it's about time you wear one," she interrupted. "You're at the beach, Ellie. You're supposed to be having fun, not dressing like a nun and there is a smoking hot cowboy who would love to see you in this suit."

I sighed but didn't argue. Instead, I let her pile swimsuit after swimsuit into my arms, ranging from safe, neutral tones to things that barely qualified as clothing.

After what felt like an eternity, she finally declared we had enough and dragged me toward the fitting rooms.

I slipped into the first suit —the black one I had picked out— figuring I should at least start with something comfortable. The top of the suit fit well, hugging my curves without making me feel too exposed, and the bottom hem sat high on my hips, giving the illusion of longer legs.

Olivia didn't even wait for me to fully step out of the fitting room before letting out a loud whistle. "Holy Crap! Ellie. Colton's going to lose his mind when he sees you in that."

I felt my face heat instantly. "Stop it."

She grinned, completely unbothered. "I'm just saying. You've been dancing around your feelings for him. Maybe it's time you give the guy a little push."

I rolled my eyes, but deep down, I couldn't deny the thought sent a thrill through me especially after the way he was looking at me last night. Still, I refused to give her the satisfaction of admitting it.

"Okay, you need to try on the next thing, or we are going to be here all day," she said, shoving another bikini into my hands. I glanced down at it and immediately groaned. It was an electric blue color with red trim, making me feel like the Fourth of July.

"Liv, no." It screamed tacky in a way that I wasn't expecting.

"Oh, yes." She practically shoved me back into the fitting room. "Just try it on."

I held up the tiny triangle top and the even tinier bottoms, already regretting everything. But still, I slipped it on, took a deep breath, and stepped out.

Olivia's jaw dropped before she let out a victorious squeal. "Oh, we're buying that one."

I groaned, covering my face with my hands. "This is a mistake."

"Nope. This is perfect." She grabbed her phone. "Hold on, I'm texting Colton a picture."

I grabbed her wrist before she could finish, glaring. "You wouldn't dare!"

She just grinned. "Fine. But you're wearing that when we go to the beach." Her bright smile only shined brighter as she teased me. "You can even tell him that you picked it because the blue and red colors are associated with police."

I exhaled, already accepting my fate. "I hope you know that I hate you."

"Oh, shut up, you love me."

Unfortunately, she was right, I did love her even if she had a bad habit of pushing me out of my comfort zone.

She let me get redressed in my jean shorts and t-shirt—staples I had added to my Clinton wardrobe at my mom's insistence. The linen shorts I had packed with the intention of looking effortlessly classic and put together were now forgotten, tucked away in a drawer at home in favor of the simple, practical summer clothes including flip flops.

Mom and I had practically cleared out everything Walmart had to offer in my size, and at first, I had protested. But now, as I tugged on the soft cotton of my t-shirt, I realized I was grateful for Mom's insistence.

After what felt like an eternity of Olivia trying on swimsuits, we finally made our way to the checkout where we found a large cage of hermit crabs with a for-sale sign.

"Are those real?" I questioned, watching as one with a peace sign shell walked from one side of the cage to the other.

The teenager working behind the counter shrugged. "All of the Sunsations sell them. Kids love them for a souvenir."

Olivia shuddered, looking at the crabs like one might break free and try to get her. She tossed a bottle of sunscreen onto the counter alongside our swimsuits, giving me a pointed look.

"Because I know you forget to bring any, and I refuse to listen to you complain about a sunburn all night," she said, smirking.

I rolled my eyes but didn't argue. She wasn't wrong, I had a history of sunburns.

With our bags in hand, we stepped out into the bright afternoon sun, the heat already settling on my skin. The salty breeze rolled in from the ocean, and for the first time, excitement bubbled in my chest.

"You're actually looking forward to this, aren't you?" Olivia teased, nudging me as we walked toward the beach house.

"I don't know what you're talking about," I said, keeping my expression as neutral as possible.

She snorted. "Uh-huh. Sure."

By the time we finished our shopping adventure and got back to the house, the energy was buzzing. The boys were loading up the cooler with drinks, Kenna and Addie were already in their swimsuits, and Mom was making sure we had enough towels and that the beach chairs were packed up.

"There you two are," Mom said when we walked in. "Go get changed—we're heading out in ten."

Olivia tossed me a knowing grin before disappearing into our assigned bedroom, and with a deep breath, I followed.

I held up the swimsuit I had ended up with—Olivia's top pick, of course. The electric blue fabric looked a little too daring in my hands, but before I could talk myself out of it, I changed quickly and grabbed the white cover-up we had also purchased.

By the time we all piled into the cars, my nerves again settled, replaced by something else entirely. Excitement.

Maybe Olivia was right. Maybe I really was looking forward to this.

And maybe—just maybe—the beach was about to be more fun than I'd expected.

* * *

Mom and Mitch moved around us like seasoned pros, packing chairs and the cooler into the sand.

"Do I really need to apply sunscreen now?" I asked sounding like a little kid as Mom handed me a bottle. "Can't I get a little sun first for a base tan?"

"Absolutely not! You need sunscreen now," she replied, her tone no-nonsense, more maternal than I had ever heard it. "And make sure to put extra on your shoulders. You always burn there first."

I sighed but obeyed, knowing arguing would only waste my time.

Colton and Mason had just finished setting up a large umbrella in the sand when Colton turned to me, a mischievous grin spreading across his face. "Want me to help you with that?" he asked, his eyes looking at the sunscreen in my hand.

I met his gaze with a playful smile, the heat rising in my chest at the thought of him touching me. "I think I've got it covered," I replied with a smirk, carefully squeezing the sunscreen into my palm and moving to run it up and down my arm. I still had my cover on and that was keeping me from being too embarrassed meeting his eye.

Colton took a step closer, his presence a mix of warmth and tension, and raised an eyebrow. "Are you sure? I'm really good at this."

I tried to keep my composure as I ran the sunscreen over my arms, my skin tingling with the thought of him brushing his hands over me. "I can manage," I said, my voice a little lighter than I intended. I still couldn't believe I had let my sister convince me to buy a suit that would have me so exposed and the last thing I would be able to handle is his hands on my body.

He watched me for a moment, his grin widening. "Does my helping make you nervous?"

"Nope." I finished covering my exposed skin, my heart racing for reasons I wasn't quite ready to examine. Without overthinking it, I yanked off my cover-up and tossed it aside, finishing the sunscreen job as quickly as I could.

Before Colton could say anything else, I turned and made a break for the ocean, hoping the waves would cover the way my skin burned with more embarrassment than the sun ever could. I could already feel the heat creeping up my neck, but at least the cool ocean breeze would help me pretend I wasn't completely flustered.

But as I sprinted toward the water, I couldn't ignore the way I felt his eyes on me, watching every move. The pulse of excitement that ran through me was undeniable, and I started to think the ocean might not be enough to wash away the heat from Colton's attention.

Olivia had already claimed a spot by the chairs, curled up with a book in her hands, the picture of serenity. It always seemed like she was the calm one in the group. Addie and Kenna were in the water, laughing and splashing around, their carefree energy contagious. Every now and then, they'd toss water back and forth, trying to dodge the waves crashing against their legs.

I found myself watching them for a moment, the sound of their laughter blending with the rhythm of the ocean. I felt a tug to join in, but for a moment, I stayed back, letting the water lap at my legs as I debated. The whole beach, the entire afternoon, felt like a brief escape from everything else.

Colton's voice broke through my thoughts, pulling me back to the present. "You going in, or are you just going to stand there all day?"

The water lapped around my ankles as I stood at the shoreline, watching as Colton waded in deeper without hesitation. The sun gleamed off his tanned skin, making him look even more effortlessly confident. The ocean was calmer than it had been yesterday, but the waves still rolled in strong enough to make my stomach flip.

Colton turned back to me, his hair already damp from the ocean spray. "Come on, Ellie, you can't just stand there and admire me all day."

His teasing grin made my heart stutter, but I rolled my eyes, stepping forward until the water swirled around my calves.

"I wouldn't say I was admiring," I said, tipping my chin up, though I knew the lie was painfully obvious. In the dim light the night before, I had only gotten a glimpse of how attractive a shirtless Colton was. Now, in the sunlight, he looked like something straight out of a magazine—a Greek god with his tan and chiseled muscles.

He smirked. "Sure, you weren't."

Another step forward, and the water climbed up to my thighs, the cool rush making me shiver. Colton held out his hand, and after only a moment's hesitation, I took it, letting him guide me farther out until the waves started rolling in strong enough to push against us.

"Okay," he said, squeezing my hand. "Rule number one of wave jumping: you can't fight the ocean."

"That sounds ominous," I muttered, eyeing the wave cresting in the distance. We had talked about wave jumping during the drive up, and Colton had eagerly volunteered to teach me. But now, standing in the strong water with the waves crashing in front of me, I wasn't so sure this was something I wanted to attempt.

Colton laughed. "You just have to work with it. When the wave is small, you stand your ground. When it's big, you jump with it—use it to lift you instead of letting it knock you over."

"Sounds simple enough," I said, but my grip on his hand tightened as a wave rolled toward us, taller than I was ready for.

"Alright," Colton coached, eyes locked on the water as he felt out how strong the next wave would be. "Get ready... jump!"

I pushed off the sand as the wave hit, but I was a second too slow, and instead of lifting me, it crashed into my stomach, sending me stumbling backward.

Colton caught me, laughter bubbling from his chest as he steadied me. "Not bad for a first try."

I coughed out saltwater. "I think the ocean disagrees."

He grinned. "The first time Brendan taught me to do this the water took my shorts clean off, so you are doing much better than I did." Colton tightened his grips on my hands and gestured toward the incoming waves. "Alright, let's try again. This time, trust me and jump with me."

I let out a breath, nodding, and we waited as another wave built in the distance. This time, Colton didn't just hold my hand—he shifted closer, his hands moving to rest on my waist. With nowhere else for mine to go, my hands found their way to his shoulders, the contact with his bare shoulders unexpectedly sending a rush of warmth through me.

"Ready?" His voice was lower now, the playfulness still there but something softer layered beneath it.

I nodded, and when he said, "Jump," I followed his lead.

The wave lifted me effortlessly, my feet leaving the ocean floor for a weightless second before I came back down, still standing, still in Colton's arms.

He grinned. "See? You're a natural."

I smiled back, my heart beating faster than it should have from just jumping waves. Maybe it was the thrill of it, or maybe it was the way Colton was still holding me, the ocean swirling around our legs, the rest of the world fading into the rhythm of the waves.

Before long, Mason and Olivia came to join us. While Mason waded straight into the deeper water where Colton and I stood, grinning as he waved for us to come further out than we already were, Olivia took her time getting into the water. She stayed closer to the shore, moving gracefully through the shallows where the waves lapped at her ankles. She joined Addie and Kenna, who had wandered down the water's edge looking for seashells. They were bending over, their fingers gently skimming through the sand, trying to find the perfect shells as their laughter rising above the rush of the surf. Olivia knelt beside them, her laughter joining theirs as she pointed out a particularly large shell she'd found.

I watched them for a moment, enjoying the carefree rhythm of their movements, but Mason's call to the deeper water pulled me back. I glanced at Colton, who was still holding onto me, his fingers lightly gripping onto my waist as though he was making sure I wouldn't slip away. His eyes met mine, and he gave me that familiar, warm smile.

"We can go out with him, or we can stay right here," he said, his voice easy and steady. "It's wherever you feel most comfortable."

I let his words settle over me, the gentle pull of the waves at my feet mixing with the warmth of his gaze. I wasn't entirely sure what I wanted. Part of me wanted to take the challenge, to join Mason and Colton and feel the strength of the ocean lift me, but the other part of me just wanted to linger in this peaceful space, the shallow water swishing at my legs, safe and calm.

The decision felt bigger than just water. I was always the one to weigh the pros and cons, to calculate and figure out the best course of action. But here, with Colton beside me, I was realizing that maybe it wasn't about making the perfect choice.

I took a deep breath, meeting his gaze again. "Let's go with Mason," I said, the words feeling lighter than I thought they would. The truth was, with Colton beside me, I didn't need to know exactly what was going to happen next. I trusted him more than the need to analyze all the options.

His smile widened, and without another word, he began guiding me toward the deeper water, his hands still securely holding onto me. The pull of the waves grew stronger, and I could feel my heart rate quickening—not from fear, but from the anticipation.

We stayed out there, jumping waves for what felt like forever. The rhythm of the ocean, the push and pull of the water, felt like it could go on endlessly, and for a while, I let it. Each wave carried a little bit of the tension that had built up over the past few days, each jump a reminder that there was nothing to do but enjoy the moment. Colton was right beside me the entire time, his presence grounding me as much as the water moved around us. We didn't speak much other than his reminder to 'jump' when the wave came near, but every time my eye caught his, there was that easy, unspoken connection between us.

Eventually, though, the sound of Mom's voice cut through the laughter and the crashing waves. I turned to see her and Mitch standing up from their chairs, their hands waving at us in the air.

"Come on, you kids! Time to hydrate and add another layer of sunscreen!" Mom called out, her voice firm but kind.

I groaned, but I couldn't deny she was right. I could already feel a tightening over my cheeks when I smiled, a reminder that the sun had been beating down on me for hours. It wasn't painful yet, but I knew it was coming if I didn't listen and apply another layer.

"Alright, alright," I muttered, giving Colton a teasing smile. "She's acting like we are all teenagers." He just laughed, shaking his head, but his hand still found mine as we made our way back to the shore.

The warm breeze felt refreshing as we stepped out of the water, and I was grateful to feel the sand firmly beneath my feet again. When we reached the umbrella and the chairs, I could already see Olivia, Addie, and Kenna lounging around, each of them enjoying their own version of the beach day. Olivia had her book open again, her eyes flicking up occasionally to watch the water, while Addie and Kenna were talking, laughing, and passing a beach ball between them lazily through the sand.

Mom handed me the sunscreen bottle, giving me a pointed look. "You know where this goes," she said with a raised brow, already starting on Mitch's back.

I sighed, taking the bottle from her. "Yes, I know, Mom," I muttered, applying another layer of the thick white paste to my shoulders.

Colton watched me for a second before grabbing his own bottle and applying his own sunscreen, his movements smooth and effortless. "Can't have you turning into a lobster out here," he teased, his eyes twinkling as he added sunscreen to his arms.

"She's just trying to keep me from turning red," I commented back, still feeling the heat in my cheeks from more than just the sun. "As history shows, it's not my best look."

Colton's grin grew as his eyes went from the top of my head to my toes and back up. Suddenly I was feeling a heat that was hotter than the sun, "You're right, this blue and red look is much better."

Mom spoke up again, this time more seriously. A strong mothering tone coming through her words. "Alright, kids, don't forget to drink water. We brought plenty. We don't want anyone getting dehydrated out here."

I nodded, grabbing mine from where it sat in the sand, and settled back into my chair, the cool shade offering a little reprieve. Colton sat beside me, and for a moment, we both just relaxed, letting the noise of the waves and the chatter of our family fill the space around us. He reached for my feet and started gently massaging them as Mason tore into the cooler, passing around some of the snacks we had packed.

* * *

"Want to get away for a bit tomorrow?" Colton asked, his voice casual, like it was natural to suggest an adventure. "I have a place I want to show you."

"Where?" I asked hesitantly. The last time he'd suggested something spontaneous, I'd ended up one step away from skinny-dipping, so I had every reason to be suspicious.

Like the night before, Mom and Mitch had gone to bed early, leaving the rest of us sprawled around the living room, half-watching some action movie Mason had thrown on. But Colton and I weren't paying attention. We sat in the corner, passing a bowl of popcorn back and forth, whispering.

"Ocracoke Island," he said. "It's not far from here. There's a lot of pirate history—you'd love it."

I blinked up at him, surprise written across my face. "Pirate history? I read a little about the islands around North Carolina before I came, but I didn't realize it was close enough we could visit."

Colton grinned. "Yeah. Blackbeard the Pirate wrecked off the shores there, and legend says his treasure is still buried somewhere on the island. The whole place is themed around pirates, and a lot of the original history is still standing. It's pretty cool to explore."

That piqued my interest. "You're serious? You'd take me there?"

He shrugged, like it was no big deal even though it was. "Of course. I know the area, and you seem like the type who'd appreciate it. It's mostly silly, but it's worth the drive."

There was something about the way he offered the experience— no pressure, no expectations. I smiled, this time with genuine gratitude.

"I'd like that," I said softly.

Chapter Fourteen

The next morning, long before the sun rose, Colton and I set off in the big van, leaving the others behind at the beach house. The road stretched ahead in peaceful quiet, the hum of the tires blending with the steady crash of waves beyond the dunes. Outside, the world was still half-asleep, painted in soft shades of blue and green, the horizon just beginning to lighten with the first hints of dawn.

Our first stop was Breeze Thru, a small gas station with a drive-through setup that worked like a car wash—except instead of soap and water, you rolled through a covered lane while workers fetched your order. Colton insisted it was a must-do, claiming you couldn't come out to the Outer Banks without experiencing it at least once. I wasn't sure how a gas station qualified as an attraction, but Colton seemed amused by the whole thing, so I played along.

We had been driving for hours when Colton suddenly pointed toward the line of houses on the shore, his arm shooting out across the dashboard. "Right there—that's the house from that Nicholas Sparks movie!"

I followed his gaze, spotting a large brown house perched right on the shore. "I didn't realize you were a Nicholas Sparks guy."

He let out a laugh. "Not at all. But my mom used to point it out every time we drove past, so I figured it was something you would want to see."

I turned to him, unable to stop the smile tugging at my lips. "So, what you're saying is, you're a closet romance movie fan?"

Colton scoffed, shaking his head. "Not a chance." But the grin threatening to break free told a different story. "I just have a good memory. And you did say you wanted to see everything the island had to offer."

"Well, for the record," I said, glancing at him, "I appreciate the effort."

He shot me a sideways look, eyes gleaming in the dim light. "Noted."

The road stretched ahead, long and open, the kind of drive that felt forever in the best way. The hum of the tires against the pavement blended with the occasional burst of music from the radio, neither of us feeling the need to fill the silence with words. It was comfortable, easy—just like it had always been with Colton.

After a while, he reached across the console, his fingers finding mine with an effortless familiarity. "We'll need to catch the ferry over," he said, his thumb brushing lightly over my knuckles. "Shouldn't be too long of a wait."

I nodded, already feeling a flicker of excitement. "I've never been on a ferry before. It sounds exciting."

Colton glanced over, his smile widening like he was pleased to be the one to change that. "Then you're in for a treat."

"Do you think we could stop and grab something to eat before we get on? I worry a little about getting sick." I had a history of occasional car sickness, and while I'd managed to keep it at bay by focusing on the steady blast of the air conditioning, I knew the boat ride could make it worse.

Colton shot me a knowing grin. "What would you say if I told you I already planned for that? There's a coffee shop right before the ferry, and I was going to stop there anyway."

I blinked at him, surprised. "I'd say you're either scarily perceptive or you just really wanted an excuse for coffee."

He laughed but didn't confirm or deny it. A few minutes later, he turned into a small parking lot in front of a charming bungalow with a large wooden sign: *The Dancing Turtle.*

Before I could even unbuckle, he was already out of the van, jogging around to open my door.

I stepped out slowly, glancing up at the sign, *The Dancing Turtle,* with a hesitated glance over at him. "I thought you said it was a coffee shop."

"It is." He took my hand without hesitation, leading me toward the entrance. "And they have the world's best coffee."

Inside, the scent of fresh coffee and warm pastries wrapped around me, the kind of comforting warmth that made me want to linger. The place was quiet, still waking up with the morning, and Colton walked me straight up to the counter.

"What are you thinking?" he asked, eyes flicking toward the menu.

Their board was full of interesting drink names. I always gravitated toward cookie-flavored coffees, so the grasshopper Latte was an easy choice. "That one," I said, pointing to the small *Latte of the Day* sign. "And a raspberry scone."

Colton grinned and threw in his own order for the Almond Joy Latte without missing a beat, quickly paying the woman before moving his hand to the small of my back. "Let's take a seat while we wait."

The table we picked had a painted-on checkerboard and a small bag of colored seashells beside it for the game pieces, inviting customers to play if they wanted to stay for a while.

"So, how did you hear about this place?" I asked, settling into my seat. As soon as I did, his hand reached across the table, wrapping around mine.

He chuckled. "A few years ago, we were heading out to the island, but Lucy was pregnant and needed to pee first. This was one of the few places with a bathroom. Ever since then, it's became tradition to stop before the ferry."

Before I could respond, the barista called out Colt's name, and we both jumped up to grab our drinks and my croissant. Our plastic cups were drizzled with thick chocolate syrup, topped with swirls of whipped cream and a small brown sack with my scone.

I lifted my cup, eyeing him over the lid. "So, you're telling me this stop was originally a bathroom emergency?"

Colton smirked, bumping his cup lightly against mine in silent cheers. "All good traditions have to start somewhere."

We returned to the van, placing our drinks in the cupholders as Colton eased the vehicle into the ferry line. Since we'd left so early, only a few cars were ahead of us. He gestured toward the massive ferry waiting at the dock, its ramp lowered, ready to load as soon as the captain gave the command.

"Some ferries are for cars only, like this one, but others carry passengers too. Those usually have big indoor seating areas where people can sit and watch the water as they cross."

I glanced at the boat, my curiosity piqued. "How long will we be on the water?"

"Just under an hour," he said, drumming his fingers on the steering wheel. "Enough time to take in the view but not long enough for you to get sick. Especially now that you've got some food in you."

I gave him a look, but he only smirked as the line inched forward. When it was our turn, Colton smoothly pulled onto the ferry, following the attendant's signals until we were parked between a Jeep and a small sedan. He cut the engine as directed and stretched, then turned to me with a grin.

Once all the vehicles were on the ferry, and the boat started to move an announcement comes out that we were free to wander the ferry. Colton opens his door, "Come on, let's go up top."

The moment we stepped out of the van, a salty breeze wrapped around me, cooler than I expected. I inhaled deeply, letting it fill my lungs, the scent of the sea fresh and sharp.

We climbed the metal stairs to the upper deck, stopping at the railing where the view stretched forever in every direction—open water, a pale blue sky, and the distant strip of land we were heading toward.

Colton leaned against the railing, his eyes flicking to me. "Still feeling, okay? We can go back to the van if you need us to."

I nodded. "It's actually kind of nice out here."

His smile was full of satisfaction. "Told you."

The ferry gave a small jolt as it moved further out to the middle of the water, the waves causing the boat to slightly bounce. The rhythmic churn of waves against the hull filled the quiet between us.

Then Colton nudged me. "Since this is your first ferry ride, I should probably warn you about the ghosts."

I blinked. "Excuse me?"

His expression was pure mischief. "It's true. Some say that on foggy mornings, you can see the spirits of old sailors wandering out here. Ones who never made it back to shore."

I narrowed my eyes, though a smile tugged at my lips. "You're messing with me."

He shrugged, feigning innocence. "Maybe. Guess you'll just have to keep an eye out, just in case."

I shook my head, laughing softly as I turned my gaze back to the water. The horizon was beginning to brighten, streaks of gold breaking through the clouds.

There was something about this moment—the quiet, the easy teasing, the way Colton always knew how to make everything feel lighter.

Maybe it was the morning haze, or maybe it was just him, but for the first time in a long time, I felt completely at ease.

I grip my coffee as I settled beside him. I leaned against the railing, watching the waves ripple in our wake, the gentle movement oddly soothing.

Colton stood close beside me, his arm brushing mine. "Are you still doing, okay?" he asked, his voice quieter than usual, like the hush of the morning had settled into him, too.

"Yeah." I took a slow sip of my drink, letting the warmth settle in my chest. "I think I was expecting the ferry to be rougher, but it's actually kind of... peaceful."

He rested his arms on the railing, staring out at the open water. "For a little while, there's nowhere to be. No distractions, no calls, no responsibilities. Just the ocean and the ride."

I studied his profile, the way the wind ruffled his hair, how the morning light caught the sharp lines of his jaw. It was rare to see him this still, this peaceful. I reached out, my fingers brushing over his where they rested against the railing. He didn't hesitate—he turned his hand over, lacing his fingers through mine like it was second nature.

We stayed like that for the rest of the ride, letting the quiet speak for us.

The ferry captain announced we needed to return to our vehicles, the ferry quickly docked, and the second we drove off, I could feel the difference in this new place.

Ocracoke wasn't like the other beach towns we had driven through. It felt older, like history was woven into the air itself. The streets were lined with small shops and restaurants, their signs weathered but charming. Bicycles and golf carts wove between cars on the narrow roads, and I caught glimpses of pirate flags hanging from porches and store windows.

We stopped at the edge of town and Colt parked the car, announcing that we should get out to explore. After walking a good mile or so, Colton glanced at me, a smile playing on his lips. "So, what do you think?"

I turned in a slow circle, taking it all in. "It's like stepping into a different world."

"That's why I figured you'd like it." He gestured toward a wooden sign pointing toward a historic site. "Come on, I have something to show you."

I followed him down a sandy path lined with twisted oak trees, their branches stretching low overhead, casting dappled shadows on the ground.

"The first stop on our pirate tour," Colton announced, stopping in front of a small, fenced-off area. A plaque stood nearby, detailing the history of Blackbeard's last stand.

I scanned the words, my heart picking up speed. "This is where he was killed?"

Colton nodded. "Legend says his head was cut off right out there in the water before the man who killed him took it as a prize." He pointed past the dunes toward the open sea. "Some say you can still see his ghost searching for it on foggy nights."

I shivered, but not from the wind. "That's crazy." I shook my head, trying to remove the nerves. "What is with you and ghost stories?"

"You're know they are your favorite bedtime stories," he teased, bumping my shoulder. Colton laughed, reaching for my hand again. "Come on, there's more."

We wandered down the narrow streets of Ocracoke, the sound of seagulls overhead mixing with the chatter of tourists. The island had a charm that felt entirely its own—weathered wooden buildings with brightly painted signs, golf carts zipping past instead of cars, and an undeniable love of all things pirate-themed.

Colton slowed his pace, glancing at a small shop ahead. A massive wooden pirate stood outside, one hand gripping a sword, the other hand curved in an exaggerated "Arrr!" gesture. The sign above the door read *Blackbeard's Booty: Souvenirs & Oddities*.

"You up for some treasure hunting?" he asked, nodding toward the entrance.

I gave him a look. "You mean overpriced T-shirts and questionable décor choices?"

He grinned. "Exactly."

With an amused sigh, I followed him inside. The store smelled of salt and old wood, and every inch of space was filled with pirate paraphernalia—weathered maps, fake gold coins, and an absurd amount of eye patches.

Colton strode straight to a rack of T-shirts, holding one up. It was black with a cartoonish skull on the front and bold letters that read: *Surrender the Booty!*

I snorted. "Absolutely not."

He ignored me, draping it against my torso like he was sizing it. "I don't know, Ellie. I think this is your new look." He leaned back and seemed to evaluate me. "This would make a great swimsuit cover for when we go to the beach tomorrow."

I batted his hands away. "If you want it so bad, you wear it."

He grinned and slung it over his shoulder like he was seriously considering it. Then, before I could react, he grabbed a pirate hat off the shelf—a massive, feathered monstrosity—and plopped it on my head.

I gasped. "Colton!" I adjust it so that it's no longer covering my eyes. "What are you doing?"

His laughter echoed through the store. "Oh, you looked good."

I narrowed my eyes, grabbing the nearest accessory—a foam cutlass—and pointing it at him. "Say that again and I'll make you walk the plank."

Colton raised his hands in surrender, still chuckling. "Alright, alright. No need for violence, Captain Ellie."

A voice from the register called out, "Everything alright back there?"

I turned to see an older man watching us with mild amusement. Quickly I pulled the hat off my head and moved to put the cutglass away, my cheeks burning with embarrassment.

"We're great," Colton assured him, before lowering his voice to me. "But we should probably leave before you start a mutiny."

I rolled my eyes but smiled.

"Fine," I said, moving to leave the store. "But if you buy that T-shirt, I'm never speaking to you again."

Colton just laughed, draping an arm over my shoulder as we walked toward the register. "Come on, it might just be my best look yet."

Chapter Fifteen

The midday sun hung high in the sky as we gathered outside the rental shop, picking out bikes for our ride through the Outer Banks.

"Alright, everyone ready?" Mitch asked, adjusting his helmet with a dramatic tug, taking over as the leader of the group. "Remember, we obey the rules of the road. I don't want to see any reckless driving."

Mason scoffed. "Come on, Dad, we're just riding bikes, not entering the Tour de France."

Mom shot him a look. "No injuries, please. That goes for all of you." Her eyes lingered on Colton and Mason the longest, which made sense given their competitiveness in the waves yesterday.

We took off at a steady pace, the group loosely sticking together as we moved through town. Small shops lined the roads, their porches draped in colorful signs advertising fresh seafood, handmade crafts, and souvenirs.

Colton rode beside me as we pedaled along the quiet streets. "So, what's the verdict? Does Outer Banks live up to the hype?"

I smiled, breathing in the salty air. "It's charming. And not nearly as touristy as I expected."

Up ahead, Mason suddenly yelled, "Race you all to Surfin' Spoon!" and took off like a shot, his tires kicking up a small cloud of dust.

"Absolutely not," Mom called after him, her voice thick with an authoritative tone, but it was too late.

Addie whooped, launching forward. Kenna, Olivia, and Colton quickly followed suit, laughter ringing out as our bikes sped down the narrow road. I hesitated for half a second before deciding—what do I have to lose? I pumped my legs harder, chasing after them.

Olivia, determined to win, nearly veered into a bush trying to dodge a slow-moving golf cart which managed to throw Mason off balance, making him drop from his place at the front of our group.

"Watch out!" I yelled, half-laughing, half-terrified for her life.

"I'm fine!" she called back, swerving dramatically but managing to stay upright with an array of skills I wasn't expecting.

Olivia, ever the menace, nudged my handlebar just enough to throw me off course. I threw my feet down to the ground so that I didn't fall over.

"Hey!" I shot her a glare, but she just grinned, looking entirely too pleased with herself.

"Oops," she said innocently.

The ice cream shop came into view, a small cottage with a line forming outside and the sign on the front said *Surfin Spoon*. Olivia got there first, jumping off her bike to do a victory dance with Addie and Kenna ending right behind them. At the last second, Colton slowed down just enough to let me cross the imaginary finish line beating him.

"Did you just let me beat you?" I asked, breathless as I hopped off my bike.

He smirked giving me a once over. "Guess I got distracted."

I rolled my eyes, but my stomach flipped anyway.

Mom and Mitch came up behind us, Mason right behind them.

Mason had only been off his bike for a second when he dramatically collapsed onto a bench.

"I demand an official rematch," he huffed, wiping nonexistent sweat from his forehead as if it had been a fight for his life. "I should have been the winner."

"Oh, shut up," Kenna said, reaching out and poured the water from her bottle onto his head.

Mason jerked back, scandalized. "You did not just do that!"

Addie doubled over laughing while Olivia quickly snapped a photo of the soaking wet Mason.

I settled onto an adjacent bench, watching as the group dissolved into playful chaos. The easy laughter, the warm sun, the salty air—it all felt perfect.

Colton nudged my knee with his. "See? I told you the Outer Banks is the best."

I gave him a sideways look. "Okay, fine. You were right."

Mom and Mitch finally caught up with us, and together we joined the long ice cream line. By the time we stepped inside the air-conditioned building, the cool air was a welcome relief from the sticky heat outside.

As we waited, I glanced around, noticing coins and dollar bills tucked into the wooden walls, wedged into every available crevice. Without a word, Mason, Addie, and Kenna reached into their pockets and slipped their own money into the slats, their movements casual, like it was some kind of unspoken tradition.

Mom, ever prepared, pulled a crisp dollar bill from her purse and handed one to both Olivia and me, just like a mother handing out pennies for a wishing well. She smiled knowingly. "Go on, put your money in the wall."

Olivia grinned, smoothing out her bill before carefully tucking it between the wooden planks. "So why did we just do that? I imagine my wish for unlimited ice cream won't come true," she declared dramatically.

Mason snorted. "That's a waste of a wish when we're literally in an ice cream shop."

I laughed, rolling my eyes as I wedged my own dollar between two boards. "Okay, but seriously—why did we just do that?" I asked, smiling when I caught Colton watching me.

Without hesitation, he slipped his own dollar into the wall and shrugged. "I love that you're asking now, after you've already done it. You must really trust us."

"Always," I shot back, nudging him with my elbow.

"They donate all their tips to helping special needs kids play sports," he explained. "In the winter, when the boards shrink, all the money falls to the ground. They say it sounds like rain on a tin roof when it drops."

Something about that image brought me joy. I glanced around at the walls again, imagining the sound, the way all those tiny, unnoticed contributions added up to something bigger.

The line inched forward, and soon we were standing before the massive menu board, debating flavors while Mitch announced he was getting the biggest sundae on the menu.

"Are you seriously about to eat a sundae the size of your head?" Kenna asked, eyeing him skeptically.

Mitch grinned. "No, I'm about to share a sundae the size of my head." He slung an arm around Mom's shoulder. "Right, honey?"

Mom gave him a sweet but knowing smile. "You're on your own."

The whole family erupted into laughter as we stepped up to order, the ease of the moment settling over us like a well-worn blanket.

With our ice cream in hand, we made our way to a row of picnic tables outside the shop, the warm afternoon air filled with the hum of conversation and laughter from other families enjoying their own treats. The wooden benches creaked as we all settled in, Mason already halfway through his cone while Addie and Kenna debated whether to go back for a second scoop.

Mitch, true to his word, sat in front of an enormous sundae, spoon in hand and a determined gleam in his eye. "You all laughed, but in approximately ten minutes, I will be the champion of the ice cream competition."

Mom shook her head, sipping her milkshake. "You know, just because you can eat that much doesn't mean you should. I don't want to hear you complaining later when you have a stomachache."

Colton leaned forward on his elbows, eyeing the sundae with awe in his eyes. "You need a strategy, Mitch. Are you going for speed or endurance?"

Mitch pointed his spoon at him. "A little bit of both. Can't let the frozen yogurt melt but also don't want to pass out from brain freeze."

I laughed, shaking my head. "This is a ridiculous conversation."

Mason grinned. "Oh, come on, Ellie. There's a science to this." He leaned close to mock whisper, "Dad's greatest weakness is ice cream."

Olivia nudged me with her elbow, a mischievous glint in her eye. "I say we time him. Make it official."

Kenna pulled out her phone, setting the stopwatch. "Ready... set... go!"

Mitch dove in, taking an enormous bite while everyone watched in anticipation, our own ice cream so much less important than Mitch's. A few seconds later, he froze, his eyes squeezing shut as he clutched his head. "Brain freeze—brain freeze!"

The table erupted into laughter, Mom rubbing Mitch's back while he groaned dramatically.

Colton leaned close to me; his breath warm against my ear. "See? There's a lesson in there somewhere."

I smirked up at him. "Yeah. Don't try to eat a giant sundae."

As the laughter died down and conversations overlapped, I found myself watching everyone—Kenna and Addie sharing a ridiculous story from childhood, Olivia happily stealing spoonfuls of someone else's ice cream after not getting any of her own when we were inside, Mom and Mitch bickering over whether he should take a break when he tried to keep eating.

The afternoon felt perfect, full of warmth and the kind of easy joy that only came from being surrounded by family. I let myself sink into it, savoring every moment, I leaned into Colt and relaxed into his side.

* * *

After we got back to the house, everyone scattered—some retreating to their rooms, others lingering on the porch to enjoy the warm night air. I stayed behind in the kitchen, rinsing out the last of the lunch plates that we had thrown into the sink before our ice cream run, needing a moment of quiet after all the laughter and chaos of the evening.

The tap water ran warm over my fingers as I scrubbed out the remnants of food. I heard soft footsteps behind me, then the quiet rustle of a dish towel being unfolded. Mom settled in beside me, wordlessly taking the first clean bowl from my hands and drying it.

For a while, we worked in companionable silence, the only sound the clinking of dishes and the distant hum of the conversations outside. There was something soothing about it like we had done this a thousand times before. Maybe we had, back when I was younger, before things had changed.

Mom finally broke the silence, her voice warm but thoughtful. "You look happy, sweetheart."

The words caught me off guard, and I glanced at her. "What?"

She smiled knowingly, folding the towel neatly over her arm. "I mean it. I've been watching you, and you seem... lighter here. More like yourself."

I let out a small breath, turning back to the sink. "It's been nice," I admitted. "Being here, away from everything heavy in Vegas. It's different."

"Different how?"

I hesitated, rinsing off a fork, watching the water swirl down the drain. "I don't know. It's just... quieter. Slower. There's space to think." I paused, realizing how true that was. "Back home, it feels like I'm constantly running. Like if I stop for too long, I'll fall behind."

Mom studied me, that careful way only a mother could, seeing past my words to something deeper. "And is that what you want? To always be running?"

I blinked at the question, because I hadn't really thought about it like that. I had just assumed that was the way life was supposed to be —always pushing forward, always chasing the next thing. But here, in this place, with Colton, I had stopped moving. And for the first time, I wasn't sure if I wanted to start again.

Mom must have seen something shift in my expression because she softened, nudging me lightly with her elbow. "Does this have anything to do with a certain young man?"

Heat crept up my neck. "Mom—"

She chuckled, shaking her head. "I'm just saying... I see the way he looks at you. And the way you look at him when you think no one's paying attention."

I sighed, setting the last dish on the drying rack. "Maybe, but it's complicated."

Colton and I had started this "relationship" with the idea that it was only for the summer and yet here I am, realizing I'm wanting more.

Mom nodded like she understood. "Love usually is."

I stiffened at the word, my heart thudding in protest. "Dating has never been like this before."

She raised a brow, her knowing look cutting right through me. "You sure about that?"

I swallowed hard, gripping the edge of the counter. "It's just... temporary. I knew that going into this. I came here to spend time with you, not to get caught up in—" I exhaled, hesitating.

Mom dried her hands and turned to face me fully. "Ellie, I know you. You overanalyze everything. You think if you just keep running the numbers, breaking things down logically, you'll find the right answer. But some things in life don't work like that."

I stayed quiet, because she wasn't wrong.

She reached for my hand, squeezing it gently. "Sometimes, the right answer isn't about what makes the most sense—it's about what makes you feel at home."

My throat tightened, emotion welling in my chest.

"I don't want you to walk away from something good just because it scares you," Mom continued. "You deserve something real, Ellie. Something that doesn't make you feel like you always have to be chasing the next thing."

I swallowed, nodding even though my thoughts were tangled.

She squeezed my hand once more, then let go with a soft smile. "Just promise me something?"

I slowly met her gaze. "What?"

"Don't be so in your head that you talk yourself out of something you know you want."

Her words settled deep inside me, threading through the confusion and fear I hadn't yet voiced.

I let out a slow breath, my grip on the counter loosening. "I'll try."

Mom studied me for another moment, then nodded, satisfied. "Good. Now, come on—let's head outside before those boys eats all the good snacks."

I let out a small laugh, shaking my head as I followed her. But even as I stepped onto the porch, surrounded by the warmth of family and the laughter of people I loved, thoughts of Mom's words lingered because deep down, I already knew she was right.

Chapter Sixteen

By the time we left the beach, the sun had dipped low, casting long shadows over the water. The salty breeze clung to our skin as we packed up, trading the sound of crashing waves for the familiar hum of family chatter as we drove back to Clinton.

Our first night back in Clinton they had planned another family dinner, this time at Mom and Mitch's place. Colt's parents brought all the food, making it feel more like their gathering than ours.

When Roseanne and Thomas arrived, their truck packed with enough home-cooked dishes to feed a small army, Mom threw her hands up in exasperation. "Roseanne, I told you; you didn't have to bring anything! We were just going to order some pizza tonight."

Roseanne just smiled sweetly, unloading a large, covered dish into Mom's waiting arms. "Oh, hush. You know I'd never show up to a dinner empty-handed. Besides, I figured you'd be tired after the trip. This way, all you have to do is sit back and enjoy."

Mitch peered over Roseanne's shoulder at the stack of aluminum-covered trays still waiting in the truck bed. "Good heavens, Roseanne, are you feeding the entire town?"

Thomas chuckled, grabbing another dish. "You know my wife. She believes no meal is a real meal unless there are leftovers for days."

I watched the exchange, filling with warmth. The easy way our families meshed, the laughter, the teasing—it all felt so seamless, like this had always been our normal.

Colton caught my eye from across the room, sending me a small, knowing smile. He could read me too well.

"You going to stand there all night, or are you going to help?" Kenna teased, nudging my arm as she passed with a basket of biscuits.

Pulled from my thoughts, I grabbed a tray and followed her into the kitchen.

As we started setting the table, conversation flowed easily. Mason and Mitch were already bickering over who would get the last biscuit before the meal even started, while Olivia and Paisley talked about some boutique trend that I only half-followed.

I caught snippets of Thomas and Mom's conversation as they worked side by side in the kitchen.

"Hard to believe they all came back in one piece after a week together at the beach," Thomas joked, helping Mom set out silverware.

"Oh, don't be fooled," Mom said with a smirk. "There were *definitely* a few near casualties. I think Mason was about three seconds from getting tackled into the ocean at least twice."

Mason, overhearing, grinned. "To be fair, I deserved it."

Kenna snorted. "That's the understatement of the year."

Colton slid into the seat beside me, his knee brushing mine under the table. "Are you doing alright?" he murmured, keeping his voice low so only I could hear.

I nodded, but something about the night felt... different. Maybe it was reality settling in now that we were back in Clinton. Maybe it was the way Roseanne and Thomas looked at me like I was already part of their family.

Or maybe it was the way Colton kept looking at me—like he was hoping I was starting to feel like I belonged here, too.

Dinner was lively, filled with laughter, stories from the trip, and good food. And yet, beneath all the joy, I couldn't shake the feeling that something was shifting. That, whether I was ready or not, my time here was running out.

* * *

That night after dinner, Olivia asked me for some alone time with Mom, the two of them slipping off to Walmart together with the excuse of wanting to look around. The rest of the family stayed behind, lingering around the house after dinner, the warm hum of conversation trailing behind us as Colton led me toward his truck. He didn't have to say anything—I already knew where we were going.

The ride was quiet, but not uncomfortable. The occasional flicker of streetlights illuminated his profile, highlighting the sharp angles of his jaw, the way his hands rested easily on the wheel. He didn't rush the drive, as if drawing out these quiet moments between us. Maybe he sensed it too—that inevitable pull, the fragile tension stretched tight between us.

When we finally pulled up to his house, the truck rumbled to a stop, the familiar creak of the gear shift breaking the silence. He helped me inside before flicking on a lamp, its golden glow spilling over the room, casting long shadows on the walls. It was cozy, lived-in, and so distinctly him. He tossed his keys onto the counter, stretching his arms above his head before turning to face me.

"You want a drink?" His voice was low, casual, but something flickered in his eyes—an unspoken question beneath the words.

I hesitated for only a second, still not sure if coming here with him was a good idea. "Sure."

I sank onto the couch, pulling a throw blanket over my lap, watching as he moved through the kitchen. There was something about the way he existed in his space. That kind of certainty, that deep-rooted sense of home, was something I didn't ever feel in my own apartment back in Vegas.

He handed me a glass and settled beside me, his knee brushing mine. It was such a small touch, but it sent a slow, steady heat curling through me. I took a sip of the ice water, the chill going all the way through me.

Colton turned toward me slightly, draping his arm over the back of the couch, his fingers barely grazing my shoulder. "You looked comfortable tonight," he murmured, his voice thick and rough around the edges. "With your family and especially with my family. I liked seeing that side of you."

I swallowed; my throat suddenly tight. "Yeah?"

He nodded, his gaze never wavering. "Yeah." His fingers brushed against my shoulder again, a deliberate, lingering touch that made my breath hitch.

This was dangerous territory.

I should pull away. I should put distance between us. But instead, I let myself lean into it, let myself sink a little deeper into the warmth of him, just for tonight.

Because the truth was, I loved being here with him. And that was exactly what scared me the most.

"Did you have fun tonight?" Colton asked, his voice low and easy as he stretched out on the couch beside me.

I exhaled a soft laugh. "Yeah. Your family is warm and really love each other. It was nice seeing our moms together like that. Mom never talked about any friends, she only ever mentioned spending time with Addie or Kenna."

Colton nodded; his expression thoughtful. "She's been close with my mom since she arrived, but I get why she wouldn't talk about it. She didn't want you to think she was building a life without you."

I traced the rim of my glass, my thoughts swirling. "And I guess I let myself believe she had. That she was out here, moving on, while we were somewhere else, trying to figure things out without her." I let out a slow breath. "But that wasn't fair to her, was it?"

Colton reached over, his fingers brushing against mine, grounding me. "She loves you, Ellie. That much is obvious. She glows when she talks about you and you sister."

I swallowed past the tightness in my throat and nodded. "I understand that better now."

For a moment, silence stretched between us, comfortable yet thick with unspoken thoughts. Then, a slow country song drifted through the speakers of the old radio he always kept on the mantle of the fireplace —the beat of it soft and familiar.

Colton jumped up from the couch, holding out a hand for me. "Dance with me."

I arched a brow. "Here?"

"Here." No hesitation. No doubt.

I had studied human behavior in school and throughout my career, learning the triggers that made people act the way they did and what could change their behavior when pushed. Yet, no textbook or theory had ever prepared me for the force that was Colton Bennett tonight. His alpha-male, take-charge attitude was impossible to ignore, and every ounce of that energy seemed to be directed toward me in a way that both overwhelmed and intrigued me.

I rolled my eyes but slid my hand into his anyway, letting him pull me up and against him. My arms looped around his neck as his hands settled at my waist, warm and steady.

We swayed, the movement unhurried, the world outside his living room fading into nothing. His thumbs traced slow, lazy circles at my hips, a touch so simple yet so consuming.

I sucked in a breath, my voice barely above a whisper as I tried not to let it waver with my sudden rush of emotions. "You make me want things I shouldn't want."

Colton's grip tightened, his forehead dipping to rest lightly against mine. "Like what?"

I swallowed hard, my pulse skittering. "Like staying."

His fingers flexed at my waist like he was restraining himself, his breath fanning warm across my skin. "Then stay. I know we haven't talked about it, but you have to know that I want you to stay."

I closed my eyes, letting myself sink into the moment, into him. But deep down, I knew—staying longer than the summer had never been part of the plan, and my plans couldn't change for a boy even though I desperately wanted too.

The soft hum of the country song still lingered in the air, its faint echoes wrapping around us as I pulled away from Colton, breaking the intimate silence, we'd shared. The weight of his words still hung between us like threads, each one tied to something that made my heart ache.

We stood there for a moment, the quiet of the room pressing in around us, and I felt the pull between my longing for him. My gaze drifted to the porch doors, where the night outside felt vast and endless, offering escape, yet I couldn't seem to take that step. Not with Colton standing beside me.

Colton's hand found mine again, his touch warm and sure. He didn't speak, but the look in his eyes was soft, understanding, but persistent. "Come with me," he said quietly, leading me toward the back door, his grip tightening ever so slightly.

We stepped out onto the porch, the cool night air greeting us with a gentle breeze that brushed against my skin. The porch light above us cast a soft glow, but it wasn't enough to fully illuminate the weight in the air between us.

I shifted my feet, uncertain. "Colton..." My voice trailed off as I stared down at my hands, unsure of what I was even asking. I wanted to stay with him, to be here in this moment, but I couldn't ignore the loud voice in my head screaming that this wasn't part of the plan and that I needed to get out of there.

He stood in front of me now, his hands resting at his sides, but there was no mistaking the intensity in his eyes as he watched me carefully. "Ellie, I need you to listen to me," he said, his voice low but unwavering. "I know this wasn't what either of us planned. But right now, standing here with you... I can't imagine us walking away from each other."

I swallowed hard, my chest tightening. "A part of me wants to stay, but I also know that my life has to return to Vegas and my life there." The words felt heavy in my mouth as I said them aloud.

Colton stepped closer; his voice firm yet gentle. "I'm asking you to choose. Not between your life and mine, but between living your life with or without me." He reached for my hand, his thumb brushing against my skin with a tenderness that made my heart ache. "I'm not asking for all the answers right now, Ellie. I just need you to know that I'm here. I'm here, and I want us to find a way to be together."

I closed my eyes, trying to breathe through the rush of emotions that threatened to consume me. "I want to stay," I whispered, more to myself than to him, but the words felt right. Our relationship, as short as it has been, suddenly was being hit with the most intense of growing pains.

He stepped closer, his voice dropping to a whisper. "Then stay."

I took a breath, opening my eyes to meet his. The rawness in his gaze, the vulnerability that matched my own, made it impossible to look away. "But what if staying means I lose everything I've worked for?"

Colton's fingers gently cupped my cheek. "What if everything you've worked for has already led you to this moment? What if you're exactly where you need to be?"

I could feel the pull between us intensifying, and in that moment, I realized that no matter how much I tried to convince myself otherwise, there was no turning away from this connection, from him. I didn't have the answers, and maybe I never would. But for the first time in a long time, I didn't feel like I had to have everything figured out.

I leaned into his touch, my lips brushing his in a kiss that was soft but full of promise—and for the first time in my life, I wondered if maybe—just maybe—I didn't need to know everything. Maybe I just needed to follow where my heart led me.

* * *

With Olivia here, family dinners became a regular thing—big, lively gatherings where Mom did her best to bring everyone together while also holding onto whatever quiet moments she could get with her daughters, never sure when, or if, we'd be back.

The kitchen was always buzzing with conversation, the clatter of dishes, and the rich aroma of home-cooked meals filling the air. Mom flitted between the stove and the table, her eyes flicking to Olivia and me every few minutes as if trying to memorize our faces before we left.

"Ellie, can you grab the cornbread?" she asked, a tight smile on her face as she pulled a roast from the oven. "Just bring it over to the table for me."

I nodded, grabbing the warm dish and setting it on the table before taking a seat. Olivia sat across from me, deep in conversation with Kenna, their laughter filling the room. Colton was beside me, his knee brushing against mine—a small, steady reminder of his presence.

Mom finally sat down, looking between Olivia and me, her expression soft but searching. "I am so grateful to have both my girls here. It has been a long time since we have had this opportunity to all be together. This summer has been so special for me."

Olivia smiled. "It does feel nice, doesn't it?"

Mom nodded, but there was something wistful in her eyes, something unsaid. I felt it too—the weight of time lost, of distance not just measured in miles but in years where my sister and I had been too stubborn to come and visit.

Olivia looked to me hesitantly. "We should do this more often, maybe we can plan a visit every year."

Mom nodded enthusiastically. "I'd like that."

The conversation moved on, shifting between ranch work, town gossip, and old memories. But beneath it all, I couldn't shake the feeling that Mom was holding on too tightly, afraid that the moment might slip away too soon.

And maybe, deep down, I was afraid of that as well.

It was a few hours later and the laughter and clinking of dishes from dinner had faded, leaving only the soft murmur of voices in the kitchen. I lingered in the hallway, absently running my fingers over a framed photo of Colton and my step siblings as kids. He looked the same—just younger, wilder, a grin permanently etched onto his face.

I turned to find him in the other room, standing near his mom. I should've gone in. Should've made my presence known. But then I heard her voice—

"Do you think she's the one?" his mother asked, her voice quiet but not nearly quiet enough. "The two of you have barely left each other's side since she arrived."

I found myself frozen to the spot.

Colton exhaled, the kind of breath that sounded like he was weighing his answer carefully. "I don't know," he admitted. "I want her to be."

My stomach twisted, but I silently continued to listen, unsure of what I wanted his answer to be.

His mom hummed. "But?"

Colton ran a hand over his face. "But I don't think she's ready for what I want. She always seems ready to make a break for it, especially when I try to move the relationship forward."

I took a step back, like I could physically remove myself from the words. Like I hadn't already felt the pressure of them pressing down on me for weeks.

He thought that I wasn't ready? He wasn't wrong. But hearing it said out loud, hearing him acknowledge that, hurt more than I expected.

I turned on my heel and slipped outside, the cool night air doing nothing to soothe the ache in my chest. I had known this would happen.

Minutes later, the screen door creaked open, and Colton stepped onto the porch. His gaze found mine instantly, concern flickering behind those warm green eyes. "Ellie? What are you doing out here?"

I forced a smile, crossing my arms over my chest. "I just needed a little fresh air."

He studied me for a long moment. "What's wrong?"

I shook my head, plastering on my best attempt at indifference. "Nothing."

He didn't believe me. I could see it in the way his jaw tightened, the way he shifted his weight like he was debating whether to push me for the truth.

I beat him to it. "I'm starting to think it is time I should go home."

Colton's brows pulled together, his jaw tightening as he restrained how he really felt. "Now?"

I nodded, my fingers gripping the railing a little too tight, the cool metal grounding me. "When Olivia leaves, it might be a good idea if I go with her."

His expression darkened, and before I could step away, his hand reached out, warm and firm, closing over mine. "Ellie don't do this," he said, his voice low but edged with something that made my chest ache. "Don't leave so soon. You said you'd stay through the summer."

I swallowed hard, my pulse thrumming in my ears. "I know what I said."

"Then what's changed?" His grip tightened slightly, not enough to hold me there, just enough to make me feel him.

I looked away, my eyes fixed on the heavy tree line, searching for an answer that wouldn't hurt either of us. The problem was, there wasn't one.

"I don't know if I can stay, Colton." My voice was barely above a whisper. "The longer I'm here, the harder it's going to be to leave."

His thumb brushed against my skin, gentle despite the tension radiating off him. "Then don't leave."

I wanted to listen to him. Wanted to believe it was that simple. But nothing in my life had ever been simple.

I took a shaky breath, forcing myself to meet his gaze. "It's not that easy."

A muscle ticked in his jaw. "It could be so easy for you to stay here, stay here with me."

The words hung between us, heavy and full of possibilities I wasn't sure I was brave enough to chase. We let the weight of it settle, neither of us willing to pick at the unraveling threads between us—because we both knew that if we did, if we tugged too hard at the fragile seams, we might come undone completely.

Colton exhaled sharply, his grip on my hand loosening just enough that I could pull away if I wanted to. But I didn't. Not yet.

Instead, I stayed, my fingers tightening around his like they could anchor me in place. Like holding onto him could somehow silence the part of me that kept insisting I should go. My heart was at war with itself—one side pulling him closer, the other trying to push him away.

And the worst part? I didn't know which side would win.

Chapter Seventeen

The sun had just begun to dip below the horizon, casting a golden glow over the landscape as Colton pulled the truck to a stop in front of the lighthouse. My breath caught as I took in the sight—the towering structure bathed in the warm hues of evening, standing tall against the endless stretch of sky and sea.

When he'd shown up at the house earlier, he'd only said he had another surprise for me—one that required a bit of a road trip. Colton enjoyed surprising me and considering one of those times, it had involved hours of tearing through the fields on a four-wheeler, so I'd been hesitant to agree. But now, staring at the lighthouse, I was glad I had trusted him.

"I can't believe we're here; this is even better than I imagined." I whispered, more to myself than to him, but Colton heard me anyway.

"You mentioned it was something you wanted to see before you left," he said, his voice low, the look in his eyes softening into something warmer. "Figured we could cross it off your list since you are planning on leaving soon."

The way this man remembered even the little things I had mentioned meant more than I could put into words—especially now, when we were both starting to feel the weight of summer slipping away, the unspoken reality of time running out pressing in on us.

Colton casually mentioned the Oak Island Lighthouse. Almost without thinking, I told him it had been on my list since I first decided to visit North Carolina—though I never really expected to see it, not when I'd only planned to stay a week. So, when he said he had a surprise for me, I never imagined it would be this.

"Thank you," I said, turning to face him, my voice filled with emotion. "You didn't have to do this, but I'm very glad you did."

He smiled and opened the door for me, offering his hand as I stepped out of the truck. "Getting a smile like that from you makes it worth it."

The lighthouse loomed ahead, its black and grey patterned tower standing proud. We walked side by side toward it, the sounds of the waves crashing on the rocks below the only sound in the air.

"I've always thought the idea of a lighthouse was so beautiful," I murmured as we reached the base of the lighthouse, my fingers reaching out to trail along the rough stone. "The idea that there is a large bright light out there, acting as a beacon for those who are feeling as though they are at the end with no hope."

Colton's hand brushed against mine as we made our way up the winding path toward the Oak Island Lighthouse, the salty breeze tugging at my hair and carrying the distant cry of gulls. The tall, weathered tower rose ahead of us, its black-and-white stripes bold against the soft blue sky. The crunch of gravel beneath our feet was the only sound for a few moments, comfortable and steady, like us. As we got closer, I tilted my head back to take in the full height of the lighthouse, its presence steady and unmoving.

Colton watched me, his expression mixed as I traced the cool, weathered stone beneath my fingertips. "They stand through every storm," he said after a moment, his voice softer than usual. "No matter how bad it gets, that light still shines."

I turned to face him, something about his words held a deeper meaning. He wasn't just talking about lighthouses.

"Yeah," I said, my voice barely above a whisper. "I guess that's why they have always fascinated me. They don't give up on people, even when everything else feels lost."

Colton took a step closer, reaching out to tuck a stray strand of hair behind my ear. His fingers lingered, brushing against my cheek, and for a second, neither of us spoke.

"You ever think about what your light is?" he asked.

I swallowed, unsure where to go with how loaded any possible answer would be. "What do you mean?"

He shrugged, his thumb grazing my jaw before dropping his hand. "Everyone's finds what keeps them steady. Something that pulls them through when they're lost. Just wondering if you've figured out what yours is yet."

"Maybe," I admitted shyly, lowering my head slightly.

Colton studied me, like he was trying to read between the lines of what I wasn't saying. Then, with that easy confidence of his, he took my hand, lacing our fingers together.

"Come on," he said, gripping my hand tighter. "Let's see the view from the top."

The climb to the top of the lighthouse was steep, each step echoing in the enclosed space as we made our way up. By the time we reached the top, my breath was uneven—not just from the climb, but from the anticipation of what waited beyond the door.

Colton pushed it open, and a cool ocean breeze rushed in, surrounding us as we stepped onto the narrow balcony. Then I saw the view—and it stole what little breath I had left.

The horizon stretched as far as I could see, the last streaks of gold and pink fading into the deep blues of twilight. Below us, waves rolled against the shore in a steady rhythm, their quiet crash blending with the distant hum of the town. Tiny lights flickered in the distance, warm and inviting against the night.

I gripped the railing, taking in the moment. "This is..." I exhaled, shaking my head with a small laugh. "It's incredible."

Colton leaned against the railing beside me, his shoulder brushing mine. "Figured you'd especially like it up here."

"Like it?" I turned to him, my heart swelling. "I love it. This is perfect."

His expression changed, the warmth in his eyes deepening into something more certain, more intent. He reached out, again tucking a loose strand of hair behind my ear, his fingers lingering just long enough to send a shiver down my spine. I had worn my hair in a long braid down my back— because, at some point, he'd mentioned in passing that he liked when I wore it that way.

"I love you, Ellie," Colton's voice was steady but raw, like he was letting go of something that had been buried deep. "I know we've rushed this summer, stealing every moment we've had together, but I can't imagine walking away from this, from us, when the season ends."

His words filled the air between us, reminding me of everything I hadn't said, but had quietly felt for the past few weeks. My heart raced, each beat pulsing with the uncertainty of what do when summer ended and the undeniable pull that had drawn us together in such a short time. He was right—our time had been brief, a summer that felt like it was slipping through our fingers. But in that short time, everything between us had deepened, and now I couldn't even imagine a life without him in it.

I opened my mouth to respond, but no words came out. I couldn't find the right ones to express what was swirling in my chest—how conflicted I was between my old life and the possibility of something real here.

He chuckled softly. "You keep looking at me like that," he murmured, his lips turning into a half-smile. "And I'm going to have to kiss you again."

His gaze locked with mine, a soft intensity behind his eyes. And for a moment, everything outside of us—the beach, the distant horizon, the world at large—faded away as his lips fell to mine.

"I don't know what comes next, Colton," I whispered, my voice barely audible, even to my own ears. My indecision was there, hanging between us. But the feelings of my heart told the truth. I couldn't shake the tug I had toward him, the way everything seemed to make sense when he was near.

He didn't answer right away. Instead, he continued to be a constant anchor holding on to my hand like a silent promise.

"You don't have to know right now," he said, his voice full of certainty. "We don't have to know all the answers this minute. All I know is that I want to be with you, no matter what."

His words settled over me like a blanket of warmth. They didn't answer everything, but they gave me something to hold onto, something real in a sea of uncertainty. And as the breeze stirred around us, I leaned closer, my heart beating faster in my chest.

Colton's hand slid to my cheek; his touch gentle but firm.

"I think I'd like that," I said, my voice a soft confession.

Colton's hand slid to my cheek, his touch gentle but firm as he closed the distance, his lips brushing against mine in a kiss that spoke of promises and possibilities, of all the things we were ready to face together.

When we finally pulled away, both of us breathless, I rested my forehead against his and enjoyed the sounds of the ocean in the background. "This summer," he whispered, "doesn't have to end with the season."

I didn't need to know exactly what that meant. All I knew was that with him, maybe—just maybe—I could find my place.

Colton closed the space between us, his hand sliding to the small of my back as he tilted his head, his lips brushing against mine in a slow, deliberate kiss. The world around us faded until there was only him.

His lips moved against mine with the perfect mix of softness and certainty. My hands gripped the front of his shirt, pulling him closer, needing more. He responded instantly, his other hand settling at my waist as the kiss deepened.

He turned our bodies slightly so that my back was pressed against his chest, a perfect way for his arms to wrap around me.

"Now that," he murmured, "was worth the climb."

I couldn't help but laugh. His presence, so steady and real, made all the tensions, the doubts, the unspoken things we still needed to sort out fade into the background. I just let everything go and leaned into him, letting myself be lost in the warmth of his arms, in the way everything felt simpler with him.

"Definitely made the climb worth it," I whispered, my fingers tightening around his arm as it draped across my chest. Colton's friend worked at the lighthouse and had graciously agreed to open it up for us, but only for a short time since it was still a functioning lighthouse. Before I could fully process everything that we had discussed, Colton was already reaching for my hand, guiding me back down the stairs and toward the truck. Once we were inside, he drove us to a nearby beach.

When we pulled into a small parking spot, Colton turned to me with a playful grin, pulling out a small basket from the floorboard. "I know you said you were hungry, so let's have a picnic on the beach," he said, his voice laced with excitement.

The simplicity of the moment pulling at my heartstrings. A picnic on the beach—just the two of us, the ocean's rhythm in the background, and the fading golden light around us. It was perfect.

As always, Colton helped me out of the truck, his hand warm in mine as we made our way to the beach. The sand was cool beneath our feet. Without a word, he spread out a blanket for us to sit on, the fabric rustling gently as it settled.

I couldn't help but smile at the way he moved—efficient, confident, always thinking ahead. As soon as the blanket was down, he gestured for me to sit. The ambience making everything feel peaceful and just a little bit magical.

We sat in comfortable silence for a moment. The view before us was stunning, the coastline stretching endlessly, the colors shifting as the day transitioned into evening. It felt like the world had paused, like time itself had slowed down to give us this one perfect moment.

"This place is beautiful," I murmured, my voice barely above a whisper as I turned toward him, still mesmerized by the scene in front of us.

Colton's lips curled into that signature smile, the one that made my heart skip a beat. "You're a little breathtaking yourself," he said, his voice low and intimate. He was looking at me. And for a brief, breathless moment, I couldn't think of anything else.

For a long moment, we were quiet, simply enjoying the serenity of the place. The world around us seemed to disappear leaving just the two of us in our own little bubble.

"I love this," I whispered, resting my head against his shoulder. "I love being here with you."

As the words left my mouth, a thought struck me cold and sudden. I had come to Clinton with the intention of reconnecting with my mom, to make sense of the mess she had left behind.

I felt a knot tighten in my stomach as I pulled away slightly, my gaze drifting over the waves, trying to distract myself from the mess I could already feel starting to unravel inside me.

"So, what's your plan here?" I mused aloud, my fingers weaving through the sand, feeling each piece slip through my grasp in a way that felt representative of how fast the days here had flown.

Colton's brow furrowed, the familiar cluster of wrinkles appearing between his eyebrows—something I had started to fall in love with. "What do you mean?"

I hesitated, trying to gather my thoughts. "What's your plan?" The question felt heavier than I expected. Truthfully, I wasn't entirely sure what I was asking either. I knew a small part of me was asking what his long-term vision for *us* was. We had gone on a few dates, and he had casually mentioned big plans for the two of us, but neither of us had used the big, scary words yet. Those three words had stayed suspended between us, and I was willing to let them hover there for as long as possible. "I guess I'm asking, what's your plan for *us*?"

His expression shifted, the easygoing warmth in his eyes giving way to something more serious, more deliberate. Slowly, his hand found mine, fingers intertwining, his touch comforting. He always did this when the conversation turned deep—like he was reminding me that we were in this together. "I want true love," he said, his voice low and certain. "I want an old farmhouse, somewhere with space to breathe. I want land where we can grow our own vegetables, watch our kids grow up, and see them run through the grass. I want too many animals, including a dog who sleeps at the foot of our bed."

He paused, his gaze locking onto mine, something unshakable in the way he looked at me, like he already saw that future laid out in front of him. His voice softened, but the significance of his words pressed into my chest. "I want to sit on the porch every night, watching the sun set. And I want to do all of it with you, wrapped in my arms, because nothing feels right unless you're here."

My breath caught. My heart ached, torn between the impossible beauty of the life he described and the sharp edges of reality pressing in, threatening to kill any happiness his words could bring me.

I could see it—the farmhouse, the land, the warm glow of porch lights as the day faded into night. I could almost hear the laughter of children, feel the press of Colton's arm around me as we watched them chase fireflies in the yard.

Could it be me beside him in those porch swings?

I swallowed hard, forcing my voice to stay steady even as my emotions threatened to betray me. "That sounds perfect in theory, but I can't just drop my entire life and stay here. What if I get bored after my busy life in the city with so much to do?"

Even as I said the words, I could feel the wedge between us, something fragile that might break if either of us pushed too hard.

I tried to pull my hand away, but Colton's grip tightened—a silent reminder that he knew how I worked as well as I did. Always on the edge of running. Afraid of getting too close. He'd once compared me to a rainbow, something beautiful but fleeting, always slipping away before he could truly hold me. His gaze softened, and I could see him searching for the right words—the ones that might make me stay. But maybe there were no right words. Maybe this was something that went beyond words.

A part of me wanted to settle into this life with him. Wanted the stillness of warm summer nights on a front porch, the comfort of a love that didn't have to chase the next big thing. But another part of me couldn't shake the pull of the city—the energy, the opportunity, the life I had built for myself before I came here.

"This life might be slower," he admitted, his voice steady but laced with emotion. "But I'm here for it. I love the quiet, the way there's always time for family and helping a friend. It might not be exciting all the time, but it's real. I want that to be enough for you."

He bit his lip, his fingers fidgeting with my rings, an unconscious sign of his own inner struggle as he processed the conversation—and the conclusion I was coming to. His Adam's apple bobbed as he swallowed, his next words softer, more careful.

"Ellie, I want this life with you. But if you can't stay, I understand."

His words took my breath away the weight of them, the sheer love in them, made my stomach twist into so many knots.

I looked at him—really looked at him. The man who had taught me how to slow down, how to see beauty in simplicity. The man who had somehow slipped past my walls one moment at a time.

I wanted to give him the answer he deserved. The promise he deserved. But I couldn't lie to him.

"I don't know if I can stay here," I whispered, hating the way the words tasted in my mouth.

And the worst part? I wasn't even sure who I was hurting more—him or myself.

He didn't pull away or shrink back. Instead, his hands reached up to gently cupped my cheeks, his thumbs brushing over my skin.

Without another word, he leaned in and pressed a kiss to my lips—soft, tender, with promise.

"Ellie," he murmured between kisses, "if you can't stay here, I'll go with you. I'd follow you to Vegas, if it meant staying together."

His words broke something open inside me, a flood of clarity. I didn't have to make a choice between my life and his when he was offering to change his entire life for me. But we both knew that it was futile, he had his friends and family were here. We both had separate lives outside of this magical moment in time when they came together.

His offer—to follow me to Vegas, to uproot his life—was beautiful and selfless. It felt like both a dream and an impossibility all at the same time. But it also made the reality crash down around me about the changes it would bring to either of our lives. It was easy to want to stay in the quiet, in the simplicity. But what would I be giving up? What would he be giving up?

"I don't know," I murmured, my voice barely above a whisper. "I just don't know if I'm ready to walk away from everything I've built. And I could never ask you to do that either. Your family, your friends—your whole life is here. I couldn't ask you to leave all of that."

I could see it in his eyes—the understanding, the frustration, the way he wanted to fix it but didn't know how because there wasn't a win-win solution.

"I just need some more time to figure it out," I added, my hand slipping from his to press against my chest, trying to quiet the racing of my heart. "I don't want to make the wrong choice."

Colton's face softened, and for a moment, I saw the vulnerability in him that he usually kept hidden. He wasn't just a man who loved the idea of a simple life—he was someone who loved me enough to give it up.

"We'll figure it out together, Ellie," he said, his voice steady despite the uncertainty swirling in both of us.

I nodded, the truth in his words sinking in like a slow tide.

But for now, I let the evening settle around us, the ocean breeze keeping a steady rhythm as we sat side by side, neither of us moving forward, but neither of us pulling away either.

I wanted to lean into him, to allow myself to be swept away by the intensity of it all. But the rational part of me—the part that always kept my feet firmly planted—knew that indulging in this would lead us down a path neither of us could walk without pain. I could feel it in the pit of my stomach, the inevitable conclusion hanging in my peripheral vision.

I smiled up at him, drawn to him by a pull stronger than anything I'd ever felt. In that moment, everything felt right—like we had found something real, something steady, as constant as the waves crashing below us.

As the stars began to peek through the inky sky, I didn't want to move. Didn't want to let go of the warmth of his arms; the steady way he held me like he never wanted to let me slip away.

I lifted my head and kissed him gently, the soft press of our lips a promise I couldn't yet say. His fingers curled against my waist, holding me there, as if he could keep me anchored in this moment forever. When we pulled away, our breaths mingling in the cool night air.

"You're my favorite adventure, Ellie," Colton murmured, his voice rough with emotion. "As short of an adventure as it might be."

I had spent so much of my life chasing something bigger than myself, always searching for the next horizon. But standing here, wrapped in his arms, I realized adventure wasn't just about growth—it was about feeling. About finding something, someone, worth holding on to.

My heart fluttered in my chest. "I think you're mine too."

Chapter Eighteen

The drive back was quiet, but with Colton it was never the uncomfortable kind. The quiet gave me time to ponder. The lighthouse and picnic had been a dream. But now, as the miles stretched between us and the shore, reality started creeping back in that our heavy conversations about the future still unresolved.

Colton's hand rested on the console, palm up, an open invitation. Without thinking, I slipped my fingers into his, letting him thread them together. His thumb brushed over the back of my hand, slow and steady. It was a simple touch. Comforting. Familiar.

But my chest ached with the knowledge that I might not be able to stay wrapped up in this forever.

My phone buzzed from my lap. I hesitated before glancing at the screen.

Olivia: Hey, are you on your way home yet?

It was a simple text, but it snapped me back to reality. A reality where time was running out, a sharp reminder of the very thought I was desperately wanted to avoid.

Colton must have felt the way I tensed because his grip on my hand tightened.

"You okay?" His voice was soft, like he already knew the answer.

I swallowed, staring out at the darkened road ahead. "Yeah. Just tired." Lying was easier than trying to explain and I was tired from all my thoughts.

He didn't push, just gave a small nod before turning his eyes back to the road. But there was a shift between us, despite both of us trying to pretend it was okay.

By the time we pulled up to Clinton, I felt the weight of the night settling into my bones. I needed sleep, but more than anything I needed to breathe. I needed to stop thinking about how easy it would be to fall for Colton completely and how desperately I needed to get out of this small town.

We pulled up to the house, and I noticed that the kitchen light was on, casting a glow through the front windows, and I knew someone was still awake.

Before I could open the door, Colton caught my wrist, keeping me in the cab of the truck.

"I meant what I said, Ellie," he murmured. "About wanting this life. About wanting you in mine more than anything else. I am yours."

A lump formed in my throat. I swallowed hard and nodded, slipping out before I could say something I wasn't ready to.

Inside, the house was dim, the only light coming from the kitchen. Olivia sat at the table with her hands wrapped around a mug. She looked up as I stepped in, her gaze instantly narrowing. "You look..." she waved a hand at me, "like you've been through some *things*."

I let out a laugh, dropping into a seat at the table beside her. "That obvious?"

She nudged my shoulder. "So, spill. Get it off your chest."

I hesitated, chewing my lip as if the repetitive motion would help clear my heavy thoughts. "He took me to the lighthouse."

Her eyes widened. "The one you were talking about at dinner the other night?"

I nodded. "Yeah. It was more than perfect."

Something softened in her expression as she tried to read me. "And that's bad because...?"

I let my head fall forward against the hard wood of the kitchen table, exhaling. "Because it makes everything harder. Because he keeps giving me reasons to stay and I don't know if I can."

Olivia set her mug down and turned to face me fully. "Ellie. You have to ask yourself something—do you *want* to stay?"

I swallowed, my stomach twisting. "I don't know."

"Yeah, you do." Her voice was gentle but firm, the younger sister sounding older and more mature than ever before. "You're just scared to admit it."

I closed my eyes, recognizing the truth of her words.

Because she was right.

I knew exactly what I wanted, but I just didn't know if I was brave enough to take it.

* * *

The next morning, I woke with the weight of last night still pressing heavy on my chest. The lighthouse, the kiss, Colton's words—I needed space. I needed to think without the pull of Colton's steady hands and the way he always seemed so certain we could make it work.

Slipping out of bed, I scrawled a quick note for my mom and Olivia, letting them know I was heading out for a run. I didn't wait for anyone to wake up—I just grabbed a pair of my mom's old sneakers and slipped outside, needing space before I said or did something I couldn't take back.

Olivia had thankfully packed more practical clothes than I had, and I'd borrowed a pair of her leggings and a sports bra, knowing she wouldn't mind or even notice they were missing considering she had brought as much clothes as I had. She always understood me better than I expected, sometimes better than I understood myself and would understand my need to move my body to clear my mind.

The familiar crunch of gravel under my feet was oddly soothing as I made my way toward the trail behind the house, one that cut through the fields and led down to the water, the very same one that Colton had taken me down on the four wheelers. The morning air was crisp, carrying the scent of damp earth and fresh pine. This place had settled into my bones more than I cared to admit and that smell made me feel more comfortable than it should have.

When I was young, whenever Mom and Dad fought, I'd grab my tennis shoes and run—fast and far, until the weight of their anger couldn't touch me anymore. Back then, it was the only way I knew how to escape, to outrun the heavy energy that settled over our home like a storm cloud. And ever since, running had been my best source of stress relief—the only thing that made me feel like I had control when everything else felt uncertain.

I reached the end of the path before I had even worked through a single thought, so I just kept running. My feet hit the dirt road in a steady rhythm, but my mind was anything but steady. The town was still a few miles ahead—not an impossible distance, though I hadn't exactly planned for the return trip. Since I'd left my phone at the house, I could always find a payphone or borrow one if I decided I didn't want to run back.

The logical part of me knew I should pace myself, conserve energy, make a plan instead of running aimlessly toward nowhere in particular. But logic wasn't what had me out here before the sun had fully risen, my pulse racing for reasons that had nothing to do with exertion.

Maybe I thought the movement would shake something loose—some answer, some clarity that had evaded me last night when Colton had looked at me like I was the only thing in the world that mattered. When he'd told me what he wanted, so plainly, so honestly.

A farmhouse. A quiet life. A love that was steady, unwavering.

I sucked in a sharp breath, my chest tightening, though whether it was from the run or the thoughts pressing in, I wasn't sure.

Because the problem wasn't that I didn't want those things. The problem was that I wanted them too much.

I had no idea how long I had run before the sound of tires crunching over the dirt road behind me made me pause. I turned just as Colton's truck rolled to a stop a few feet away. He climbed out, his eyes locking onto mine immediately.

"Your mom called when she found your note," he said, shoving his hands into the pockets of his jeans. "She was worried about you and figured you had run to my house."

I exhaled, looking away. "I just needed some air."

Colton took a slow step closer, watching my face as if he could see the words I wasn't saying. "Or space from me."

I didn't answer right away because, honestly, I wasn't sure. Maybe it was both.

I looked ahead to the path I had been running on and got the twitch to take off again.

His jaw tensed, but his voice stayed even. "Are you going to take off running again if I asked you to talk to me?"

I swallowed hard. "No. I just... I needed time to think. I might still need time."

He nodded, kicking at a loose rock with the toe of his boot. "You come to any conclusions yet?"

I crossed my arms, staring out at the horizon. "I don't know."

Colton let out a breath, the sound heavy, frustrated. "Ellie, I need to know what you want. Because last night, it felt like we wanted the same thing even if you weren't admitting it out loud like I was. And now?" He shook his head. "Now, you won't even look at me."

My throat tightened as I finally turned to face him. "I don't want to hurt you, Colton."

His expression softened, but the hurt was still there, just beneath the surface mostly because he was trying to not show it. "Then don't."

The silence stretched between us, thick with words we weren't ready to say. And for the first time, I wondered if I was about to lose him before I even figured out if I wanted him enough to change my whole life.

I exhaled sharply, my arms wrapping around myself like I could physically hold in everything threatening to spill out. Suddenly my outfit of leggings and sports bra made me feel very vulnerable, since I was unable to hide in any manner. "It's not that simple, Colton."

His eyes darkened with heavy emotions I had never seen before. A sadness like he could already feel me slipping away. "It *is* that simple."

I shook my head. "No, it's not. You—this—" I gestured between us, struggling to find the right words. "You make me feel things I never planned for. And one minute that feels amazing and the next it scares the hell out of me."

Colton's jaw tensed, but he didn't speak. He just watched me, waiting for what I was going to say next.

I swallowed hard, knowing I owed him more than silence. "I've spent my whole life making decisions based on logic. What makes sense. What's practical. I built a career, a future, and I did it by always thinking three steps ahead. And then I came here, and suddenly, none of that matters because you make me *feel* something I can't explain." My breath came out unsteady. "But I don't know if I can build a life on feelings alone."

Colton's expression didn't change, but something in his stance did—like he'd just accepted something he didn't want to.

"So, what?" he asked, his voice rough. "You're afraid of getting stuck here? Afraid you'll wake up one day and realize you made a mistake?"

"I'm afraid of making the *wrong* choice." My voice barely rose above a whisper. "And I don't want to hurt you in the process."

For a long moment, he didn't say anything. Then he nodded, slow and measured, before looking away, his fingers flexing at his sides like he was holding himself back from reaching out to me.

"I get it," he finally said, his voice flat. "You don't know if this is enough for you. You don't know if I am going to be enough for you."

"Colton—"

"No," he cut me off, shaking his head. "I needed to hear it. And I'm glad I did, because now I understand." He let out a hollow laugh, running a hand through his hair. "You're always waiting for some grand realization, some moment where everything just clicks into place and makes sense to you. But love doesn't work like that, Ellie. It's not a formula. It's not a strategy. It's just *choosing* someone, every day, because you can't imagine your life without them."

I opened my mouth, but no words came.

He studied me for a moment longer, then took a step back, his jaw clenching like he was bracing himself. "I can't keep waiting for you to decide if I'm worth staying for especially when I told you that I'm willing to do anything to make you happy, even going to Vegas with you." His voice slowly became quiet, making what he said final.

Then he turned and walked away, leaving me standing there, my heart pounding, my mind racing—because for the first time, *I* wasn't only hunting myself.

Chapter Nineteen

"Ladies and gentlemen, please lift up your trays and return your seats to the upright position as we prepare for our final descent at the Las Vegas airport."

The captain's voice crackled through the speakers, but I barely registered it. As the plane descended, the air blowing from the vent above me shut off, as if the cabin itself was bracing for the dry Nevada heat waiting outside.

I swallowed hard, my fingers gripping the armrests as the wheels hit the pavement with a jolt. The seatbelt light flicked off, and immediately, the plane erupted into chaos. Passengers unbuckled, springing up from their seats despite knowing we'd be stuck here for another fifteen minutes. Olivia shifted beside me, watching the rush of movement with a sigh.

"Every single time," she muttered. "It's like they think they can make the doors open faster if they are standing."

I forced a small smile, but it barely held. My stomach was in knots. Wasn't this what I wanted? To be back? To leave everything behind before I let myself get in too deep?

Olivia nudged me lightly. "Are you okay?"

I didn't answer as I flipped my phone off airplane mode. The flood of notifications came instantly, my screen lighting up with missed calls and more than a dozen unread texts.

Mom had sent half a dozen messages and left five voicemails I wasn't ready to listen to. Mitch had sent a few texts of his own—short, direct, but still laced with concern. Kenna and Addie had checked in, their words light but filled with worry after I sent them a brief text stating that Olivia and I were leaving.

But it was Colton's messages that made my chest ache.

> Colton: I didn't mean to scare you off this morning. I just wanted you to know that I'm willing to try and that I do see a future with you. That I'd do anything to make you happy.
>
> Colton: Sweet dreams, beautiful woman.

There was a gap between those messages and the ones that followed in the morning—when he still thought I was in Clinton. When he had no idea, I had already slipped away before the sun came up.

> 5:15 AM Colton: Good morning, sweetie. Can we meet up for lunch today? I'd love to talk about last night. I feel like we need to clear the air. I hate the way we left things.
>
> 7:48 AM Colton: Jen said you left. Why did you leave?
>
> 9:09 AM Colton: I wasn't trying to scare you away. I was trying to give you options, not decide your future for you.
>
> 12:02 PM Colton: Please just let me know that you're okay.
>
> 3:27 PM Colton: Please, Ellie. I just need to know that you're okay.

I stared down at my phone, reading each message repeatedly.

Olivia sighed beside me, pulling out her own phone. "Mom's freaking out. She called me, like, five times." She scrolled, then made a face. "Oh great. She's gone as far as to contact Dad! Our parents are so worried about us that they resulted in speaking!"

I didn't respond. I couldn't.

Because the truth was, I didn't know what to say.

Last night, I had *almost* stayed. I had let Colton's words sink into my bones, had let the idea of a life with him settle in my heart. I had pictured it—porch swings and sunsets, small-town laughter, the weight of his arms wrapped around me.

And I had wanted it.

But I had also felt like I was biting off more than I could chew. That kind of love, that kind of commitment—it wasn't something I could promise when I wasn't even sure who I was in this new version of my life.

The people in our row began filing out, grabbing their bags from the overhead compartment before moving down the aisle. Olivia and I stood, following suit. She stayed close, watching me carefully as we moved down the narrow aisle and into the jet bridge. I knew she wanted to ask more, to dig deeper, but she held back—for now.

We walked through the terminal, the storm of the past twenty-four hours filling me with uncertainty and chaos. Each step took me further from Clinton, from Colton, from the life I had started to imagine belonging in.

By the time we reached baggage claim, Olivia had had enough of my silence.

As we waited for our suitcases to appear on the carousel, she turned to me, crossing her arms. "Okay, I'll bite. What exactly happened? Because I know you, Ellie, and there is *no way* you just woke up and decided to come home, especially when you had been making excuses to stay for weeks."

I swallowed, my grip tightening on the strap of my carry-on. "It was time to leave."

She scoffed. "That's not an answer. A few days ago, you were so happy. I thought for sure you'd end up staying. And now? You caught the first flight out. What changed?"

I grabbed the first of my suitcases as it slid past, yanking it off the belt with more force than necessary. Olivia grabbed one of hers too, still staring at me expectantly.

I chose not to answer as we waited for the rest of our bags, partly because I didn't know what to say and partly because everything felt heavy. After packing early this morning and racing to the airport, I was too exhausted to have this conversation.

We walked toward the parking garage in silence, the unanswered question hanging in the air. She popped the trunk of her small car, and together, we loaded our bags. But as soon as she pulled out onto the road, the floodgates opened.

"So, what did he say?" Olivia demanded, her voice sharp but tinged with concern. "Because I know that's what this is about. I saw how you looked when we left." She cast a quick glance at me. "And honestly? You look worse now."

I stared out the window as the neon glow of the Strip blurred past. My chest tightened.

Because the truth was, I didn't know what to say.

And I wasn't sure if I had made the right choice.

* * *

My apartment felt cold and unfamiliar.

I had lived here for years, but after weeks spent in Clinton, surrounded by sprawling fields and the easy cadence of small-town life, the walls seemed to close in around me with their sad grey color. The neon lights outside my window flickered against the glass, a constant reminder that I was back in the city—the place I had always believed I belonged.

So why did it suddenly feel so suffocating?

I dropped some of my bags by the door, too drained to take them to my room to unpack. Olivia had already retreated to her own apartment, and for that, I was grateful. I just needed a second to breathe.

Crossing the living room, I collapsed onto the couch, kicking off my shoes. The exhaustion from the travel, from the emotions, from the way my mind hadn't stopped *running* and the way I couldn't stop thinking about a certain cowboy, but I still didn't move. Instead, my fingers idly reached for my carry-on, the only bag I carried with me to the couch, unzipping it as if muscle memory had taken over.

And then I saw it.

Tucked between layers of my clothes was Colton's sweatshirt.

I hadn't even realized I packed it in my rush to leave, but there it was, a faded blue hoodie with the logo of some farm supply store on the front—something I had stolen one night at his house after I complained about the evening chill. I had meant to give it back. I had *planned* to.

But I had taken it with me instead.

Slowly, I lifted it, my hands gripping the worn fabric as I pulled it onto my lap. It still smelled like him—like cedar and the faintest hint of laundry detergent, somehow smelling warm and safe.

My chest tightened, a lump forming in my throat.

I had spent the entire flight telling myself I had done the right thing. That leaving was the only choice. That staying would have been reckless, would have been *too much*.

But as I sat there, Colton's sweatshirt draped over my lap, the resolve was weakening.

Then my phone rang.

I flinched at the sound, my heart leaping as I grabbed it from the coffee table. But the name flashing across the screen wasn't the one I had been hoping to see.

Mom.

I hesitated for only a second before answering. I had ignored all her previous calls and leaving at the crack of dawn from her house was not the way to handle things.

"Hey Mom," I said, trying—and failing—to sound normal.

"Oh, Ellie," she breathed, relief flooding her voice. "You're safe. Thank heavens."

Guilt curled in my stomach. "Yeah. We just landed a little while ago and we both made it back to our apartments."

"I was worried sick," she admitted. "I didn't even know you were thinking about leaving until Olivia texted me this morning. You should have said goodbye, sweetheart."

I squeezed my eyes shut, letting her maternal tone to add to the shame I was already feeling. "I know."

A pause. Then, softer, "Was it because of Colton? He came here looking for you when you didn't answer your phone this morning."

I exhaled slowly. "It was a lot of things."

Mom didn't push, but she didn't let me off the hook, either. "Honey, I know you. And I know the way you looked at him when you thought no one was watching. You love him."

I didn't respond, I couldn't.

Instead, my fingers absently twisted the hem of Colton's hoodie, tracing the small, frayed holes that had formed in the once-perfect fabric. Somehow, that made me feel better—that nothing stayed perfect. Not clothes. Not places. Not people.

And definitely not love.

"What did he say?" I whispered.

"He just wanted to know if you were okay." Mom sighed, when her voice came out it was thick with emotion. "He sounded heartbroken, Ellie."

I swallowed past the lump in my throat. "I didn't mean to hurt him."

"I know." A pause. "But did you mean to leave him?"

I didn't have an answer for that.

Mom let out a slow breath, sensing my hesitation. "You don't have to figure it all out tonight. Just... don't bury this, okay? Don't let fear make the choice for you. You were so close to something real, to someone who truly cares about you. Don't let that slip away before, you're sure."

Another moment of silence stretched between us before I finally found my voice. "Thanks, Mom."

"I love you, Sweet Pea." She sighed, the sound felt like she was holding herself back from saying more. "I already miss you."

"Love you too." I ended the call and set my phone on the table, then walked to the other side of the room, as if getting distance from the phone could quiet the pounding of my pulse.

I wasn't ready to think about Colton. I wasn't ready to face the weight of what I had done.

But then my phone buzzed again.

I glanced down, expecting a text from Mom or even Olivia.

But it wasn't.

Colton.

I stared at the screen for a long moment before finally opening the message.

> Colton: Take care of yourself, Ellie. I hope you find whatever it is you're looking for back home.

My vision blurred.

I read the messages once. Then twice. Then again, my breath coming shorter with every pass.

This wasn't like the others. This wasn't *please call me* or *tell me what I did wrong* kind of text.

This was a *goodbye*.

My fingers trembled over the keyboard, but I didn't type anything. What would I even say?

That I missed him? That I wanted him? That I had made a mistake?

Or worse—that I *didn't know* if I had?

I let the phone fall back onto the couch beside me, my hands shaking as I curled into myself, Colton's hoodie still clutched in my grip.

And for the first time since leaving Clinton...

I let myself cry.

Chapter Twenty

The apartment was silent except for the hum of the air conditioning, the artificial chill doing little to settle the unease always in my stomach. Olivia had planned to come over for dinner—stopping on her way to grab Chinese food, and we were going to stream a rom-com, something light and mindless. Something that would require nothing from me.

But as I sat curled up on the couch, laptop open, halfheartedly scrolling through my emails, I knew exactly how this night would go.

I would pretend to listen as Olivia talked about work, about her clients, about some drama she was dealing with Dad since they were still in the complicated steps of growing the boutique. I would push food around my plate, force out a few laughs at whatever ridiculous movie we put on, and pretend I was fine.

Because that's what I did now.

I worked. I smiled. And more than anything else, I pretended.

I had buried myself so deep in the structured chaos of my life in Las Vegas, drowning in deadlines and projects and late nights at the office, that I convinced everyone—including myself—that I was moving on.

But no matter how many hours I logged, no matter how many distractions I chased, I couldn't shake him.

Colton.

The name alone sent a sharp ache through my chest that tore me to pieces.

I pressed my fingers to my temple, exhaling slowly. I wasn't supposed to be thinking about him.

And yet, my phone sat beside me on the couch, the dark screen taunting me.

It had been weeks.

Weeks since I had left Clinton.

Weeks since I had left him.

And yet, I still hadn't deleted his messages.

I had told myself to. I had hovered over the delete button more times than I could count. But each time, I couldn't do it.

Because the moment I erased them, it would be real.

So instead, I opened them again. The texts I had told myself to delete, the ones I had read a hundred times long since memorized and yet still sat unanswered.

The thread stretched out before me, a timeline of regret.

> Colton: I didn't mean to scare you off this morning. I just wanted you to know that I'm willing to try and that I do see a future with you. That I'd do anything to make you happy.
>
> Colton: Sweet dreams, beautiful woman.
>
> 5:15 AM Colton: Good morning, sweetie. Can we meet up for lunch today? I'd love to talk about last night. I feel like we need to clear the air. I hate the way we left things.
>
> 7:48 AM Colton: Jen said you left. Why did you leave?

> 9:09 AM Colton: I wasn't trying to scare you away. I was trying to give you options, not decide your future for you.
>
> 12:02 PM Colton: Please just let me know that you're okay.
>
> 3:27 PM Colton: Please, Ellie. I just need to know that you're okay.

Then, the one that broke me. The one I read repeatedly, like a punishment and maybe that was why I kept rereading it, because I deserved to hurt just as badly as I had hurt him.

> Colton: Take care of yourself, Ellie. I hope you find whatever it is you're looking for back home.

I swallowed hard, my fingers tightening around my phone. The finality of that last message felt like a punch to the gut.

I had thought ignoring it would make it easier. That I could pretend I had moved on, that leaving had been the right choice.

But all it did was make me feel like I was slowly suffocating.

I closed my eyes, trying to shake the image of him telling me he would follow me anywhere. Trying to shake the thought that I had left behind something I wasn't sure I could ever replace.

I didn't hear Olivia come in. One second, I was still staring at my phone, at the last thing Colton had ever said to me. The next, she was snatching it right out of my hands.

"Liv!" I yelped, reaching for it, but she danced back easily, raising an eyebrow.

"Are you serious right now?" she asked, scrolling before her expression twisted in frustration. "You've been staring at his texts for weeks, Ellie. I saw you doing it in the office, at home, even in the freaking parking garage last night. *How long are you going to torture yourself before you admit what it means?*"

I swallowed hard, wrapping my arms around myself. "It doesn't mean anything."

She scoffed. "Oh, right. That's why you look like a ghost. That's why you keep replaying his messages in your head instead of answering them."

I pressed my lips together, but Olivia wasn't done.

"Ellie, I know you. You don't get like this over just anyone. You're in love with him, and the fact that you're still here, pretending you're fine, is the biggest lie you've ever told yourself."

I sucked in a sharp breath. She had never said it out loud before and the worst part was that I didn't deny it.

But Olivia wasn't finished. "You left because you thought staying would trap you. But let me ask you this—how free do you feel right now?"

I sat there in silence.

Because the truth was, I had never felt more lost in my life.

And then Olivia said the words that cracked something inside me. "If you were really happy, you wouldn't be trying so hard to convince yourself that you were."

I inhaled shakily, looking away.

Because deep down, I knew there was truth to what she was saying.

We didn't sit in that silence long. My sister moved the conversation forward, her voice deliberately light, steering us away from the heavy cloud that had settled around me. It was Olivia's way of offering a lifeline without making it too obvious.

She plopped down onto the couch beside me, kicking off her heels with a sigh. "Okay, I got extra egg rolls because I knew you'd steal mine, and I—" She paused, her brow furrowing slightly as she looked at me again, this time with more scrutiny. "Have you even eaten today? You're looking thin."

I rolled my eyes, reaching for the takeout bag. "Yes, Mom."

She made a skeptical noise but didn't push it, instead pulling out the containers and setting them on the coffee table. "Well, I hope you're hungry, because I got enough food to feed an army."

A small, forced smile tugged at my lips. I appreciated her effort. The last thing I could take right now was another deep dive into my emotions, and Olivia seemed to sense that.

For the next few minutes, we focused on the food—unpacking cartons of fried rice, orange chicken, dumplings, and, of course, egg rolls. Olivia turned on the TV, some romantic comedy neither of us really cared about, and we settled into a rhythm of eating and pretending this was exactly how the evening was supposed to be.

It almost worked. Almost. But I wasn't the only one distracted. Olivia was watching me.

She waited until I had taken a few bites before she spoke again, her tone softer. "Ellie."

I swallowed, staring down at my plate. "Liv, can we just eat?"

"We are eating." She leaned forward, elbows resting on her knees. "But you're barely talking, and you keep glancing at your phone like you're expecting something."

I froze for half a second before forcing out a casual, "I'm just waiting for a work email."

Olivia didn't buy it.

Not even a little and I couldn't blame her. Even with my phone face down on the couch I still desperately wanted to pick it up and look at it, make sure that I hadn't missed a message from Colton even if it was obvious by his last text that he had no need to contact me again.

She grabbed another egg roll, but her next words held deep meaning the small talk of food obviously over. "You know that you could go back to him so easily. He would welcome you with open arms. They all would. Addie and Kenna have both texted me that they miss us."

I stilled, my chopsticks hovering over my plate. I hated how much I missed him and that she was willing to call me out on it.

I took a slow breath and reached for my water, buying myself a few seconds. "It doesn't matter."

Olivia made a disbelieving noise. "It doesn't?"

I didn't answer. Because the truth was, it did matter.

I felt like I was stuck. Like I had left a part of myself behind in Clinton, and no matter how hard I tried to fill the space with work, with distractions, nothing worked.

Olivia watched me closely, her expression softening even more. "You love him, don't you?"

My fingers tightening around my napkin. "Liv..."

"Ellie." Her voice was steady, unwavering. "You love him."

I didn't deny it.

Because denying it wouldn't make it any less true.

* * *

I still hadn't responded to Olivia's huge question.

Not when her words were still ricocheting through me, bouncing off all the walls I had built around my heart.

You're in love with him.

How free do you feel right now?

If you were happy, you wouldn't be trying so hard to convince yourself that you were.

I let out a shaky breath, my fingers twitching with the urge to grab my phone again.

But instead, as the credits to the movie rolled before us, I turned away from Olivia, brushing past her as I walked toward my bedroom.

"I'm tired," I murmured, a lie as big as the one I'd been telling myself for weeks. "You can crash in the guest room if you want."

She let out a sigh but didn't push me further. Not yet. "Get some sleep, Ellie," she said softly.

I closed the door behind me and leaned against it, squeezing my eyes shut.

I was so tired of thinking about him yet the moment I crawled into bed; Colton's voice was all I could hear.

I rolled onto my side, staring at my phone where it sat on the nightstand. The screen was dark, but I could still see his last message in my mind like it was burned there.

> Colton: Take care of yourself, Ellie. I hope you find whatever it is you're looking for back home.

I swallowed hard and reached for my phone before I could talk myself out of it.

For the first time since leaving Clinton, I opened our message thread to type something back.

I hesitated before typing out the first words.

> Ellie: I miss you.

I stared at them for a long time before shaking my head and deleting them. Too much. Too soon.

I tried again.

> Ellie: I'm sorry.

But that didn't feel right either.

Colton had never asked for an apology. He had asked for honesty.

I took a deep breath, then typed something else.

> Ellie: I don't know what I'm looking for. But I do know that I was happy with you.

I hovered over the send button, my heart pounding. I could end this right now. I could bridge the gap, open the door, give us something.

But my thumb never moved.

Instead, I let out a heavy breath and locked my phone, tossing it onto the nightstand as if that could make it disappear.

I rolled onto my stomach, burying my face into the pillow, but sleep never came.

Because deep down, I already knew that I had gone to Clinton to find something. To figure out my relationship with my mom and find some solid ground.

But all I had done was leave the best thing that had ever happened to me behind.

* * *

I stayed in bed longer than I should've the next few days, the Vegas sunlight streaming through the blinds in thin, judgmental lines. The noise of the city filtered in from the street below—honking, music, life moving on around me like I hadn't just unraveled the best thing that had ever happened to me.

I thought leaving would help. That putting distance between me and Clinton—between me and him—would clear the noise in my head. But it hadn't. The silence here was worse. It wasn't peaceful—it was hollow.

I tried to go through the motions. I went to work. I answered emails. I stared at the marketing reports piling up on my desk and told myself I was doing the right thing. That I was focused. That I was back on track.

But the more I told myself I was fine, the more I buried myself in the kind of busy that left no space to feel.

By the time evening rolled around, I was still at the office, pretending it was by choice.

The office was nearly empty, the kind of quiet that only settled in when the sun had long since disappeared, and everyone with a normal work-life balance had already gone home.

Not me.

I sat at my desk, fingers flying across the keyboard, my eyes locked on the screen as I pored over a presentation I had already reworked twice. There was nothing wrong with it. The data was solid, the formatting sharp, the delivery polished. But the silence pressed in around me, and I needed something—anything—to keep my mind occupied.

I had been doing this for days and while I wanted it to help, I was starting to think that there was no chance.

Throwing myself into work, taking on extra projects, showing up early and staying late until I was the last one in the building. It was easier this way. If I kept moving, kept thinking, I wouldn't have to feel the ache sitting heavy in my chest.

The ache of leaving Clinton.

The ache of leaving *him*.

I clenched my jaw and focused on the screen, forcing my mind to stay present. The numbers. The strategies. This was what mattered. *This* was my life.

Not Colton.

Not some small-town fantasy I had no business entertaining.

Not the way my phone sat dark and silent beside me, confirming what I already knew—he had meant what he said.

He wasn't reaching out anymore and I wasn't sure if that made it easier or worse.

I pushed the thought down, fingers tightening around the mouse as I clicked through the slides, mindlessly tweaking details that didn't need fixing. The numbers blurred together, offering a temporary distraction—until a deep voice cut through the silence, sharp and deliberate.

"How long do you plan on hiding in here?"

I startled slightly, turning just in time to see Dad standing in the doorway. No knock. No hesitation. Dad standing with his arms crossed over his chest, the hard lines of his face unreadable.

I blinked, caught off guard. "What are you doing here?"

Dad stepped inside, the soft click of the door shutting behind him making the walls feel smaller. "Maggie mentioned you've been staying late. She was worried, figured someone should check in."

Of course, Maggie had noticed. She had been Dad's assistant for years, had practically watched me grow up, and had always been too perceptive for her own good when it came to Olivia and me.

"I'm fine," I said flatly, turning back to my computer. "Just catching up on some work. A lot of things got pushed aside while I was gone."

Dad exhaled a deep breath; the kind that told me he wasn't buying it. "Ellie." His voice was firm, but not unkind. "You don't have to prove anything to me. You already have this job. You don't need to run yourself into the ground."

I scoffed, clicking my pen a little too aggressively as I scribbled a note on my never ending to do list to buy a coffee machine for my office and a lock for my door. "I'm not." The sharpness in my tone surprised even me, but I didn't care. "I just want to get caught up from when I was gone."

Dad moved closer, pulling out the chair across from my desk and sinking into it. He studied me, his eyes sharp and knowing—the same way they had been in boardroom meetings, in investor calls, in every high-pressure situation which had taught me to push aside my emotions and focus on the next goal.

Then, finally, he said it.

"You're running."

I let out a dry laugh, shaking my head. "I'm sitting at my desk, working. If that's running, then I guess I can cancel my gym membership."

Dad didn't flinch at my sarcasm. He just leaned forward, resting his elbows on his knees. "You left without telling anyone, you've ignored your mom's calls for days, and now you're practically living at the office. I know running when I see it, Ellie. Because I've done it too."

I swallowed hard, my fingers tightening around my pen. "I didn't run. I reevaluated my priorities." I nodded my head as if to cement the statement between us. "I came home."

"Did you?" Dad tilted his head slightly. "Or did you just run back to what was safe? To the one thing you know how to do—work?"

His words hit hard.

The air in the room felt heavier. I exhaled sharply, turning my chair away slightly, as if I could physically block him out. "Why do you even care?" I muttered. "You've spent most of my life buried in your own work. Why does it bother you that I'm doing the same thing?"

Dad's jaw tightened, but he didn't snap back. Instead, he sat there, looking at me in a way that made my stomach turn. "Because I know exactly where this road leads, Ellie. I built my whole life around work. I chased success so hard that I lost time with the family, the people I cared the most about. I thought I was doing what was best for everyone, but I missed everything. And by the time I looked up, it was too late to get it back."

His words left a crack in my armor, but I refused to let the crack grow. I squared my shoulders and returned my attention to the computer. "That's you, Dad. Not me."

He sighed, rubbing his hands over his face, like he was debating how much further to go. "Ellie, I'm not saying don't work hard. I'm saying don't let this be the only thing you have. Because one day, you'll wake up and realize that the things that matter. The things that make life *mean* something. They're already gone."

I swallowed past the lump in my throat. "I have plenty of things that matter," I lied.

Dad studied me for another long moment before sighing, pushing himself up from the chair. "If you say so."

He turned to leave, but before he reached the door, he hesitated. "For what it's worth, I think you're making a mistake."

I stiffened. "Excuse me?"

He looked over his shoulder. "With Colton."

My breath caught, my tone sharpening instinctively. "What do you know about Colton?"

Dad shrugged, unbothered by the edge in my voice. "Enough. When you and Olivia took off in the middle of the night and wouldn't answer your phones, your mom called me. She thinks he's the reason you left." His eyes narrowed slightly. "And from what I can tell, your sister was all too ready to come home. But you? You were happy out there, Ellie."

The statement hung between us, heavy and undeniable.

I clenched my jaw, forcing myself to look away. "You wouldn't know that."

"I don't have to. I can see it written all over your face now."

My chest ached, but I forced my expression to stay blank. "I am happy," I said evenly, the words tasting hollow even as I said them.

Dad studied me for a beat, then gave a slow, measured nod. "I hope you figure out the truth before it's too late."

He turned toward the door but hesitated, glancing back at me with a look There was something different in his eyes—something weary, almost resigned. For the first time, he looked *old*.

"Letting love and happiness slip away is a hell I wouldn't wish on my worst enemy."

And then, just like that, he was gone.

I sat there, staring at the door long after it had closed, my heart pounding, my hands shaking.

I wasn't sure how long I stayed like that, but eventually, my phone buzzed.

I picked it up, half-expecting another email or work notification to come through, since working late that had become a regular thing.

But my stomach dropped when I saw the name on the screen that I never expected I would see again.

Colton.

It was just a text message.

I hesitated before opening it, my pulse roaring in my ears.

A photo filled the screen—Colton, standing in the hospital, a baby wrapped snugly in a soft blue blanket nestled in his arms. His expression was a mix of quiet awe and something softer, something almost reverent. Below it, his message was simple.

> Colton: Brendan finally got his boy. The girls wanted me to share this with you.

I had to breath as my fingers gripped the phone too tight as my eyes scanned the picture, searching. For what, I wasn't sure—some background detail, some hidden message, some *proof* that he missed me as much as I missed him.

But there was nothing.

No lingering sadness in his eyes. No sign that he was breaking the way I was. Just Colton, holding his nephew, wrapped in the warmth of his family.

The breath I'd been holding left my lungs in a shaky exhale.

My father's words echoed in my mind.

"One day, you'll wake up and realize that the things that matter. They're already gone."

I stared at the message, my heart pounding, my chest aching with a hollow kind of longing.

Because for the first time since I left Clinton, I wasn't just missing him.

I was missing the future I would never get.

Chapter Twenty-One

The city lights stretched endlessly, neon colors reflecting against the pavement as I stepped out of my office building days later. The air was dry, the heat still lingering even as the night settled in, but none of it made me feel grounded. Not in the way that it used to.

I had thrown myself into work, into structure, into the familiar—but none of it stopped the ache in my chest. None of it filled the void I hadn't realized I was creating when I left Clinton.

I had told myself I'd made the right choice when I left. That I had done what was best for me. But as I stood there, watching people move past me on the busy sidewalk, I felt more lost than ever.

And then I saw him.

At first, I thought I was imagining it. I had to be. Because there, leaning against a truck parked along the curb, was Colton looking remarkably out of place in his wrangler jeans, worn in boots, and the black cowboy hat he had worn on our date to the rodeo.

I froze. My breath hitched in my throat, my pulse roaring in my ears. He was standing there looking very uncomfortable, hands tucked into his pockets, but there was something *different* about him.

He looked the same and yet... not. He looked like a man who had been through hell and made it out the other side.

And his eyes? They were locked on me like he had just found what he'd been searching for.

He pushed off the truck, stepping onto the sidewalk. The sounds of Vegas—the honking, the chatter, the chaos—faded into nothing.

"Colton." My voice barely worked.

He let out a slow breath, his lips twitching like he wasn't sure if he should smile or get mad. "Ellie," he muttered, running a hand through his hair. "You really weren't going to talk to me again, were you?"

I swallowed hard. "What are you doing here?"

He tilted his head, giving me a *really* look. "You *really* have to ask?"

I should've looked away. I should've turned and walked back inside, back to the life I had built before him. But I didn't. I couldn't.

Because Colton Bennett was standing in front of me in the middle of Las Vegas, and for the first time in weeks, I could breathe again.

Colton looked tired in a way that had nothing to do with work. It was in his eyes, in the way his shoulders sagged just a little. When he looked at me, it wasn't just longing—it was relief, like he'd finally able to catch his breath.

"I thought you were done," I whispered, my throat tight as I tried not to let my emotions show. "Your messages..."

"I meant what I said," he admitted, his voice quieter now, rough around the edges. "I wasn't going to chase you forever, Ellie. But I had to see you. I had to look you in the eye and see you—one last time."

His gaze swept over me, but not in the way I was used to.

This wasn't the teasing smirk he wore when he checked me out in my bikini at the beach, or the knowing glance he'd thrown my way before the rodeo when he thought I wasn't looking.

This was different.

This was Colton looking at me like he was searching for something—proof that I was okay, even if he wasn't.

His brows pinched together, his throat bobbing as he swallowed. "I just... I couldn't take it anymore, Ellie." His voice cracked slightly, and that tiny break did something to me—made my breath catch, made my chest ache. "I got in my truck and started driving. I didn't have a plan. I didn't know what I was going to say or do when I saw you again." He let out a slow, unsteady breath, raking a hand through his hair. "I just needed to see you."

I clenched my hands at my sides, fighting the urge to reach for him. Because if I touched him now, if I let myself sink into his warmth, I knew I wouldn't be able to pull myself away again.

"Colton..." I whispered, but I didn't know what to say.

Because in that moment, I wasn't sure if I was more heartbroken that he had come all this way... or that I had made him feel like he had to.

He stepped closer, close enough that I could see the way his chest rose and fell, the way his hands clenched like he was holding himself back. "Tell me you're happy."

The words hung between us.

I blinked, caught off guard. "What?"

His jaw tensed. "Look me in the eye and tell me you're happy. That you don't think about Clinton, about us. That you don't miss me the way I miss you." His voice was raw now, edged with frustration, desperation. "If you can do that, Ellie, I'll walk away. But if you can't..."

He didn't finish the sentence. He didn't have to.

I opened my mouth, the words "I am happy" sitting on the tip of my tongue. But when I looked up at him, at the man who had loved me without hesitation, at the man who had shown me a life I never thought I'd want—I couldn't say it. Because it would be a lie.

Colton saw the truth before I could even say it. His shoulders sagged slightly, his throat bobbing as he exhaled. "Then why are we standing here like this? Why are we putting ourselves through this when we are both miserable apart?"

Tears burned the back of my eyes, but I refused to let them fall. "Because I don't know how to fix this."

His hands shot up, gripping my face gently, firmly. "Then let's figure it out. Together."

And then he kissed me.

Not softly. Not cautiously.

It was desperate, urgent—like a man who had been starving for weeks and had finally found something to eat.

And I kissed him back just as fiercely.

Because Colton Bennett had just shown up in the middle of Vegas to fight for me and help me back to him.

And this time I wasn't going to let him go.

* * *

My office was quiet except for the faint hum of the city beyond the glass windows. Everyone else had gone home hours ago, and yet, the room didn't feel empty.

Colton stood in the doorway, hands in his pockets, his eyes locked on me like he couldn't quite believe I was real. The Vegas skyline stretched out behind him—bright, bold, buzzing with life—but inside this office, everything had gone still.

I had imagined our reunion a thousand times. But none of those imagined moments had prepared me for the steady calm that settled in my chest the second I saw him standing there.

His green eyes held so much—relief, hope, a quiet kind of longing that mirrored my own. And for the first time in weeks, I didn't feel like I had to brace for impact.

I hadn't asked him to come. I hadn't even sent a message saying I needed him, but somehow, he knew.

"I wasn't sure if I was ever going to see you again," I said softly, rising from the edge of my desk.

Colton's mouth curved into a faint smile. "I just needed to see you."

That pulled a quiet laugh from me—nervous, but real. "So, you just showed up?"

He shrugged. "I needed to see you. I was okay with you moving on if you were happy, but when you stepped out of the building, I knew that I had made the right choice to come find you."

My heart clenched in the best way. He hadn't just come to see me. He'd come *knowing me.*

"I've missed you," I said, my voice barely above a whisper.

His eyes softened. "I've missed you every day since the second you left."

I moved toward him, my heels quiet on the carpeted floor, until we stood a breath apart. "I kept trying to go back to who I was before you. Back to this life. But nothing fits anymore. Nothing feels right without you in it."

Colton's hand brushed gently along my arm, grounding me. "That's because it wasn't supposed to. We weren't meant to leave it behind—we were meant to build something new."

My breath hitched. "You came all this way..."

"Because I needed you to know," he said, his voice low, steady. "I didn't come here to make you choose Ellie. I came because I already have. I want you. However this looks, wherever it takes us. I want the life we create—even if we have to figure it out as we go."

Tears welled in my eyes, but this time I didn't hide them. "I want that too."

"No more running?" he asked gently.

I shook my head. "No more running."

He stepped closer, cupping my face in his hands, his thumb brushing softly across my cheek. "Say it again," he whispered. "Just so I know it's real."

I leaned into his touch, smiling through the emotion tightening in my chest. "I want us. I want this. Whatever it looks like—I'm in."

His forehead pressed to mine, and for the first time in forever, I felt whole again.

Epilogue

The sky was streaked with soft hues of pink and orange, the last remnants of daylight casting a golden glow over the fields behind Colton's house. The air was warm, thick with the scent of freshly cut grass and the distant hum of crickets, a familiar symphony of spring in Clinton.

I sat curled into Colton's side on the back porch swing, his arm draped around me, his fingers tracing lazy circles against my bare shoulder. The steady rhythm of the creaking wood beneath us was soothing, lulling us into the kind of comfortable silence that only seemed to exist in places like this—with people like him.

Six months.

That's how long it had been since I packed up my apartment in Vegas, traded the neon lights for starlit skies, the chaos for something steady, something real. Since I came back here. Since I came home to live with Mom and Mitch. Since Colton and I decided to give this a real shot.

My job looked different now—I still managed projects, choosing to work remotely, but I finally had balance. I finally had a life outside of work and it was a life I loved.

And Colton? He was still the same stubborn, wonderful man who had fought for me and for the life he knew we both needed.

"Y'know," Colton said, breaking the quiet, his voice low and thoughtful, "we might not have that big ole' farmhouse yet, but this view's pretty good while we wait."

The back porch was just barely big enough for the swing, but it had been my one request when I came back to Clinton. I had moved in with mom and Mitch, but I spent more time here at Colton's house than anywhere else.

I smiled, tilting my head up toward him. "I think this is perfect just the way it is."

His lips twitched, but his eyes held something else—something deeper, something knowing.

Before I could ask, he reached into his pocket, and my heart stuttered. I had seen the indentation of a box in there after he had gone into the house for a drink and had been on edge ever since.

"Colton."

He took my hand, turning me so I was facing him completely. His fingers were steady, but his voice was soft—raw in the way that only he could.

"Ellie, I don't need a big house, or a perfect life plan, or even a huge yard with dogs—"

I laughed, already feeling the sting of tears behind my eyes.

"I just need you," he murmured, his thumb brushing over my knuckles. "Every day. For the rest of my life."

And then he pulled out the ring.

It was perfect with its elegant and timeless—exactly what I would have picked for myself.

He didn't kneel. He didn't get the chance to because I was already falling into him, hands clutching his as I whispered, "Yes."

His grin was slow and knowing, as if he had never doubted my answer for a second. He slipped the ring onto my finger, his touch reverent, deliberate—like he was sealing something unspoken between us.

And then he kissed me.

It was deep, unhurried, lingering, filled with the kind of promise that didn't need words. A kiss that tasted like forever.

Because that's exactly what we had.

Forever.

Inspiration for the Novel

My family is from North Carolina, and throughout the years my family often spent our summers visiting the Outer Banks—a place that holds some of my most cherished memories. In the summer of 2024, I was thrilled to share that magic with my husband and son, creating unforgettable moments as we explored my favorite spot for the first time as our little family.

Now, I'm so excited to share this special place with you through The Charm of a Cowboy! Because this is a real place, I pulled inspiration from many of places that I have loved to visit. Included are a list of locations mentioned in the book, just in case you want to visit!

Breeze Thru Convenience Store and Gas Station
40374 North Carolina Hwy 12, Avon, NC 27915

Surfin' Spoon Frozen Yogurt Bar
3408 S Virginia Dare Trail, Nags Head, NC 27959

Sunsations
710 S Croatan Hwy, Kill Devil Hills, NC 27948

Dancing Turtle Coffee Shop
57196 Saxon Cut Dr, Hatteras, NC 27943

Meet your Author

Trena VanHoff has been telling stories since childhood, always with a book in hand and a notebook brimming with ideas waiting to be brought to life. Today, she writes in her spare time while working in the medical field. Trena lives in Utah with her husband, two sons, and four dogs (yes, it's a full house!), but she will always be a California girl at heart.

Though she dreams of seeing her name on the bestseller list, what excites Trena most is the thought of her books passing through the hands of many readers—dog-eared pages, worn spines, and all— tucked onto the shelves of a thrift store for someone else to discover. After all, that's how she's found many of her own favorite books.

Trena writes heartfelt, gripping stories that explore romance and the dynamics of large families, often inspired by her own experiences. Whether delving into contemporary relationships or the complexities of family life, she aims to create narratives that linger in readers' hearts long after the final page is turned.

When she's not writing, Trena enjoys sipping a Diet Dr. Pepper and spending time with her family, often reading a good book while plotting her next novel.

Keep an eye out—her next story promises to be one you won't want to put down!

Find her on Instagram, Facebook, and TikTok for book updates @trenavanhoffbooks

Or her website www.Trenavanhoffbooks.com